THE GUARDIAN LIST

A novel by

Lawrence Montaigne

Lawrence Montaigne

Copyright © 2012 Lawrence Montaigne

This is a work of fiction. Names, characters, places, and incidents are the product of the author's imagination or are used fictitiously. Any resemblance to actual persons, living or dead, events, or locales is entirely coincidental.

All rights reserved.

ISBN-13: 978-1478242260
ISBN-10: 1478242264

The Guardian List

Acknowledgments

Without the encouragement of the membership of the Anthem Authors Book Club in Henderson, Nevada, this book never would have come to fruition. Their enthusiastic criticisms were supportive of my efforts throughout the writing of this work.

I wish to thank Dr. Mary Shramski who took me by the hand and lead me through the publication process.

My thanks to Carol von Raesfeld for her editing and care in preparing the text for publication and Dorothy Hardy for her work on the cover.

A special thanks to Officer Jeremy Levy of the Las Vegas Metropolitan Police Department for sharing some of his experiences, many of which I have used in this book.

And finally, my heartfelt thanks to my wife, Patricia Ann, for sharing with me those lonely hours of isolation during the creative process of putting this work together.

Lawrence Montaigne

THE GUARDIAN LIST

BOOK ONE

Preface

"Plato proposed the establishment of an additional class of citizens, <u>The Guardians</u> who are responsible for management of the society itself.

Plato held that effective social life requires Guardians of two distinct sorts: there must be both soldiers whose function is to defend the state against external enemies and to enforce its laws, and rulers who resolve disagreements among citizens and make decisions about public policy. <u>The Guardians</u> collectively, then, are those individuals whose special craft is just the task of governance itself."

                    Plato — *The Republic*

Chapter 1

Father Nathan Ignatius had served at St. Ann's Parish for almost forty years after serving as Chaplain with the Armed Forces for six years. He had planned to stay in the military but when he got word that Father Maloney, his mentor all through school and the seminary, succumbed to a fatal heart attack and that the parish was in need of a priest, (preferably one familiar with the Georgia community of Marietta located just north of Atlanta,) the good Father took his leave from the military. Born and raised in the North Atlanta area, Father Ignatius knew most of the congregation that attended St. Ann's, and still claimed some relatives living in the area. It was not an easy decision to leave the military but with an ailing mother, the ministry of St. Ann's appeared to be the most prudent move to make at the time. And the congregation of St. Ann's opened their arms in gratitude for their new pastor whom they considered a part of the Marietta family.

It was a prophetic move to make at the time and as the years quickly slipped away, St. Ann's grew from a rural congregation of five hundred to a major Catholic community serving over seven thousand members as the physical church expanded to accommodate the growing congregation. A community center, gym and theatre with meeting halls and craft rooms were added to the church grounds, followed by a new rectory that housed the offices and living quarters for Father Ignatius. There was a separate wing that housed the four nuns who were assigned to the newly created St. Ann's School certified to teach children between the ages of five and fourteen. Under the guiding hand of Father Ignatius, the Catholic community of Marietta flourished and became a spiritual beacon for those of the faith. "Father Iggy," as he was sometimes lovingly referred to, (but not to his face,) encouraged community participation in the management of the various church activities throughout the area. There were community collections of money and clothes to aid the poor, a kitchen that served three meals each day to the elderly and homeless, and classes to help those needing help in preparing for job interviews and finding employment. Father Ignatius reached out his hand also to other denominations when they were in need and encouraged mutual civic responsibility. St. Ann's Parish was a model for all the other denominations in and around the Atlanta area.

As a man of vision, Father Ignatius knew how to relegate duties to those within the church ranks. "None of what we have accomplished here could have been done without the leadership I share with Mother Therese, our most capable and endearing partner in Christ," said the good father in a sermon acknowledging her twenty years of service at St. Ann's. It was truly most fortuitous the day when Mother Therese arrived at St. Ann's with a simple valise in hand and a heart she opened wide to the welfare of the entire community. It was her vision that laid the groundwork for the St. Ann's School; it was her vision for the charity works in which the church was so involved. Father Ignatius was always the first to give credit where credit was due.

Mother Therese, a woman of grace as well as unusual stature, stood just over six feet tall with piercing blue eyes and a smile that melted even the most immoveable adversaries when it came to getting things done within the community. "Never say 'never' to Mother Therese," warned Father Ignatius. He could never have foreseen the consequences of her unrelenting dedication to St. Ann's.

At the monthly gathering of the staff after Sunday evening mass, she said in her subtle manner, "I was thinking perhaps we could do something different this year for our Christmas pageant."

"But tradition dictates that we continue to present the usual Nativity play," offered Sister Barbara. "The community expects to see something in which the children can experience a living rendition of the marvelous birth of our Lord Jesus." She was not trying to be arbitrary; it was just her way of looking at issues from both sides of the coin.

"Oh, I wasn't suggesting that we change our program and eliminate the Nativity play, but wouldn't it be fun for the children if we could put on a production of the musical, *Annie*? And wouldn't it be a wonderful opportunity to include some of the parents in the adult roles where they could participate with the children? Of course, it was just a thought..."

Sister Barbara had to admit that it was a very ambitious idea. She looked to the other Sisters for their reaction and was not at all surprised at the positive feedback.

"We could do our usual presentation of the Nativity, say on Sunday evenings for three weeks prior to Christmas. Then, on Friday and Saturday evenings, over the Holiday season, we could also do our production of *Annie*..."

Father Ignatius was caught up in the enthusiasm of Mother Therese's idea. He visualized how such a project could possibly enhance the church's involvement in expanding new horizons in which the children could participate.

"Why don't we have another meeting on this very subject towards the end of the week? Sister Barbara, I'd like you to work with Mother Therese on this project. Two heads are always better than one and I'd like to hear what you both come up with..."

And so the idea of presenting a production of *Annie* took wings in the chapel of St. Ann's Parish one Sunday evening three months prior to Christmas. As was her penchant, Mother Therese decided to do a bit of creative casting, over and above what the authors of *Annie* had envisioned. Among the congregants was a ten-year-old girl with a voice that rocked the rafters of the chapel. Unfortunately, she didn't have red hair or fair skin, as did the original Annie on Broadway. This talented ten-year old was black. Not only could little Ethel Horn sing with the voice of an angel, but she could also carry the role with an innate acting talent to match her singing.

"She's black," reminded Sister Barbara. "The role of Annie specifically calls for a red-headed, fair Caucasian. That was the author's intent…"

"Where does it say anything about the author's intent in the script?" asked Mother Therese. "Annie is an orphan. What's to say she can't be a black orphan? What's to say that Daddy Oliver Warbucks can't be black, too? Or white, for that matter? What's color got to do with the meaning of the play? As I see it, it's a play about orphans, not race."

Sister Barbara had to think about that one. She backed down and decided to check the script. At the next meeting of the Sisters with Father Ignatius, the question of race was raised regarding the casting of the leading role of Annie. He took a minute to mull the idea over in his mind and when Mother Therese expounded on the talents of young Ethel Horn, Father Ignatius saw an opportunity to open wider the door of racial equality that had only been opened a crack since the Johnson administration back in the Sixties. There were still parts of the South that prided itself with closet racial discrimination that was only whispered among those diehard racists still fighting to enforce the obsolete Jim Crow laws. St. Ann's Parish was integrated, but only about ten percent of the congregation was black, another ten percent Hispanic. If there was closet discrimination among the congregation, it was never addressed in the presence of the priest or the nuns. What wasn't talked about openly in public did not exist; it was the law of the South.

Ethel Horn was cast in the role of Annie by unanimous decision among the nuns. Father Ignatius did not have a say; he never interfered with any issues over which the nuns presided. If there was an issue where the four nuns were deadlocked, Father Ignatius might be asked to cast the deciding vote…but only if asked. He was proud to think of St. Ann's as a democracy in which the five leaders of the church were equal participants.

Chapter 2

Adam Wicker was the father of twelve-year-old Amy Wicker and husband of Diane Wicker. From all outward appearances, the Wickers were a model of a perfect Southern family. Adam worked as a heavy equipment operator and when construction in the area flourished, he managed very nicely to support his family. But when work dried up, as it usually did in the winter months and Adam was unemployed, he became sullen with time on his hands and took to heavy drinking. He was a burly man with arms the size of small hams and a gut to match. During good times he could charm a snake from a tree, but in bad times, he was abusive to his wife, Diane, who knew from past experience how to avoid confrontation. Their daughter, Amy, was the light of Adam's eye. There wasn't anything in the world he wouldn't do for her.

Adam was not a churchgoer. He was a Southern Baptist married to a devout Catholic who would have left him years before had divorce not been against her religious beliefs. Adam had been laid off from work the week before the auditions for *Annie* and he had been hanging out at Duke's Bar & Grill, returning home late each evening tanked to the gills. The night of the audition, he hung out with friends, bragging about how his daughter was a shoo-in for the role of Annie in the church play and that everyone would be expected to attend or he'd "bust a few heads." It was all said in jest, but some of the patrons weren't so sure that Adam wasn't serious. When he was drinking heavily, he was ready to take on the world and there weren't very many patrons of Duke's Bar that would stand up to him and test his mettle. He promised Diane that he would be home early to celebrate his daughter being cast in the play. So when he arrived home about ten, his wife had worked herself up into a state of high anxiety. She was in fear of how Adam would react to his daughter's disappointing audition even though she'd been cast in a lesser role.

"Are you fucking with my head?" he shouted.

She hated when he used that language in the home for fear that Amy might hear. She tried to hush him and held out her hand to indicate that he should lower his voice but she could see from the expression on his face that he was out of control with disappointment. "It's only a school play. It's no big deal, honey," she tried to pacify him. "She got a really good supporting role…"

"She had her heart set on playing Annie. She told me so herself. The guys down at Duke's are all excited about her doing the play. I must have gotten two dozen requests for tickets for opening night…" He was working himself up into a state of rage. "Who'd they give it to? Who's gonna play Annie?" he demanded.

"One of the other children," she replied. She knew how he felt about the minorities in the community, how he ranted about them taking over the town and how they were sapping the workers with higher taxes to support their welfare rolls. She could see trouble rearing its ugly head.

"Who, damn it? Who got the role of Annie?" he exploded.

The door to Amy's room opened and rubbing the sleep from her eyes, Amy came into the kitchen. "Hi, Daddy," she said as she ran across the floor in her bare feet and he grabbed her up in his arms. "Did Mommy tell you I didn't get the part of Annie?"

"Yeah, I heard. Who'd they give it to?"

"Ethel. They gave it to Ethel."

"Ethel? What Ethel? You never talked about an Ethel. Do I know her?"

"She's in one of the classes behind me…in fifth grade."

"No way," he said, his eyes wide and disbelief written all over his face.

Diane reached out and took Amy from her father's arms. This was building to a bad scene and she didn't want Amy in harm's way. "C'mon, honey, back to bed. We can talk about this in the morning…" she said as she managed to extricate Amy from her father's grasp and headed towards the child's bedroom. They had no sooner cleared the kitchen door when Amy called out, "She's black, Daddy! They made Annie black!" she cried out.

Adam stood, stunned. He was sure Amy had made a mistake. "Hold on--" he shouted.

Diane froze in the hallway. There was no way she could avoid him.

"What did you say?" he asked.

"They gave the part of Annie to Ethel and she's not even white."

Adam looked at his wife. "You knew about this?" he asked, more of a threat than a question.

"It's no big deal, Adam," she said as she tried to maneuver towards the child's bedroom. He grabbed her by the arm. She tried to pull free from his grip but he was overpowering. "Please, Adam, you're hurting me…"

"I asked you a question. They cast a nigger in the role of a white girl and you don't tell me? You don't think I have a right to know?" His voice reached a booming pitch that bounced off the confined walls of the hallway. Amy got scared and began to whimper.

"Now see what you've done. You're scaring her," Diane scolded. She pulled away and he released his grip so as not to compromise the safety of the child. She passed on down the hallway to Amy's room. Diane placed the child on the bed and pulled a cover over her. She turned on the small television set near her bed so Amy could occupy her mind with something other than the ravings of her father. Once she was convinced that the child had settled down, she returned to the kitchen where Adam was stoking the fires of his outburst with half a glass from the whiskey bottle on the sideboard. His eyes were blazing. Diane cautiously entered the kitchen and when Adam saw her, he threw the glass against the wall, shards and liquid showering Diane where she stood. Then Adam reached out, grabbed the kitchen table by one end, and overturned it, smashing it against the kitchen sink. He cleared the counter of the dishes that were stacked for drying with one sweep of his arm as Diane cowered in the corner, covering her face with her hands, expecting the worst.

"You were there and you did nothing? Did you say anything to that priest of yours?" There came no reply. "She had her heart set on playing that part. How many hours did she rehearse those songs every evening for a month? And they cast a black kid? And you said nothing!" He glared at her, waiting for an explanation but none came. He wanted to strike out and beat the hell out of her for not standing up for her own daughter. "What the hell kind of mother are you?" he admonished as he turned and grabbed up the whiskey bottle from the sideboard as he stormed out of the house by the back door, almost wrenching it from its hinges.

~~~

He hadn't attended a Klan meeting in months. His father was a Klansman before him as were his two older brothers, but Adam was not a follower. He had been raised with the Klan's diatribes against blacks and Jews, but he dissented in their lackluster ways to do anything other than bellow and rage. He wanted to see some action like when he was a kid. He and four other white kids stoned a black student to death in the schoolyard. He did ten years in juvenile detention for participating in that act of violence and upon being released from incarceration, he came away as something of a hero within the Klan community. But the laws of the land were fast changing and the leaders of the movement were turning into "pussies" and "fairies" – afraid to take any overt actions against the minorities for fear of retaliation by the courts that were no longer soft where the Klan was concerned.

~~~

During the next few days following the results of the audition, Adam continued his verbal tirade, both at home and at Duke's Bar & Grill where he could count on the patrons for their sympathy and support. And having had her fill of Adam's abuse and fearing for her safety, Diane made plans.

Adam got a call from the union office about a temporary job for a few days where they needed a dozer operator to clear a lot in preparation for the construction of a super store. Whenever there was a job on the horizon, Adam had the sense to clean up his act, get home early and cut back on his drinking. So the first day on the job, he left the house at five in the morning, kissed his sleeping daughter goodbye, having no inkling that Diane had plans of her own. By eight o'clock, she had gotten Amy dressed, fed her breakfast, and taken her to the corner where some of the children congregated, waiting for the St. Ann's school bus.

"Now remember, I'll come for you after school. You wait for me, you hear?" she said.

"I can take the bus, Mommy," insisted Amy.

"Don't you have rehearsal for the play after school?" asked Diane.

"Oh, yeah, I forgot."

The bus arrived and she kissed her daughter. "Later," she said as the bus doors hissed shut and it headed on down the road.

With a single-mindedness of purpose, Diane returned to the house where she frantically began to pack. She couldn't possibly take all their possessions so she limited her packing to two bags of clothing and personal effects of her own and two cardboard boxes of clothes and possessions for Amy. She put a few odd things in the trunk of the Mustang, the bags and boxes in the limited space of the back seat and the passenger seat, and then made one final phone call.

"Hey, mom, it's me. Just wanted to let you know I'm on my way. You sure you're okay with this?"

Her mother was well aware of Diane's life with Adam but over the years she tried to encourage her daughter to work things out. After all, the marriage had lasted for over ten years and there was the issue of committing a sin in the eyes of the church that she had been strongly devoted to her whole life. But Diane threatened to find refuge in the public assistance program for battered women if her mother didn't step up to help. Together, they sought counsel from St. Ann's Program for Battered Women and the wheels had been set in motion to serve Adam with a court order prohibiting him from coming anywhere within a hundred yards of his wife and daughter. It was the hardest thing she had ever done in her thirty years but she knew in her heart that it would only be a matter of time before Adam would be out of control and possibly do physical harm to her and her daughter.

Chapter 3

The Aryan Knights of White Supremacy met on a bi-monthly schedule, usually with no other agenda than for the members to consume vast quantities of beer, get loud and disorderly, while reproaching the minority sector of the Marietta community. The weather had turned bitterly cold: ice and sleet covered the streets and homes in and around the southern community. Construction work on the new market had ground down to a halt and Adam again found himself unemployed. When he returned home to find his wife and daughter gone, he threw a fit. But the Sheriff's vehicle that pulled up to the house caused him to keep some sense of composure as he was served with a restraining order. He signed the receipt and stood in the doorway as the Sheriff's vehicle pulled away. The blast of cold air seemed to act as a buffer against all the anger and confusion whirling around in his head. He now turned his rage not only on his wife and her parents, but also on the staff of St. Ann's and the entire Catholic community. As he threw the legal order on the kitchen table he noticed the calendar hanging from the cabinet door with the date encircled with a bold red marker. Tonight was a bi-monthly meeting of the Knights.

~~~

The meeting was no sooner called to order than Adam was on his feet, venting his anger against the liberal acts of "the Priest and his bunch of whore nuns," and although the membership of fifteen sided with Adam, no one had an inkling as to what recourse there was within the law.

"We've got to watch our asses," said Roy Patterson, the horn holder. "You want us to take on the entire Catholic community because your kid didn't get the lead in a school play? C'mon, Adam, be reasonable…"

"You're missing the bigger picture here, Roy. It's not a play I'm talking about. We've got a small minority that's got enough influence among the mackerel snappers to rewrite plays to pacify the blacks. *Annie* was written for a white girl. What's next? Do they rewrite the classics? How about history? Don't you see where this is going?" he railed. He was on his feet, his face turned beet red, his arms flailing the air like a combine machine gone awry. The fifteen members in attendance agreed with Adam's argument but in reality, there wasn't much that could be done to rectify the dilemma. Were it an issue of the blacks supporting a political candidate of their choice in an election, making speeches and having public meetings to draw attention to their preference, the Knights were always ready to take the opposing side. They would assemble with their brown shirts with the lightning bolt emblems on their armbands and their flags of the Confederacy, all the while using bullhorns to disrupt whatever peaceful gathering drew the attention of the minority community. After all, the Knights had as much right to public access as any other entity in the community and the law gave them that protection. But the Knights had to be careful not to alienate the liberal press by appearing in an unfavorable light, even if a large number in the community quietly supported their cause. Whatever action the Knights took had to appear as if they were acting on behalf of that faction of the community that lacked and needed a voice. But no matter how it appeared, the casting of a black student in a school play just didn't warrant a full-scale Knight's demonstration that would support the cause of the white community. In the end, Adam's thesis fell short for lack of enthusiasm on the part of the Knight's membership. Adam's anger now turned on the Aryan Knights of White Supremacy. If they wouldn't take action, he would come up with something to make them get off their dead asses and act like men.

~~~

After the initial shock of Ethel Horn being cast in the role of Annie, the cast and community finally accepted the church's decision and rehearsals moved ahead. Mother Therese was pleasantly surprised at how well everyone was pitching in and how well the play was progressing. They had eight weeks before the first performance and the days just seemed to fly by with school in the mornings and afternoons, then rehearsals for the play with music and choreography in the early evenings and on weekends. Everyone was excited about the sketches that Sister Margaret, "the artistic nun," did for the costumes. It was turning into a major production and with only weeks left to go before the first performance, most of the tickets had already been purchased or reserved. The money would be put into St. Ann's account to support the homeless and provide meals for the needy. It was an ambitious project and one could feel the excitement in the air upon entering the church for mass or attending classes in the center.

The Friday afternoon of the preview performance of *Annie* was filled with electric vibes that permeated the entire community. Mother Therese had performed a minor miracle in putting together such a competent cast that was turning in a performance beyond everyone's wildest imagination. No longer was there a question of Annie's racial ethnicity; tiny, vibrant, talented Ethel Horn was most definitely Annie. Everyone was keyed up in anticipation of the seven o'clock curtain that would mark a milestone at St. Ann's Parish. The bitter cold December evening did nothing to dampen the enthusiasm of the first night audience.

The theatre in the community center was quite intimate, consisting of fifteen rows of twenty seats with an aisle down the center. The three hundred seats for all the performances of *Annie* sold out as soon as the local press released the news of the show. Friday evening, three weeks before Christmas, Mother Therese circulated backstage wishing all the children and adult members of the cast "good luck" and took a moment to say a short prayer of thanks to God for "His bountiful blessings." She had made the decision to leave the preview night to Sister Margaret

The Guardian List

and the other nuns who had worked so diligently to make *Annie* a success.

While the nuns circulated backstage attending to the cast's costumes and the technical people who would work the lights and the sound, Mother Therese entered the theatre and took her seat on the aisle of the third row. Next to her was the mother of Ethel Horn, Riva, and her husband Ernest, and two of their older children.

Opening night curtain was only minutes away as the usher, Danny Whittingham, looked at the full house from his position at the rear door. He was a tall man, built like a basketball player with a sculptured, friendly face. The arriving audience had dwindled to a few latecomers as Danny was preparing to shut the doors. Only one more late arrival could be seen approaching as he stood by the door. Danny had seen this person before although he couldn't quite place him. As Adam Wicker entered the outer door dressed in a full overcoat, he headed for the door where Danny held out his hand to receive one more ticket. But instead of producing a ticket, Adam removed a twelve-gauge shotgun from under the cover of his coat and at point blank range, he fired one shot into the chest of Danny Whittingham, killing him instantly.

The sound of the blast of the shotgun drew some of the spectators from their seats, some stepping into the aisle to see what was going on. But Adam Wicker moved like a man possessed, pumping the shotgun and ejecting the spent shell, reloading and pushing people aside as he made his way down the aisle. He stopped next to where Mother

Therese was seated. Without uttering a word, he raised the shotgun and fired once into her head, pumped again and fired another shot at the Horn family. He turned, pumped the weapon again, and in a split second, as he was looking for another target, two of the larger male members of the congregation jumped Adam from behind before he could get off another shot and wrestled him to the ground. In the melee, the gun discharged with shot hitting a number of members of the audience.

In a moment, three other members joined in to subdue the physically powerful Adam, pummeling him with their fists, attempting to beat him into submission. Members of the audience were running for the nearest exits, some of the women were screaming and a number of children were crying. One of the men removed his pant's belt and as the other men held Adam, they secured his hands behind his back. Another belt was produced to tie his feet as he kicked and bucked like a raging bull.

By the time Sheriff Curran arrived, the theatre had emptied, most of the audience standing in the freezing cold outside the center. He took a moment to view the remains of Danny Whittingham, a longtime friend and classmate going back some thirty years. There was nothing anyone could do for the dead usher. The Sheriff moved on down the aisle, maneuvering between victims sprawled in various positions while other members attended to their wounds. He made his way to where a small group of men stood around the prostrate, hog-tied form of Adam Wicker who had been beaten into unconsciousness.

The Guardian List

    Mother Therese was being held by Father Ignatius who was gently rocking her back and forth, impervious to the sea of blood that covered his vestment, incanting a prayer for the dead as tears streamed down his face. Little Ethel Horn leaned over from the row behind to comfort her mother who was bleeding profusely from her face and neck as her husband, also wounded, was trying to calm her. The sounds of crying could be heard from some of the members backstage as well as the gathered audience outside.

    Sheriff Curran got on his portable phone and called for police support as well as medical assistance from one of the North Atlanta hospitals. A number of other audience members that were not lying in the aisle had remained in their seats and were suffering from superficial wounds from the shotgun pellets that had been fired when Adam Wicker had been taken down. The carnage inside the theatre was the worst Sheriff Curran had ever encountered in all his years in his service to the community.

    Father Ignatius had all he could do to keep some semblance of calm among the cast and crew in the backstage area. He asked the members of the congregation to pray for the soul of Mother Therese and those who had been victimized by this random act of violence. He turned his attention to the twelve-year-old Amy Wicker who appeared dazed, her eyes fixated, unblinking, as if unaware of what was happening all around her. Her mother knelt by Amy's chair, held her hand and covered her with kisses of comfort.

How would this child ever survive this terrible ordeal? thought the Priest. *To go through the rest of her life with this scar brought about by this dreadful deed of her father would be forever insufferable.*

Chapter 4

The news coverage of the St. Ann's massacre was covered on the front page of the *New York Times. The Daily News* carried the story along with a graphic photo of Father Ignatius with his arms encompassing the deceased nun, the tears cascading down his face. John Brown could not put down the paper. He was mesmerized with the photo of the grieving priest. The longer he stared at the tormented face and tear-filled eyes before him, his mission became clear.

It was a month since the tragedy at St. Ann's Parish. The rental car, a black Mercedes sedan, pulled into the parking lot between the church and the community center. John Brown emerged from the car, retrieved his topcoat from the hook by the rear door, draped the coat over his shoulders and headed for the side door of the sanctuary. He could see an acre of flowers and religious icons lining the fence along the front and side of the church. He stopped at the side door to momentarily view the floral offerings of the community, some fresh and others wilted from the passage of time. He could not help but feel touched by the ongoing display of charity. He felt his throat constrict in sympathy with the bereaved. He removed a handkerchief from his pocket, touched it to his eyes, gently blew his nose and headed for the side door.

Inside the building, to the right of the door, was a glass window behind which was seated a receptionist. She looked up as John approached. "May I help you?" she asked through the hole in the glass window that separated them. On the counter on her side of the window was a placard with the name Dolores Sutton. She was a slightly overweight woman close to middle age with a pleasant smile and demeanor. She appeared to be a lay person; definitely not a nun.

John moved up to the window and spoke inches away through the circular hole. "I was wondering if I might have a few moments with Father Ignatius," he asked.

"Do you have an appointment?"

"I'm afraid not. I was passing through the area on my way to Atlanta and when I saw the sign, Marietta, I realized that this is where that terrible disaster took place…"

"You're a tourist?" she asked with no small amount of disappointment.

"Oh, no, I wouldn't be so insensitive to impose upon Father Ignatius at a time like this," he attempted to explain. "My mission is more of one who would like to offer my services to the church in the form of a small donation. If I could have a few moments with the good Father to determine what would be adequate to help out at this time…"

"If you like, I can give you one of the envelopes we use for donations at the end of each mass."

"I was thinking of something a bit more substantial than a weekly contribution. If the good Father could spare me a few moments of his time..."

Dolores had to think about this for a moment. It had been less than a week since the halls and surrounding area outside the church had been flooded with a constant flow of strangers stopping by to pay their respects. Now, as things were getting back to normal there was still a good amount of tension and curiosity about strangers on the part of the community. Dolores looked up at John Brown, regarded his gentle smile, the crinkly lines around his eyes and mouth and decided that he looked harmless enough. She picked up the phone and buzzed the adjacent office. In a very subdued tone she explained to Father Ignatius the request of the gentleman at the reception desk. After a few moments, she hung up the phone.

"If you don't mind waiting, Father Ignatius will be with you shortly."

There were no seats in the hallway so John bided his time looking at some of the sketches the children had produced that were on exhibition and taped to the walls. Many depicted childish renditions of Mother Therese as she ascended to heaven with Christ holding out his hand to receive her. Some of the drawing were very insightful and had obviously been influenced by some of the teaching staff, capable of bringing out the talents of their tutelage. After a few moments, the office door swung open and the Priest came into the hallway, his hand extended in greeting.

"I'm Father Ignatius," he said as he shook the hand of his visitor.

"John Brown." The Priest furrowed his brow. John immediately picked up on the priest's show of skepticism. "No, really, that's my name, although you're not the first to question it. Can you spare a few moments, Father?"

"Please, come into my office…"

He lead the way past the reception desk and into a rather austere office with minimal amenities —a simple, old-fashioned, wooden school desk and chair, a worn leather couch showing signs of age, two straight-back guest chairs, a simple glass-top coffee table in front of the couch, and a high-boy cabinet cluttered with books, file folders, and a few academic and sport awards. The Priest motioned for John to take a seat across from him in front of the desk as he relieved John of his topcoat and placed it over the back of the other chair. As he settled into his place, he leaned back and folded his hands over his slightly paunchy stomach.

"I read about your ordeal some time ago and wanted to contact you sooner, but the timing just didn't seem right. First, let me say how sorry I was to learn of the unfortunate demise of Mother Therese. From all accounts, she appeared to have been something of a saint in her dedication to this church and the community…"

"Thank you for your considerate thoughts, Mr. Brown. I doubt that St. Ann's will ever recover from the loss."

"I was deeply touched when I read about your family here at St. Ann's Parish. I felt a compulsion to contribute in some small way to the memory of Mother Therese, if you think it would be appropriate." He reached into his jacket pocket and produced a plain, white envelope that he carefully placed on the edge of the desk and gently pushed it to within reach of the priest. "I hope this will help to continue the work to which Mother Therese was so dedicated…"

Father Ignatius looked at the envelope without making a move to retrieve it. *Is this some trick, some bribe leading up to some illegal act?* He looked across at his guest, questioningly. John merely nodded as if to say, 'go ahead.' The priest picked up the envelope and held it in his hand as if trying to ascertain the contents by its weight. Finally, realizing the envelope was not sealed, he flipped up the flap to reveal its contents. He was momentarily stunned and caught off guard.

"That's a great deal of money, Mr. Brown," he said without counting the contents. The envelope was filled to capacity with hundred dollar bills, probably close to ten thousand dollars, the priest surmised.

"Did you know Mother Therese, Mr. Brown? I mean, had you known her previously before she took her vows?"

"No, sir…"

"Are you a member of our church? I know it's an absurd question since I know most of our congregants but once in a while someone quietly attends, preferring anonymity."

"I'm not from around here, Father. Let's just say that it's my small way of offering my condolences."

"Well, I can assure you that candles will be lit as a blessing to you. Is there anything our small parish can do for you?"

"I know this may sound a bit bizarre, but I have business in Atlanta after which I'll be heading north. I was wondering if you would do me the honor of dining with me this evening. My curiosity abounds and there are many questions on my mind."

"Are you a reporter, Mr. Brown?"

"Hardly. Just your average, retired business man who was fortunate enough to have had some financial success and now I find it rewarding to share my good fortune with some of those less fortunate."

"I would have to say that you're a very generous individual, Mr. Brown…"

"Please, Father, call me John."

"As you wish. What time will you be passing back this way, may I ask?"

"Would seven this evening be convenient?"

"I think I could manage that. We have a very good restaurant at the Marietta Country Club to which I have an open invitation. I'll have our secretary confirm a reservation…"

The two men rose in unison, John retrieved his coat from the other chair and together they walked out of the office. "Dolores, would you call the Club and make a reservation for two for seven-thirty this evening?"

"Yes, Father…"

They walked out of the reception area, down the hall to the exterior door where Father Ignatius stopped and offered his hand. "I'm looking forward to our dinner this evening. I'm sure I have an equal number of questions as to your visit."

They shook hands, John exited the rectory, and the Priest watched him as he headed for his parked Mercedes. There was something mysterious about this stranger that had the priest's curiosity running wild. Who walks in off the street without so much as a phone call or appointment and hands over to a stranger that much money? *Dinner will indeed be most interesting*, he thought.

~~~

The Catholic community at large rarely took time to consider what went on in the inner depths, the deepest thoughts that percolated within the mind of a parish priest. It was a foregone conclusion that in times of emotional strife, the good Father merely turned to God for advice and consolation. That's what priests were trained to do. After all, a priest was first a messenger of God and second, a man. His emotions had been tempered with his faith and devotion. He did not react or feel the same way that lay people did. It was just assumed that Father Ignatius merely turned to God to ease the gut-wrenching pain he endured upon the death of his sister in Christ, Mother Therese.

No one could ever imagine the possibility that the good Father could carry a deep-seated hatred so imbedded in his heart that it monopolized his waking hours and deprived him of his nightly repose and sleep. He prayed. He asked God's forgiveness for the evil thoughts that dominated his consciousness. He said ten, twenty, fifty Hail Mary's each day to atone for his sin of hating the man who took the life of the nun who for twenty years shared his theology and his devotion to God. Had they not been married to their devotion to God and the church, in lay terms, they would surely have found each other in a more personal relationship.

In the month since her passing, Father Ignatius had weighed, day and night, his earthly, personal passions against his devotion and religious vows. He could not reconcile one with the other. He could not, in good conscience, preach from the pulpit about the goodness and forgiving nature of God when he himself was wracked with hatred. It was time, he concluded. He would leave the ministry. He had been in the process of formulating his resignation to the Bishop when John Brown paid him that first visit.

Chapter 5

The sixty-eight year old therapist, known only as John Brown among the members of the Society, had never been associated directly with law enforcement. He had been a very successful printer by trade, making his fortune mostly in the legal field. The Supreme Printing Company, located a few blocks west of the Village, had the distinction of printing almost every major legal brief in the New York City court system. Like most of the Society members, he was widowed with very few personal responsibilities or obligations. His wife had died in her late sixties of cancer that had been genetically prevalent in her family.

He spoke sporadically to his three children that were spread out across the country. Their occupations determined their geographic preferences; the eldest boy was a lawyer with a Chicago firm, the second son worked in Silicon Valley in California, and the youngest, a daughter, was serving with the Armed Forces and preparing to ship out for Iraq. John thought how fortunate he was not to be living in close proximity to his kids and their families where his activities, his constant traveling and unusual hours, could be subject to question or scrutiny. If one were to research the name of the founder of the Supreme Printing

Company, the name of John Brown would not be in evidence in the company's history.

Contrary to his physical appearance, (one might say slightly corpulent), Martin Wolfson was quite agile for a man of his sixty-eight years. He possessed unusual talents as an organizer with a unique ability and penchant to get the job done. He was tenacious when it came to finishing what he started with an almost hypnotic single-mindedness. He had always been politically motivated, having donated large sums of money to candidates of his choosing. In return, the political contacts and their court affiliations were the financial source behind the success of John's business. "Like casting bread upon the waters," he would muse. Within ten years of the end of the Korean War, he had expanded the one room, single press operation to include ownership of the three-story building with twenty presses operating on a 24/7 schedule.

It was this same political activist who conceived of "the list." His accomplishments in his field were unique, but as he watched the years slip away, experiencing the early passing of his wife, along with numerous friends and associates, there grew in him an urgency to accomplish something beyond his wildest imagination, something so bizarre and exceptional, that for the longest time he doubted his ability to pull it all together, doubted whether his organizational talents were so refined and developed that he could possibly make it work. He had always considered himself a man of the law. He paid his taxes religiously, never got a speeding ticket or traffic violation in the fifty years he was licensed to drive, never used drugs, and was a model citizen in every sense of the word.

Only one isolated incident that happened outside the law haunted him for some thirty years. It occurred almost ten years after his wife, Monique, gave birth to their third child. She was a beautiful woman who attracted the attention of a twenty-four year old box-boy at the local supermarket, Danny Wilder. Danny was a quiet kid, one of those people that blended in with the crowd, someone who no one would normally notice as he went about his daily chores of restocking shelves and packing groceries. But Danny was, in truth, a disturbed young man with a wild imagination and the first time he set eyes on Monique Wolfson he could not get her out of his mind. There had been other women about whom he had fantasies but this one was special. She was tall and rangy with good looks and a Madonna-like smile and she greeted the clerks behind the checkout counter as if they were old friends. On numerous occasions, Danny had assisted Mrs. Wolfson with her groceries by pushing her shopping cart out to where she parked her Cadillac. He helped her unload the cart and place the bags onto the passenger seat, all the while taking the precaution of not letting his eyes rest too long on her full bosom or making eye contact. She always tipped him generously and always with that same infectious smile. It wasn't long before he became possessed with the idea of having her. He stalked her...and when the timing was just perfect, he struck.

The police were convinced that Mrs. Wolfson knew her assailant, but she refused to cooperate with the authorities. The case was finally closed for lack of the victim's cooperation. She had been in fear for her life and the safety of her children had she revealed the identity of the man who entered her home through the open back door while Martin was at work and the children were with their sitter in the park. The police were right — Monique did know the identity of her assailant and only after an extended period of psychiatric care was she able to reveal to her loving husband the identity of her rapist. Only her husband, Martin Wolfson, shared her knowledge of the identity of her assailant and quietly, in his own meticulous way, he hunted down Danny Wilder and killed him. There was never any association between the dead rapist and the Wolfson family, no trail that could possibly lead them to Martin Wolfson. The entire incident was taken with her to the grave when she finally passed.

The day he conceived of "the list," it scared Wolfson beyond his wildest imagination. "Are you nuts?" he asked himself out loud. "What kind of a depraved mind could ever entertain such an idea?" But upon careful evaluation he was able to conclude that the idea was not his alone but an accumulation of ideas born of a legal system that in many ways was near to inept, powerless, weak, and riddled with corruption. The law lacked teeth, gumming its way through the unlawful elements of the society and at the same time, permitting those with money and power to function outside its boundaries. For as many who were apprehended, tried, and convicted, there was a whole population functioning outside the restrictions of the system who thumbed their noses at the concept of an effective legal system. Over the years he had accumulated a mental list of numerous offenders who could and did manipulate the system. The idea of meting out justice to those who circumvented the principles of the law was an exciting concept in the mind of Wolfson, now John Brown, the man who lived a duplicitous life.

For a full year prior to taking the first step to implement the concept of "the list" he devoted hours to the documented creation of the fictitious John Brown. He was amazed at how simple it was. With access to court records and secreted government documents, Wolfson meticulously created the documented, living person of John Brown. He was able to duplicate forms and legal documents thereby giving life to his fictitious creation. The difficult part would come later, the part where he had to sell his idea to people that had a predilection to send a message to those in the system that violated the concept of the law to protect the weak and disenfranchised.

That's when Wolfson turned to the priest, Father Ignatius.

Chapter 6

If John Brown had miscalculated, he could be telling the priest more than he wished to divulge to anyone on the outside. The dinner at the Country Club had been excellent. Their small talk had been intended to break the ice to where John could find an opening where he could broach the very sticky subject in question. It was over coffee and a light dessert that John was able to maneuver the conversation to open the door.

"I know this may be very personal, Father, but I was wondering if you had found forgiveness in your heart towards Adam Wicker for the crime he had committed."

"You're right, John. That is very personal. I don't know you well enough to give you any insight into my personal theology. Let us just say that I am still working on it."

"I understand." John took a sip of coffee and savored the bitter taste. "If someone were to tell you something outside the protection of the confessional, would it still be considered confidential? I mean, by virtue of the fact that you're still a priest, whether within the sanctity of the church, or outside in the real world, you still would be sworn to secrecy. Isn't that a fact, Father?"

"There is a fine line between the confessional and 'the real world' as you refer to it. Are you a Catholic?"

John repressed a smile. "No, Father. I am what might be referred to as a disenfranchised, rabid Jew."

This was a new one on the priest. He could not refrain from smiling. "Now I think I've heard it all…"

"I don't follow the Jewish faith, haven't for some years. I married a woman who was a non-Jewess and we had a lasting and loving relationship for her entire life without any religious intervention. I've tried to live a moral existence. I've worked hard, I was faithful to my wife, and when we had money we tried to help those who were less fortunate. I guess in my own way I'm a religious person."

"I'd have to agree, John, although in the eyes of the church you've denied God and that in and of itself is a mortal sin."

"Then I guess I plead guilty."

"I understand the part about being disenfranchised, but what in the world is a 'rabid Jew?' I understand orthodox, conservative, and reform, but 'rabid' escapes me."

"Quite simply, let anyone say anything against the Jews and I respond like a mad dog."

Father Ignatius smiled. He expected nothing less from this man who sat across the table. "You understand that I cannot hear your confession outside the faith. It's just not done. As for anything you feel you would like to tell me, I would have to weigh its severity before I could decide if it comes under Canon Law. It's a very fine point wherein I cannot give a non-Catholic absolution or forgiveness, nor can I guarantee the sanctity of the confessional…"

"I understand, Father, so let's just say that I have a hypothetical case. Someone I know committed a heinous act many years ago. Since that time he has carried around the guilt of his crime that has weighed heavily on his conscience for decades. Could you hear the details without divulging to the authorities what is said across a dinner table?"

"What you're suggesting has nothing to do with religion but rather a personal confession better reserved for a psychiatrist? Has your friend sought help in the medical field?"

"No, not really. He's torn between his guilt and the satisfaction that what he did was justified." *The moment of truth,* he thought. "He killed a man in cold blood. It was an act of revenge. The victim was a rapist who violated my friend's wife."

"Didn't the law intercede?"

"I won't bore you with the details, Father.

Needless to say, justice is served in many ways. My friend did what had to be done outside the law…"

"I believe it's called 'vigilantism.' We avoid depending on the mob mentality to avenge wrongs we think the law is incapable of handling. We have courts for that very purpose."

"I agree with you." *Now, here's the tricky part,* he thought. "Adam Wicker committed such a heinous act that it's almost impossible to comprehend what penalty the court could mete out to wipe the slate clean. What would be justice in this case? A nun is dead; the church usher is dead, the mother of little Amy is dead, numerous members of the congregation have been severely maimed for life, and a twelve year-old child will suffer for the rest of her life knowing that her father was responsible for this horrendous massacre.

"Tell me, Father, how will the courts balance the scale? First, this trial will go on for years at the cost of millions of dollars to the taxpayers, monies that could be used to feed the poor, or ease the suffering of the infirmed, or alleviate some of the pressures on our under-funded schools. Oh, yes, some people will defend the system because we're a civilized society. We don't take the law into our own hands. We're above that kind of caveman mentality, but if Adam Wicker were to perish tomorrow, believe me, aside from the clergy and a few greedy defense attorneys, no one in all of Marietta would shed a single tear..."

Father Ignatius had lost his appetite. He pushed the dessert plate away after having had only one spoonful. He knew in his rational mind that what John Brown was advocating was not only against man and God's law, but a violation of everything he believed in for his entire adult life. *So why,* he asked himself, *is John Brown making so much sense? Why in the deepest recess of my being do I long to see Adam Wicker dead?*

Chapter 7

Marge Linden worked out of the North Side of the LVMPD; the Las Vegas Municipal Police Department. She hated desk duty but with the shortage of officers, the policy of "rotation" had been implemented to serve the community as well as the force. Both the Mayor and Governor had promised additional funds during their most recent elections, but to date, neither was able to find funding that would increase the number of officers on the street. Marge had been with the department for six years, a novice compared to some of her fellow officers who had been serving well over fifteen to twenty years and had priority when it came to choice of duty.

Marge was a transplant having moved to Vegas when her marriage dissolved some ten years before. "Irreconcilable differences" was the basis for her divorce when, in truth, her husband took to heavy drinking, abusive language, and threats of physical abuse towards the end of their five-year coupling. He had lost his management position with a company that was downsizing as a result of the negative turn in the economy and unable to find employment, he took to hanging out with "the boys" until late at night. He would return home tanked to the gills, unable to face Marge with the bad news that another day had passed without finding even the most menial job. Marge's salary as a schoolteacher in the New York City school system afforded them a meager lifestyle, but after almost two years of watching her husband on the skids, they agreed to go their separate ways before they came to blows. They both agreed it was for the best and they parted as good friends.

At the end of the school year, Marge headed out to Las Vegas to stay with a girlfriend, Patty Walsh, a high school friend who was now serving with the Las Vegas Metropolitan Police Department. With prodding from Patty over a period of a couple of months, Marge decided to take the test for the police department and passed with flying colors with a bit of coaching from Patty. Now, at the age of thirty-five, Marge not only served with distinction, but she managed to gain the respect of her fellow officers as well as her superiors. Patty moved on to the San Francisco Police Department after deciding that the extreme heat of the Vegas summers was not to her liking, but like family, the girls kept in touch almost on a daily basis, either by phone or over the Internet.

Marge was a most attractive woman who took great pride in her physical appearance. She worked out at the gym three or four times a week, ran five miles each morning before breakfast with a couple of fellow officers (misery loves company they agreed), and although she was not a true vegan, she avoided the intake of any four-legged animals and ate a rounded diet of salad, vegetables, fruit, chicken, and fish. Her five-foot, eight-inch frame was well proportioned and every male officer on the West Side, married or single, had at one time or another fantasized what it would be like to bed her down at least one time. Her sandy-colored hair and her bronze colored complexion (she loved the sun) was almost "model perfect" and she drew more than a few turned heads when on duty outside the office.

~~~

It was a combination of uppers, grass, and Black Jack that pushed Arturo Bienvenides over the edge. In a drug-induced rage, at two in the a.m., he kicked in the door to his estranged wife's apartment, staggered into her bedroom where he raped and then beat her to death. In the haze that enveloped his mind, he could hear the whimpering of an infant child and as he backed away from the prostrate figure on the floor, he crashed into the crib, overturning it, causing his two month old daughter to be thrown against the wall, resulting in her instant death.

He staggered out the front door, past a small group of neighbors that had been aroused by the late night disturbance. Someone had called 9-1-1. Bienvenides staggered across the courtyard to where he had abandoned his Honda Accord in the parking area. Leaning against the car he fumbled in his pocket for the keys and as he climbed into the vehicle and gunned the engine, he crashed headlong into a carport support, knocking himself unconscious. The police had no trouble in apprehending him.

The trial lasted six weeks. Bienvenides was found guilty of breaking and entering, rape, assault, and second-degree murder. Because he had been intoxicated and under the influence of drugs, the jury found that there were extenuating circumstances and convicted him to serve ten years in Nevada State Prison in Carson City. The year was 1998.

In a review process, eight years later in 2006, the name of Arturo Bienvenides was added to the Guardian list.

~~~

Anthony Canu could not hold his liquor. That's why when out on the town with his fellow officers, his drink of choice was Ginger Ale from which he swore he got a buzz. It was almost ten in the morning when he entered the station and headed straight for Marge's cubicle. She was on the phone so he leaned on the partition waiting for her to finish.

"What's up?" she asked as she hung up.

"Have you seen this morning's paper?"

"You see this desk?" It was loaded with clutter. "I haven't had time to read a paper in a week. How much longer before the Captain is going to cut us loose? I've got bed sores from this desk chair…"

Anthony handed her a section of the day's paper with the obit face up so it would immediately catch her attention. She looked down and at first didn't see it. Then she focused in on one article and as she read, she could feel lightness overcome her and she fought to hold back the tears.

"Oh, my God," she exclaimed. "I spoke to him just two days ago. He was doing fine. His caretaker said he was getting stronger every day but that the impending trial had him on edge…"

"It was a massive heart attack," said Anthony.

Marge read the obit over again as if it was a mistake. She had known Henning since she first joined the Department. He had been long retired by the time she joined the force, but ever since the death of his wife some five years before, he had found meaning to his life as he volunteered for desk duty where he answered phones, filed papers, and did light clerical chores. The department was only too glad to have him on site where he was eager to give advice based on his expertise.

He had put in forty years on active duty, having joined the force as a rookie when he was thirty, and had been recognized many times over for his leadership and courage. He rose through the ranks and retired with a comfortable pension that afforded him and his wife, Bess, the opportunity to undertake many of the activities they had planned on over the years. Travel stood out at the top of the list and early on they decided that every year, upon his retirement, they would take a trip to some far off location. They began with China. The following year they visited Russia, followed by Australia and New Zealand. For one month each year, for six years, they traveled and for the remaining eleven months of the year, they planned.

The Guardian List

The whole travel concept was a bond that drew them closer together. His job of forty years of service had often created a strain on their marriage and more than a few times they had come close to separating, but there were the children to take into consideration – one girl and two boys. And when they finally overcame the pressures of his erratic hours, his sleepless nights brought on by the burden of responsibility, the loneliness each endured in their own charge, there was finally the relief and joy of experiencing the fruits of their labors.

Then, without warning, Bess took ill and was diagnosed with terminal cancer. They continued to travel as long as her strength allowed, but finally, the drugs and chemo took their toll and in the end, she was confined to hospice where within months she passed in her sleep.

Bob Henning had always been a strong, devoted individual, both to work and family, when suddenly he was set adrift in a sea of loneliness, alienated from the one person closest to him. In the final years of Bess's life, they had bonded in such a way where they complimented each other's opinions, likes and dislikes. With Bess gone, Bob felt he had been reduced to half a person. His waking hours were filled with memories that weighed him down like great encumbrances that he was unable to shake. He isolated himself from his children and grandchildren. He knew that he had become morose and he wanted to avoid inflicting his negativity on those closest to him. He avoided family gatherings, birthdays and communions, even funerals when they occurred within the family circle. He found his only relief was within the portals of the station where he had spent the better part of his active life. Those with whom he came in contact respected his solitude and gave him leeway to come and go on his own recognizance.

Although he had long been retired when Marge signed on with the department, she had picked up tidbits of information about Henning's background from some of the older members who knew the Captain during his years as an active leader. Marge could only surmise that her morbid curiosity regarding Captain Henning had to do with the uncanny resemblance he had to her deceased father who had perished in the 9/11 attack on the New York Trade Center. Her father stood two inches over six feet and carried himself with a military posture, quite similar to the Captain. Her father was trim of build and maintained a full head of hair that only began to show signs of graying in his later years. He had a way of shutting out the world when he focused on a subject at hand. Marge saw many of the same characteristics in Captain Henning who usually sat alone and isolated from the mainstream of officers. There were greetings but rarely did she see anyone stop at his table and offer up the time of day. She was barely three months on the force, taking her turn at desk duty, and as she was gathering up the remnants from her lunch to deposit in the trash, she noticed Henning seated alone on her way to the door.

"Good afternoon, Captain," she offered with a smile.

He looked up from his plate with a note of surprise. "Officer..." he said with a puzzled expression on his face. "We've met?" he asked.

"Oh, no, sir. But I see you here almost every day and since I'm new on the force, I thought I'd introduce myself. I'm Marge Linden," she said.

Henning was slightly caught off guard. He couldn't think of anything brilliant to offer. "Bob Henning. I'm retired," he said. That seemed to end the conversation.

"I'm still on probation," she said almost apologetically. "I never imagined how tedious it would be until I get assigned to permanent duty..."

He smiled revealing a bit of irony. "I was there just a short time ago myself, young lady. You just have to hitch up your drawers and tell yourself that tomorrow you'll be out there with the best bunch of police officers that ever graced this fine city. The optimum word is 'patience'."

"I guess so," she replied. She stole a glance at the wall clock. "Well, I'd better be getting back to my station. It's nice talking to you, Captain," she offered as she turned and with a cross between a wave and a half salute she headed out the door. Little did she realize how much she had brightened the day of Captain Bob Henning.

~~~

Over the next few years Henning became a mentor to Marge Linden and whenever an issue of department policy was not clear, she turned to the elder officer for his opinion and council. Henning thrived on the attention of the young officer, looking forward to the times when they would run into each other in the cafeteria or at a workstation. But theirs was a casual relationship and never did the eighty-two year old Henning contemplate crossing over the line of propriety. He was not impervious to Marge's sexuality and at night, when he stared blankly into the empty space of his loneliness, he visualized the similarities between young Marge and his departed wife, Bess, who possessed many of the same physical characteristics during her early years. There was warmth in the knowledge that Marge had been desirous to offer him the courtesy of his past rank without ever taking advantage of his position in the hierarchy of retired police officers. But Henning was not oblivious to his own actual loneliness and loss and it was during these flights that he contemplated just what it would be like to pack it all in, to call it a day.

~~~

The sound of the ringing phone shattered his reverie and he had to think for a moment where he had placed the portable instrument. He hoisted himself out of the comfort of his easy chair and followed the sound to where it emanated on the kitchen counter. "Henning here…" he answered with his usual formality.

"Good evening, Robert," greeted the familiar voice on the other end of the line. "It's been a while. How are you getting on?"

Henning had been contemplating when this call would come and if he was ready to enter into a dialogue with the party on the other end of the line. "I'm well," he managed to report. "I was thinking about you just the other day."

"Were you now," said the caller. "And what was it you were thinking?"

"Well, sir, I was thinking that perhaps it's getting close to that time."

"How is your health, Robert?"

"The usual. The arthritis is still acting up along with the enlarged prostate. I haven't had a good night's sleep in a couple of years but one adjusts…"

"It's probably no consolation but you're in good company…" The caller took a pause and then he asked, "Do you think it might be time for therapy, Robert?"

That was the key word that would open the door to worldly relief. "It could very well be about that time. I can't imagine there will be a turnaround in the foreseeable future."

"You're probably right. Would you like for me to set up an appointment to speak to a therapist?"

There's no use putting it off, he thought. "That's probably a good idea."

"Fine. I know you're doing the right thing, Robert. We all have to face up to it sooner or later. It's comforting to know that we have control over our final destiny. We should all think in terms of moving on with dignity."

"Yes, I do believe that sums it up."

"I'll arrange for a therapist to get in touch with you within the next few days, if that meets with your schedule."

"I believe that would be fine. I'll look forward to hearing from him."

"Be well, Robert...and God bless you."

"Thank you," he said as the phone went dead in his hand. He hoped he had made the right decision. He knew there would be no turning back.

~~~

Eight years in the state penitentiary had done nothing to reform Arturo Bienvenides. No sooner had he gone through the clearing process and walked out of the administration building, he headed straight for Vegas. All he thought about for eight years was getting a fix and latching onto some whore with whom he could relieve some pent-up desires. But first he needed to make a score. He needed money and he needed it fast. The prison authority had provided him with a one-way bus ticket to Vegas and the address of a halfway house where he could flop until he could find a job.

As he stepped from the bus, he could feel the evening summer heat almost overwhelm him. Carson City had seasons but they were unlike Vegas where it was either too damn hot or too damn cold. But the action was what he craved, what he needed most. He walked the streets of the downtown area just a few minutes from the Strip. In a local strip mall just a few blocks from the Greyhound terminal he found an all night Speedee Mart. Through the window he could see the clerk behind the counter wearing a *kaffiyeh*, a traditional Arab turban. *This will be easy*, he thought to himself, as he walked around to the rear of the building in search of a dumpster.

In a box a few feet from the rear door of the Mart were a number of bottles stacked for recycling. He picked up one that would do the trick. Looking around to be sure that he wasn't being observed, he wrapped the neck of the bottle in a few sheets of discarded newspaper to protect his hand in case it shattered. Then he brought the bottle down on the edge of the dumpster. What remained in his hand was as lethal a weapon as he could contrive. He returned to the front of the building. There were no customers inside the Mart at this late hour, so he casually entered holding the jagged bottle down by his side and out of sight. The clerk was leaning on the counter going over an inventory list and paid him no mind. Arturo walked to the cold locker, took out a beer and headed for the counter at the front of the store. Then, as swiftly and as stealthily as a cat, he slipped behind the counter and was on the clerk before he was aware of the danger.

Holding the jagged shard of the bottle up to the clerk's neck, he ordered, "Open the register!"

The clerk complied without a word. Arturo grabbed up a handful of small bills and shoved them into his pocket. Any bill over a twenty was customarily put in the slot of a secure metal safe under the counter to which the clerk did not have access.

"I'm outta here, but I've got my eye on you so if I see you reach for the phone, I'm coming through that door and cut your heart out. You understand?"

The clerk merely nodded. He was following procedure. The security camera mounted behind the counter was recording the entire action. First and foremost, the clerk's job was to stay alive. This was not the first time he had found himself in this situation. He knew that if he didn't try to do anything heroic, he could survive.

Arturo backed away from the clerk and when he cleared the end of the counter, he sprinted out the door. When the clerk could see the offender clear the parking area in front of the store, he reached down and pressed the button that automatically alerted a private security patrol that was only minutes away.

Arturo sprinted to the corner and once beyond the sightline of the store, he slowed to a casual walk, keeping in the shadows of the storefronts along the deserted street. He knew exactly where he would be able to make a score. He had checked out the best connections with other cons that had been more recently on the Vegas scene. Things didn't change all that much in only eight years. The area just east of downtown had been a ghetto then and from his contacts on the inside, he was convinced that it was still a ghetto. As he headed for the predetermined area, he could feel a sense of accomplishment, an air of freedom. He had paid for what he'd done to that bitch and now he was free. It felt good. He felt like he could fly…

As he made his way into a busier area of the downtown, he had no inkling that he was being followed. He had been tailed from the minute he had been released from the Penitentiary in Carson City.

The August heat was oppressive, the billboard above the bank on Eastern registering 112 degrees and rising. Henning parked his car in the nearly deserted parking lot of Sunset Park. Earlier in the day, before it was dangerous to inhale, the voices of children at play could be heard from the nearby playground. But once the sun reached its apex, children were loaded up by diligent mothers or nannies to return home for lunch and rest from their exhausting play. The lake looked inviting as two mallards glided over the glassy surface, barely creating a ripple. The tranquility of the park was inviting as Henning chose a bench protected by the shade of a magnolia tree and overlooking the lake where he could observe his surroundings. He could feel the sweat forming around his collar and under his arms. He opened his copy of the *Review Journal* and turned to the classified section. He smiled at the thought that he would appear to be looking for a job at his age. As he held the newspaper, he kept glancing up and down the path in the hopes he wouldn't have to wait too long. He saw a young bicyclist approaching on the nearby path, the sweat pouring down his face, his skimpy attire soaked through to the skin. *The guy has to be nuts,* thought Henning and as the bike passed on down the path, Henning turned his attention back to the paper. He was actually enjoying perusing the want ads. Perhaps he should reconsider, apply for some menial position, perhaps as a bank guard or as a casino security cop. He smiled at the thought of having to stand on his feet for an eight-hour shift in some smoky casino. *I wouldn't last an hour,* he thought. So engrossed was he in his reading, he hardly noticed the approaching pedestrian. When he focused in, he thought his eyes were deceiving him. He could ascertain an elderly clergyman come to a halt only a few feet from where he was seated. From his collar and dark vestment Henning thought how unfortunate it was that the church could not provide more practical attire for its ministers. This was obviously not the person for whom he was waiting and went back to the want ads. But the priest cleared his throat and asked, "May I join you?"

Henning did a double take. A priest was the last person he was expecting. Before he could reply, the priest settled down on the far end of the bench where he could observe Henning. "Much too hot a day to be out in the park, isn't it, Captain?"

"They could have chosen a cooler meeting place," said Henning. He folded up the newspaper and placed it between the slats of the bench. "I didn't expect a clergyman."

"I realize that. It takes a moment to adjust to the idea that a man of the cloth is privy to such a bizarre decision. I thought that before you commit, we should have a talk…"

"Then you're not the therapist?"

"Oh, heavens, no," smiled the priest. "Let's just say that I'm here as a messenger from God…"

"I don't understand," said Henning, furrowing his brow.

"Are you a Catholic?"

Henning smiled. He had not seen the inside of a church since the day he bid farewell to his wife, Bess. "I've not been to confession for a number of years, Father."

"I see," said the priest as he tried not to appear judgmental. "I felt it would be a good idea for us to talk before you see the therapist."

"Is this protocol?" asked Henning. He felt uncomfortable being confronted by this priest.

"In most cases, I take it upon myself to discuss the action each person is about to embark upon. I feel it's such a finite act that we want to be sure each candidate is aware of the repercussions, both for the postulant and his immediate family and associates as well." The priest paused and then locking eyes with Henning, he asked, "You're aware that what you're contemplating is a mortal sin in the eyes of the church?"

Henning reflected momentarily. "Isn't your knowledge of what I am contemplating also considered a mortal sin, Father? Are you and I sinners in concert or as a representative of the church are you automatically absolved?"

Henning smiled. This was truly bizarre. He would have preferred to meet with "the therapist" rather than a priest.

"I will have to answer to God as well, Captain. But for the moment, it is not my immortal soul that is in jeopardy. I'm here to discuss alternative solutions to your dilemma. You seem to have decided on a most extreme resolution. Is it possible that your decision could possibly be based on health issues?"

"Do you mean, do I believe I'm suffering from some terminal illness? No, I'm not terminally ill. Let's just say that I am terminally fed up with life. My children are grown and on their own. You're probably aware that I am widowed and I find my life to be..." He paused, looking for an appropriate word. "Drudgery, would probably best describe it. Aside from the years I spent on the force, I have no feeling that my life has made much sense. I'm bored, used up. I look around at some of my peers, men my age, and I think, 'There, but for the grace of God, go I.' I'll bet this isn't the first time you've heard that, Father."

"No, Captain, not at all. I understand what you're experiencing, but it's my duty as a priest to make sure you've covered all your options. I must ask, have you considered your children?"

"They have their own lives. They'll understand. I can't contemplate being a burden on them." Henning didn't want to discuss the children. "Let me ask you, Father, are you going to report me to some higher power to have me committed because I represent a danger to myself? Is that what this is all about?" Henning could feel that he was getting annoyed and he wasn't sure exactly why he was being subjected to this line of questioning. He leaned forward, elbows on his thighs and buried his face in his hands as if to wash away the priest's words. "Why did they send you?"

"I'm sorry if my presence offends you, Captain. I've been commissioned to make sure that we are on the same page."

"Do you want to hear my confession, Father? Is that where you're coming from?"

"That won't be necessary."

Henning smiled. "If I had something to confess, Father, it would mean that I had something to live for. Isn't that ironic?" Henning rose and closed the distance between himself and the priest. "I thank you for taking the time, Father, but you and I have nothing to discuss. Please tell the therapist that I'm ready to talk to him…" Henning turned and headed up the path towards to parking lot. There was nothing a priest could do for him. The sooner he saw the therapist the better it would be for everyone.

~~~

It was a risk that Thurman Falk took in not revealing himself or interceding when Arturo Bienvenides was robbing the downtown Speedee Mart. In a split second the clerk could have been killed, but Falk had no authority to act as a law enforcement officer. He watched Arturo's every move from the shadows of doorways and alleyways without being detected. He was merely an unlicensed private investigator who had been hired to follow Bienvenides and report back to his employer. He was paid in cash for his services and the name of the elderly gentleman who arranged for his services, John Brown, was as phony as a laughing Vulcan. He was instructed to report in on a daily basis, at the same time each evening, by placing a call to a public phone in the downtown area of the city.

Falk had first picked up the trail of Bienvenides at the Greyhound terminal the moment Arturo arrived. Falk had a reputation of being a master of deception who could blend into a crowd without detection. In his early years he had aspired to an acting career but when that didn't materialize, he used his talents in the field of investigation. As a black man with a week's growth of beard and his hair in need of a trim, he dragged his feet along the pavement as if he were twenty years older than his actual age. The remnants of a pair of tattered army fatigues hanging sloppily from his tall, angular frame helped in his deception – just another homeless black man living on the streets of the busy city. He never carried a weapon. In fact, he didn't even own one. If a job required the use of a gun, Falk was the wrong man for the job. He was merely an observer. Heroism was not included on his resume.

~~~

"The therapist" was nothing like Captain Henning had imagined. He was a short, stout, out-of-shape elderly man, perhaps a few years the Captain's junior. After introducing himself as Mr. Brown, he pushed a small note across the table of the corner café. Henning noticed that even in the heat of the summer evening, the hand that delivered the note was gloved. There would be no prints or DNA that could ever be traced back to Mr. Brown. Their meeting lasted all of five minutes; very few words were spoken. The instructions in the note were concise and self-explanatory. The Captain placed the note on the table, the therapist rose, retrieved the note which he pocketed, then without another word, he turned and was swallowed up in the foot traffic of the busy boulevard.

~~~

Three days back on the streets of Vegas and Arturo Bienvenides' daily routine was as predictable as a dog in heat. He had spent most of the few dollars he had heisted from the convenience store and it was just a matter of finding another score. He had to get out of the halfway house where he was bedded down with six other ex-cons, all of whom were in search of employment in keeping with the terms of their paroles. The small room had a smell of stale urine and sweat that made Arturo want to heave. He had slept there the first night he got into town, but the three subsequent nights, after bed check, he rose from his cot, dressed, and sneaked out the back of the unsecured building. He walked the streets in the hopes that he could find a mark that he could rob to get some extra cash. But the pickings were slim in this part of town where most of the people on the street were in worse condition than he. On the fourth day, as he was walking along a side street where a construction crew was working on an open trench, he noticed a utility van parked a few yards away. A tool bucket was conveniently sitting on the tailgate of the truck with none of the workers in sight. Certain that he was not being observed, he reached in and removed a claw hammer from the bucket which he shoved handle first down into the side of his pants. It would come in handy.

On the fourth night in Vegas, Arturo made his way south along Paradise where, during the day, he had observed a 7-Eleven across from the Hilton Hotel and Casino. By night the store appeared deserted as most of the traffic in the area was blocks away to the west on the Vegas Strip. There was very little foot traffic from the Hilton that was set back from the main thoroughfare. As he approached the store, there were two vehicles parked at the gas pumps some thirty feet in front of the store. Arturo made his way around to the side of the store where he could observe when it would be relatively safe to make his move. He hunkered down in the shadows by the dumpster.

Thurman Falk had followed Arturo from the moment he left the safe house. He placed a call from the phone on the corner out of Arturo's sightline, giving his location and then hung up and as fast as his feet would permit, he left the scene. Within minutes, a dark, vintage Mustang pulled up on the side street across from the 7-Eleven within view of the Hilton sign. The waiting game was on. A few minutes after Arturo's arrival, the two cars departed the pumping area and the store appeared deserted. He walked around the side of the building to get a better view of the interior of the store. A black clerk, somewhere in his middle to late thirties, was busy restocking some of the shelves with merchandise. Arturo took one last look around and entered the store. The clerk was out of sight working the second aisle. He looked up as Arturo approached.

"Can I help you with something?" he asked.

Arturo swung the hammer that had been hidden at his side, catching the clerk across the side of his head, rendering him instantly unconscious. Arturo reached down and removed the keys from the ring on the clerk's belt, scampered to the register which he opened with the key, scooped up a handful of bills and was just about to vault over the counter when the front door opened and Henning entered with a .38 police special in hand. He raised the weapon, pulled the trigger twice and rendered Arturo quite dead before he hit the floor. Then, returning the weapon to its holster on his belt, he turned and walked out the door as casually as if he had just made a purchase, but he could not help feeling the exhilaration that surged through his being knowing that he had made his mark, left a lasting impression for those who would walk outside the boundaries of the law. He was not impervious to the fact that what he had done was legally wrong, that vigilantism was unacceptable from any perspective. Someone had to send a message to those who thought they were above the laws of the community in which they lived and that there would be a reckoning in the here and now. He was on a high and he could feel a rush as he walked across the parking area in front of the store on his way to retrieve his car.

Suddenly, Henning was seized with a violent pain in his gut as if he was experiencing food poisoning. *What the hell could I have eaten to bring on indigestion?"* He felt out of breath as if a great weight were pressing down on his chest and then came the nausea and the sweats. He felt lightheaded and reached for a light stanchion at the curb to support himself. He had to get to his car, to get out of this neighborhood before anyone could identify him, but before he could traverse the few yards to his vehicle, he felt the world turn topsy-turvy as the pavement came up to meet him.

The next thing he remembered was the ambulance screaming in the night and his awareness that he was manacled to a steel pipe on the side of the gurney. It would be hours before the diagnosis of a myocardial infarction, a severe heart attack, was confirmed at the University Medical Center where Captain Henning would be kept under twenty-four hour surveillance, under arrest for the murder of Arturo Bienvenides who had killed the store clerk at the 7-Eleven across from the Hilton Hotel and Casino.

~~~

As soon as the news reached her, Marge made a beeline to the University Medical Center. Rumors were flying. The early edition of the *Review Journal*'s front page had the headline: VIGILANTE COP KILLS ROBBER. None of the two-column story was corroborated and the facts were sketchy at best. The three major television channels carried various accounts of the shooting, all hearsay. Henning was still unconscious when Marge flashed her ID at the nurse's station on the third floor. She was told that the Captain was resting after being administered beta-blockers and oxygen, but that he wasn't allowed visitors. The ECG showed a massive myocardial infarction, probably brought on by the sudden excitement of his confrontation and shooting of the robber. The nurse spoke of Henning in glowing terms as if she was proud to be a party to his heroic deed. The fact that Henning was eighty-two years of age made him that much more of a celebrity. Marge made her way down the hall to the waiting area and was surprised to find it overflowing with members from her department, mostly older officers who knew Henning from his active days and a number of reporters from various news organizations. No one was allowed into the Captain's room except for one of his sons, Mason, and his daughter, Elizabeth. They had flown in on the early morning flights from their respective homes – Mason from San Francisco and Elizabeth from Phoenix. There was a steady drone of muffled voices throughout the waiting area as pockets of conversation were paying homage to the fallen officer. The question of why an eighty-two year old, retired police officer had shot and killed a recidivist criminal in the act of performing a brutal crime dominated the conversations. Members of the press were trying to interview members of the department that had known the Captain but no one cooperated. The doctor in charge, Dr. Leland, was not sharing any medical information with the police or the press at the request of Henning's children until that time when details of the previous night's business had been thoroughly investigated by the police. "The Captain is resting peacefully," was the extent of any information the attending physician was prepared to share.

It was obvious to Marge that there was nothing she could accomplish by hanging around the hospital waiting room. She had been on duty all night and she needed to get a shower and some rest. She would check into the department from time to time to see if any new developments were available. As she drove to her east side apartment in the Green Valley district, questions were racing through her mind.

Her cell phone rang and she reached down and flipped it open. It was Anthony.

"I thought you were heading home to get some sleep," she said.

"I'm sorry. I should have come with you, but I was beat. When I got home I couldn't sleep. I kept thinking about Henning. Did you learn anything?"

"Nothing, absolutely nothing, but what I can't understand is what Captain Henning was doing at the 7-Eleven in that neighborhood at that hour of the night? It was nowhere near his home. And what the hell was he doing carrying a firearm? He wasn't authorized…" She was venting. "Damn it, Anthony, something isn't kosher."

"Maybe it will make more sense after you get some rest. Give me a call later and we'll grab a bite."

"Yeah, sure…we'll talk later." She flipped the phone shut. Her head ached. She needed an aspirin and a few hours sleep. She was consumed with heartache over the situation with Henning. They had been friends for over five years and although they spent time together on numerous occasions in the cafeteria, Henning revealed very few personal facts about his life. She knew he was widowed and that he had two sons and a daughter that lived out of town, but she did not know their names or anything about their families. If it had been left up to her and if it was necessary, she had no way of getting in touch with anyone related to the Captain. Of course, there were the department's sealed archival records that listed not only his service records but also personal data that included the names of next of kin and relatives with their whereabouts. It bothered Marge that for as long as she and the Captain had known each other, she really knew very little about him. Whenever they were together, they talked about department business. It made her sad to think that if Henning were to die, it would be as if they weren't friends at all but merely casual acquaintances. *What a waste*, she thought.

~~~

It was two weeks before Captain Henning was released from the University Medical Center and into the custody of the LVMPD. He had undergone triple bypass and for a while it was touch and go whether he would make it. Upon discharge from the hospital he was incarcerated in the West Side Station overnight and the following morning he appeared for arraignment before Judge Weisman. The Captain was released into the custody of his son, Mason, and confined to his home on his own recognizance when the court took into consideration his age and decided he was not a flight risk. The Captain refused counsel although he could well afford to retain an attorney to act in his defense. Being off duty, Marge volunteered her services as driver to transport the two men to the elder Henning's home. She had never been there before so the Captain had to give her directions. During the drive, the tension between father and son was overbearing. It was all the forty-year old son could do to keep from engaging in a tirade as he tried to fathom what was going on in his father's head.

"Why in God's name would you refuse a court-appointed attorney?" he asked. He was speaking to the back of his father's head as Bob Henning's gaze was fixed on the highway outside the side-rear window. He had not spoken a dozen words to either of his children during his waking hours in the hospital. What could he say? If he had his way, he would have died right there on the street from the coronary. What was happening was exactly what he had hoped to avoid. "You're going to have to start answering some questions, Father, if not to me, then to the police and the court. You do realize that you're facing some serious jail time, don't you?" The Captain did not reply.

"Perhaps now's not the time, Mason," said Marge, trying to neutralize the situation. She could see him in the rear-view mirror of her SUV and the frustration and confusion of the dilemma was written all over his face. She could empathize with him. She too was caught up in the confusion of this whole mess. She needed to talk to the Captain, to try to make some sense out of what happened. He would talk to her if they could have some quality time together, but now was not it.

Mason turned his attention to Marge. "Were you in the department when my father was Chief?" he asked.

"I've only been acquainted with him these past five years," she said.

"Then you didn't know my mother, did you?"

"No, I never had the pleasure. He didn't talk about her very much. I'm sure he misses her terribly."

"They were inseparable. I'd bet anything that all this has to do with her passing; that and his retirement from the department with little or nothing to take its place. He was so active all of his adult life and suddenly he finds himself clerking down at the station. It's got to be eating his guts out…" He was sharing these comments with Marge as if the Captain was not sitting only inches away able to hear every word. "My God, but I don't know what to do. My sister had to leave this morning to get back to her kids and I've got to get back to California before my boss realizes he can run the business without me…"

"What is it you do, Mason?"

"Computer tech. To be perfectly honest, a trained chimpanzee could do what I do. I was hoping to step up in the firm, but what with the economy, I'm lucky to have a job at all. I guess I'll have to arrange for a caregiver to come stay with Dad until I can make other arrangements. I'd take him to San Francisco to stay with me, but the court won't permit it. It's like Catch-22, isn't it?"

The conversion petered out as Marge drove in silence. Ten minutes later they arrived at the Henning home. Mason scampered out of the car to help his father who reluctantly let his son take his arm. Henning took the keys out of his pocket and Marge took them from him and ran ahead to open the front door. As they cleared the threshold, the Captain looked around as if he was seeing this place for the very first time, as if he expected someone to be there to greet him. Marge thought she detected a bit of emotion, a misting around his eyes, but that quickly abated as the Captain broke from his son's grasp and headed for the bedroom. "I wanna lie down," he announced. Mason followed him into the bedroom, turned down the covers, and despite Henning's protests, helped his father remove his jacket and shoes. Marge went into the kitchen, retrieved a bottle of cold water from the fridge and took it into the bedroom where she placed it on the nightstand next to the bed.

"Let's let him get some rest," she said as she led the way out of the bedroom and left the door slightly ajar in case Henning should call for help. She and Mason sat across from each other. "I'd make some coffee or something to drink but I don't know where anything is…"

"That's all right. I'm fine," he said. He felt weary, exhausted. He reached up and rubbed the back of his neck to try to ward off an impending headache. "I didn't thank you for your help," he said. "I heard you came by the hospital a number of times to check on Dad's condition. I know that wasn't in the line of duty."

"He and I sort of bonded over the years. Nothing personal, mind you, just a matter of respect, I guess you might call it. He was always ready to offer a bit of advice or make a suggestion if he thought I was getting off the track. It's easy to do when one is a rookie cop."

"I guess," was all he could add.

After a few moments of silence, Marge stood and held out her hand. He shook it. "I'm glad you're here, Mason. I know what a hardship this is on you, but you're doing the right thing, being with your father. I've got to get back to the station. My shift starts soon. I'll look in on him whenever I can." She took a card out of her pocket and handed it to him. "I'll help you find a caregiver if you want. I'll ask around the station. They'll know someone or I'll call the hospital. Meanwhile, when you've figured it out, you let me know your plans. I'll help in any way I can." She walked to the door and let herself out.

~~~

As Henning lay on his bed fully clothed he felt overwhelmed with the events of the past weeks. This is not the way he imagined it would turn out. He now stood on the brink of a courtroom circus in which he and his family would be held up to the scrutiny of the entire country, reviled by the press and the prosecution. He was tired. It was time to save everyone the inconvenience of a show trial wherein the department would be held up to public censure. In his heart he knew that what he did was right. He made no apologies for his act, but how would this play out in a courtroom where plain and simple, he had taken the law into his own hands? The public could not condone such behavior. In the best scenario, he would plead out to temporary insanity, his age would be an extenuating factor, as would the acts of the victim and with a good defense, he might get off with an acquittal, but not before his kids were subjected to a lengthy and costly ordeal. Would he survive the physical pressure of the daily ritual of defending his actions? Would his heart be able to take the extreme fluctuations of a jury trial, fighting for his life? What life? What was there to fight for – home and hearth? It was a joke. It was over. It was time to pack it in.

~~~

On the drive back to the station, Marge decided to go by the 7-Eleven across from the Hilton, the place where Henning had gunned down Bienvenides. It wasn't out of her way. When she pulled into the parking lot, it was business as usual. The clerk behind the counter was Hispanic. The name on the tag attached to his vest was "Ramon." She flashed her badge.

"Were you working here the night of the robbery, Ramon?" she asked.

"I spoke to the police a couple of times, officer," he said.

"I know. I just thought there might have been something that they missed when they questioned you. Anything you can think of?" she repeated.

"No ma'am," he said. "I got off at midnight, the other clerk relieved me, and that's all I know. I keep thinking how lucky I was. I mean, it could have been me who got clobbered." He shook his head. "I got a wife and two kids. I don't know what would happen to them if something like that happened to me. Man, it's scary. Real scary, ya know?"

"Yeah, Ramon, I know. I'll leave you my card," which she took from her pocket and placed on the counter. "Just in case." She turned and exited the store. As she got outside, she decided to take a look around. Henning's old Mustang had been found across the street. She walked over to the stanchion where the Captain had attempted to get his bearings when the heart attack hit. She walked around to the rear of the store, noticing the dumpster. Nothing unusual; nothing revealing.

As she got into her car and headed to the station, her cell phone cheerily played the first couple of bars of "The William Tell Overture." Even before she answered it, she had a premonition.

"We just got a call," said Anthony. "Bob Henning is gone."

She took a moment to take it in. She was not surprised. "His heart?"

"The temporary report from the coroner is suicide. They'll have a final report in a couple of hours. I'm sorry, Marge…"

Of course, she thought, *I should have anticipated it. His depression, his non-communication.* In truth, there was nothing Marge could have done to prevent him from taking his own life. In a way, it was a noble act. She felt relieved. He was at peace. There would be no more accusations, no more need to defend his actions, no more character assassination of a man who served with honor and integrity. No matter who "they" were, they could never take that way from him. She would mourn his passing, but as much as she understood his final act, as much as she felt relief from his decision to accept responsibility for his actions, there was still a buzz in the back of her mind: was Henning's act one of singularity or was she missing something?

~~~

He was waiting for Marge as she drove up. "Give me a few minutes," she said as she entered the station. On her way to the locker room she noticed Captain Peterson motioning to her from behind the glass partition that separated him from the staff. Instinctively, she checked her watch to see if she was late. He beckoned her with a wave of his hand and she walked through the line of cubicles to his office and knocked on the door. She entered as the Captain was just hanging up the phone.

"You all right, Officer?" he asked.

"Yes, sir," she replied.

"I just got the news. I know how close you were to Captain Henning. He was a good man. This whole thing is a bloody mess. I don't suppose you'd have anything that might add some light on his actions, Officer."

"No, sir. He was pretty tightlipped about his personal life. Most of our conversations were pretty superficial, if you know what I mean."

"Well, if you need to talk, I'm here. I don't want any of this negative press to affect your job performance. You and Anthony are pretty high up on the list for detective so just stay on track. You got it?"

"Yes, sir."

"That's all, Officer." He dismissed her. As she closed the door behind her, Captain Peterson breathed a sigh of relief. The death of Henning was an act of fate that was going to save the department a lot of unnecessary scrutiny and negative press. *One bad apple did not a police department make*, he mused. He was sorry to have lost a friend, but in the final analysis, he didn't need all the aggravation and lost man-hours that a trial of this nature would surely have demanded.

~~~

Marge went to the locker room where she changed into her duty uniform, checked out with the desk, and then met Anthony who was waiting outside by the patrol car. "Sorry to hold you up but I just had the weirdest meeting with Captain Peterson. I don't know why everyone thinks I'm holding back information regarding Henning's actions."

"They're shooting blanks, Marge. What Captain Henning did is casting some pretty negative press on the department. It will all blow over in a few days."

Chapter 8

The funeral of Captain Robert Henning was mostly a family affair. The local government felt that under the circumstances surrounding the Captain's pending trial and untimely death, "It would be best to let sleeping dogs lie," voiced the Mayor. Normally, the death of such a high-ranking local government official would call for a public display of respect with all the bells and whistles befitting his station, but the mayor felt that "there was nothing to gain by muddying up the waters." A few close family friends were in attendance along with Henning's two sons and his daughter. Marge Linden represented the precinct along with Captain Peterson. Most of Henning's peers had long since passed or had moved on to be with their families, wherever they had settled in other parts of the country.

Outside the funeral parlor, only one local reporter was in attendance. What was there to say that hadn't previously been dragged over the coals? The question of why Captain Henning took the law into his own hands was no longer of interest to law enforcement or the court system.

"His behavior was brought on by the frustration of an elderly retiree who could not accept the inability of the courts to act in a responsible manner in the public interest," was printed in one of the local papers, quoting an anonymous contributor. What more was there to discuss? Arturo Bienvenides was scum. He deserved to die. Henning's actions had saved the taxpayers millions of dollars in legal fees and court costs as Bienvenides would have been pampered through the legal system. Then, had he been found guilty and incarcerated again, it would have cost the state in excess of fifty thousand dollars a year for his upkeep. Everyone agreed that Henning had done the community a service for which he should have been publicly rewarded, but at the same time, how could society condone the taking of a life without legal authority? The day that Henning died was the day the impending case was closed.

Marge had heard all the pros and cons about the Henning case from her fellow officers. She agreed that the whole mess boiled down to the actions of a sick old man taking a final gasp before dying. She respected his choice when it came down to the wire, but something was bothering her — something that did not set well in her trained mind. What was the relationship between Henning and Bienvenides? The police had been unable to establish a connection between the two in any way. Did Henning just fortuitously walk in on a holdup and execute the perp? That thesis was way beyond her ability to comprehend. *There had to be a connection,* she told herself...*there just had to be."*

~~~

At sixty-two years of age, Colonel Juan Rivera-Ortega was, without a doubt, the most accomplished military officer in the entire Mexican Army. His allegiance to country overshadowed his devotion to both family and church. He was endowed with an insatiable appetite for power that was almost beyond human comprehension. There were higher-ranking military officers than he, but it was only a matter of time until he would step up and assume his rightful role as Comandante of the entire Mexican Army. There were numerous occasions when he could have assumed the role of Supreme Commander by virtue of a *coup d'état*, but Rivera-Ortega was not only highly intelligent, he was endowed with patience as well. He theorized that a government assumed by military coup created mistrust and enmity within the ranks of both the military and government, whereas a leader who assumed power by virtue of his ascension through his show of strength, skill, and initiative is a leader empowered by the majority, one who does not have to spend his waking hours looking over his shoulder in anticipation of the next assassin.

He had been born into a family of privilege and extreme wealth in the upscale, residential district of Polanco, a trendy section of Mexico City where massive estates dating back hundreds of years still survived the many political and military attempts to bring down the Mexican aristocracy. Money was power and no matter how many times the government failed, either by electoral process or military junta, Polanco's powerful masters prevailed and proliferated. The Rivera-Ortega estate on some eighty acres was located only minutes from the Paseo de la Reforma, the city's main thoroughfare lined with dozens of priceless and elegant monuments, commercial high-rise developments, embassies, luxury hotels, and colonial mansions.

The Rivera-Ortega chateau, with its twenty-four bedrooms and baths, twenty-car garage complete with auto repair shop, twenty-six stall stable complete with indoor lighted arena, eight acre lake, and numerous separate quarters for servants and guests, set back from the Paseo, was surrounded by an eight foot high stone wall with shards of glass imbedded on top. The main gate was set back two hundred meters from the Paseo where a contingent of guards patrolled on a twenty-four hour routine.

The Rivera-Ortega fortune had been made in oil for the better part of a century. In each generation, the sons in the majority stepped up to take control of the empire that flourished with the expertise of learned technicians and crewmen, most of whom had been imported from the neighboring United States. After World War II, an alliance between Rivera-Ortega and British Petroleum created one of the four leading oil cartels in all the Americas.

Juan Ortega-Rivera chose to follow a career in the military with an eye on the national political scene. As went the Army, philosophized Juan's father, so went the economy of Mexico. Juan's two brothers, Felipe and Armand, assumed control of the oil empire, having attended the University of Texas studying engineering in preparation for their positions within the family hierarchy. It was a simple arrangement: Juan needed the financial support of Rivera-Ortega/BP to further his military and political ambitions and the company needed the military support to serve his political ambitions.

On a personal note, Juan Rivera-Ortega had been married to Maria Teresa Salazar for thirty-five years. Although a marriage of convenience, the Salazar family being one of the five wealthiest in the city, Juan Rivera-Ortega admitted on numerous occasions that he would have fallen in love and taken Maria Teresa as his wife even if she had been born in total, miserable poverty. Tall, dark skinned, with black piercing eyes, there was no doubt that her beauty was unsurpassed throughout the entire city. Within a period of ten years she gave him four children – three sons and one daughter, Silvana. After completing their educations in the United States, the three boys returned to Mexico City to take their places within the family empire.

It was Silvana who turned from the family tradition of education to prepare her to follow in the footsteps of her predecessors. While attending school at the University of North Texas, she strayed from family convention after being introduced to drugs and sex by a number of her sorority sisters. By the third year of her matriculation, she found herself pregnant and in an act of desperation, she agreed to marry the apparent father of her child. With all his power in Mexico, Juan Rivera-Ortega soon learned that he was impotent in his attempt at trying to control the activities of his headstrong daughter beyond the borders of his own country. He had contemplated having her kidnapped and forcibly returned to Mexico City, but he knew that such an authoritarian act could only alienate her further from him and his wife. He had envisioned great things from Silvana, for she was not only brilliant, but shared her mother's beauty as well. Maria Teresa begged him to let Silvana have her own way. Eventually she would see the folly of her ways and return to the family and her duties where she belonged.

It had been eight years since the murder of his lovely daughter, Silvana, and his grandchild, and for eight years Juan Rivera-Ortega waited patiently for the day he would live to avenge their deaths.

The sleek black Mercedes pulled up to the gate and as the guard acknowledged the occupant, he pressed the control to open the main gate. The car glided up the long driveway to the front of the mansion where a manservant waited to greet the Colonel. Juan Rivera-Ortega mounted the steps to the great hall and entered the library. He closed and locked the door behind him, removed his tunic which he threw over the back of a leather chair, loosened his tie, and seated himself behind his desk. His hands were moist and he could feel his heart beating hard in his chest. He leaned back to gain composure, his hands folded over his chest. This could well be the day for which he had patiently waited. The private line on the phone bank rang and he picked it up.

"I have news," said the voice on the other end of the line.

"Yes," he said trying to control his anxiety.

"The contract is completed."

Juan Rivera-Ortega breathed a great sigh of relief. *Revenge is still the sweetest of man's accomplishments*, he thought. How long he had waited for this moment. "You bring me great joy, my friend. I shall be forever in your debt."

"We shall probably never speak again, Colonel, but let me assure you that it has been a pleasure to serve you. May God watch over and protect you and your loved ones…"

The line went dead as the priest hung up the phone.

Chapter 9

The view of the Strip from the twenty-eighth floor of the Wynn Hotel and Casino was spectacular. Father Ignatius stood in front of the large picture window as the sun disappeared in the west over Mount Charleston. The traffic below was like a dance of fireflies following methodically, one behind the other. The sky was crimson and yellow and orange as the billowing clouds majestically floated in the wind across the evening sky. *It is as if God is painting another masterpiece*, thought the elderly priest. A gentle knock at the door disturbed his reverie and he headed for the door across the great expanse of the main salon. He was wearing everyday attire without his vestment and collar as he opened the door.

The man known as John Brown entered the lavish suite. The men greeted each other with handshakes and John proceeded to the bar to pour himself a whiskey, straight up. "Not the conclusion I had hoped for," he said.

"I understand," said Father Ignatius. "A trial would have made sense after all the preparations and precautions were in place. Sometimes Divine Providence intercedes in an untimely manner."

"Have you given any thought to Bienvenides' replacement on the list?"

"We have numerous local candidates in mind. Making the right choice will be the order of business during this evening's meeting. I don't expect a big turnout. We'll get started just as soon as a few of the others arrive."

The priest poured himself a cup of fresh, black coffee from the thermos behind the bar and sat where he could enjoy the spectacle of the impending evening lights. John sat some distance away across the room with his drink in hand, also taking in the sight. They sat in silence until the others began to arrive. There were six in all; none of the other twenty were expected. The priest was asked to give the benediction, which he did − short, and sweet − and then those in attendance got down to the business at hand.

Of the eight men in attendance, they all had one attribute in common − they were all retired seniors in the twilight of their lives. This had been a prerequisite right from the beginning based on the philosophy that whatever time was left in the greater scheme of things, there was very little more they could accomplish regarding service to their families and communities. They referred to themselves as pragmatists, their earlier dreams of accomplishments realized or at least honorably attempted. What was left was to move on and face the end with dignity and as an extra bonus, leave word to those who survived them that murder and mayhem were not acceptable hallmarks of a civilized society.

Chapter 10

The Imam Jahl had been under the scrutiny of the CIA and the FBI since the events of 9/11 in 2001. His anti-American, anti-Israel, anti-Jew sermons were popular among some four thousand Harlem residents who flocked to the Mosque to listen to his vitriolic sermons. In the Imam's office hung a lifelike portrait of Osama bin Laden; no likeness of an American leader or an American flag were visible. If one didn't know better, upon crossing the threshold, one would think he had been transported to a Middle Eastern country.

The government of the United States had been actively harassing the Imam and many of his followers in the search for financial ties to the terrorist organization of al Qaeda but the laws of the land, the constitutional protection of freedom of speech and religion, all but reduced to powerless the effectiveness of the CIA. No sooner was a warrant served for a display of anti-American activities by the federal authorities than a score of congregants dressed in Arab attire, along with a small army of ACLU attorneys, descended upon the offices of the Justice Department protesting violations of the civil liberties and constitutional rights of free speech and rights of assembly.

Among the congregants of the Mosque of Islam, the whole American concept of freedom of speech and freedom of assembly was considered a mockery. Any freedoms handed down to man were not the results of a democracy at work but the gifts handed down by the venerable leader, Mohammed, to the Arab world, as clearly stated in the Quran. In an Islamic faction of the society that believed that religion takes precedence over government, it was easy to operate outside the law with impunity from prosecution. The very laws that set the standard for the welfare of the society were the same laws that defended the abusers of those laws.

"How naïve were the Founding Fathers? How naïve for a nation so economically privileged to try to inhibit reactionary activities intended to undermine that very economy," espoused Imam Jahl. It was easy to financially support the Brotherhood of Islam that funneled large donations through the World Brotherhood of Muslim Youth and into the coffers of al-Qaeda and the Taliban when the laws of privacy protected the church's actions.

The World Assembly of Muslim Youth was a Saudi-run organization known in international circles as the machine to funnel large amounts of money from America and Europe to support Islamic terrorism. Prior to 9/11, the U.S. State Department had turned a deaf ear on the thesis that some members of the Muslim community might be supporters of Islamic terror groups. Immediately post 9/11, the gauntlet had dropped. Too little, too late.

Max Friedman, a lawyer from the ACLU, defended the activities of the Imam Jahl and his followers by stating, "It is not in the interest of a democratic nation to prevent members of the Mosque of Islam from working for charitable organizations." And so it was impossible to bring an indictment against active supporters of terrorism even in the shadow of the events of 9/11.

~~~

Thurman Falk did not like New York. He liked Harlem even less. The streets were too impersonal, too cold, too crime-ridden for his taste. If one sought relief, he mused, there was always the upper part of Central Park where, after sundown, against the background of gently rolling hills and green pastures, one took his life in his own hands to enter the gang-infested war zone. But he had a job to do and his was not to reason why. At five in the afternoon he entered the Mosque of Islam just off Broadway and 125th Street, removed his shoes at the door, entered the great hall, bowed in supplication and knelt to pray. This was not the same persona of the street indigent from Las Vegas who tracked down Arturo Bienvenides. This Thurman Falk was dressed in conservative, casual attire, as he blended in with the faithful. It was all part of the role-playing. He began to recite the Shahada in a monotone barely audible. His mission was to observe and report; nothing more, nothing less.

~~~

Hassan Muhammad had ruled the back streets and alleys of upper Manhattan adjacent to Yorkville for over a decade. Born Jesse Lee Williams in the Harlem ghetto, he had come a long way on his good looks, his aquiline features setting him apart from most of the blacks with whom he associated. He was a magnet for Harlem women who flocked to his bed only to later end up on the streets as part of his lucrative stable of prostitutes. Pimping, pushing dope, and murder were all part of his repertoire. It was rumored that he had killed more than a dozen men in his short forty-year life, had been indicted three times for murder and had three times walked out of the courtroom a free man. He was as quick with a switchblade as he was with his mouth, able to make the transition from the language of the street to that of the highly educated. Among his associates he was regarded as something of a chameleon. For a price, he could be bought to carry out a contract. No one fucked with Hassan Muhammad. If his own hand did not dispatch an adversary, there were others in his small clutch of miscreants that served as bodyguards to do the job. Clawing his way up out of the gutters of the New York streets he learned early on that money was power and his pockets were filled to overflowing with markers from local cops and a few powerful politicians with hands on the court system that could mete out justice in his favor.

Hassan Mohammed was a religious man who took the time to pray to Allah six times each day. He attended the Mosque of Islam regularly and could find no irony or conflict between his social behavior and his religiosity. He supported the Mosque with huge financial donations. He encouraged local businesses to give generously to the World Brotherhood of Muslim Youth, that arm of Islam "dedicated to the welfare and education of disenfranchised young men whose unfortunate plight could be alleviated." That most of those young men were indoctrinated into Islamic terrorist activities was not an issue. The money collected from the American Arab community always reached its source less a large percentage "withheld for processing."

Many factions in the New York scene had considered corrective actions against both Hassan Mohammed and the Imam Jahl. Behind closed doors could be heard the words "assassination" and "execution," but law enforcement avoided these concepts like the plague. The ramifications could be overwhelming should anything go awry and always there were slip-ups and loose tongues. No, whatever justice was to be meted out against known Muslim terrorist activities would have to come from outside the framework of the U.S. legal system. The obvious proponents to take on Islamic terrorists were the Jews and their connections with the Israeli Intelligence arm known as Mossad. But after lengthy meetings, the Mossad leaders declined the opportunity to strike a blow on behalf of their allies on the grounds that history had taught the Jews that the U.S. could not be trusted to support such an Israeli covert action. The memory of the Mohammed Atta incident was still fresh in the minds of most Israelis.

Mohammed Atta had been captured by the Israelis and sentenced to a lengthy prison term after blowing up a bus in Tel Aviv. In accordance with the Oslo Accord in 1993, Israel had agreed to release so- called "political prisoners." But when Israel refused to release any prisoners with blood on their hands, President Bill Clinton and Warren Christopher intervened on Atta's behalf, forcing the release of Atta who later flew one of the planes into the World Trade Center.

Since 1948, there had been numerous occasions when the Mossad had acted within the territorial boundaries of the United States with Israel taking the brunt when there were leaks to the international press. With Iran and North Korea testing nuclear weaponry, Israel could not afford to take any actions that might justify a nuclear attack from her enemies intent on her destruction. The plans for neutralizing Hassan Mohammed and Imam Jahl were relegated to the back burner.

The Guardian List

Chapter 11

The East Side Home for the Elderly was situated on Lexington Avenue just a short walk from the 92nd Street YMHA in Manhattan. Many of the ambulatory inhabitants were thankful to have access to the "Y" where they could take advantage of daily advanced education classes and evening entertainment offered by the New York City Arts Council. Victor Vordenko was a seventy-eight year old resident of the Home, having lived there for three years since his seventy-six year old wife, Svetlana, had been diagnosed with Alzheimer's disease. Upon admission to the Home they shared a small, comfortable room for the first year, after which Svetlana became incontinent and Victor petitioned the administration to provide them separate quarters. He could not suffer the deterioration of her health over the past years to where she no longer recognized him, although he made it a point of stopping by her room each day to spend time at her bedside. It was all he could do to keep his emotions from getting away from him when he was with her. On numerous occasions he entertained the thought of putting her out of her misery.

    Victor was only a child when his family packed up their worldly goods in Odessa, Russia, and moved to the United States. They were part of the great migration of

Russian Jews fleeing the Russian pogrom, although the Vordenkos were of Russian Orthodox persuasion. They settled in the Russian ghetto of Brooklyn. Victor attended NYU where he earned a degree in Law Enforcement. As a youngster he had been attracted to the law by the demeanor of most of the policemen he saw serving the community in which he lived. He felt that they were helpful, courteous, and the uniforms were something to be admired. Victor would eventually become one of New York's finest.

It was during his tenure at NYU that he first met Svetlana Voronova, a second generation Russian immigrant who was studying Business Management with many of her classes in the same building where Victor had two of his core classes. Victor was not impervious to his own sexual needs but he was in no position to get involved in a long-term relationship. He was dedicated to achieving his professional goal in law enforcement and a long-term personal commitment appeared to be out of the question…until he found himself seated next to this tall, dark Russian beauty that immediately caught Victor's eye. It was not long before Victor and Svetlana were an "item" on campus among the undergraduate student body. A couple of casual meetings in the student café, a number of long walks around Washington Square Park after classes, a Saturday evening movie in the Village, and before he knew what hit him, Victor Vordenko was ready to abandon Law Enforcement and commit to the role of husband and father. Had it not been for Svetlana's encouragement for

The Guardian List

Victor to fulfill his early dreams as a police officer, he was mentally weighing his options in the professional world. The week after they held hands during their graduation exercises, they joined hands at the local Russian Orthodox Church where they were joined in matrimony. Victor was thoroughly convinced that their bonding was the result of some higher power and he was not about to question its meaning, such was his love and devotion to Svetlana.

He had filled out all the necessary paperwork for his entrance to the Police Academy and was waiting for the results when he received word from the Selective Service Board that he was about to be inducted into the Army. The Marine Corp was his branch of preference and the week before he was to leave for boot camp in Parris Island, South Carolina, he and Svetlana received the good news that she was with child. They barely had time to celebrate with family and friends before he was on his way to serve his country.

Upon his return to the States, after his hitch with the Marines serving in Korea during that war, he was the perfect candidate for the Police Academy. His six-foot, three-inch frame, his broad shoulders and muscular body, full head of black, black hair, and his chiseled features were all characteristics that made him the perfect NYPD candidate. Once on the New York streets, his presence was a blessing to the local merchants as he patrolled the lower East Side of the city. He was treated like some benevolent giant who gave a hand to the weary and downtrodden, and who meted out justice to those who would attempt to violate the law. He loved his work. Never did any of his fellow officers hear him complain. He was an inspiration among his peers. He was a devoted family man, the father of two beautiful, intelligent children, Sergey and Delfina, and soon to be a grandfather. But with all his positive attributes, Victor was never able to gain promotion within the department.

In his early years with the department he learned to devote his every waking hour to his duties on the force. He was developing what was later coined as "hyper vigilance" wherein he developed a keen extra sense of sight, sound, and smell. It was a normal characteristic of many police officers who learned to live their waking hours devoted to duty on the streets. These hyper-senses were merely a tool they used to stay alive. They were developing isolation from the world they previously knew. They were learning to devote their entire lives to the training they would eventually need on the streets, creating an almost automaton mentality wherein their lives beyond their duty would eventually suffer. The statistics of failed marriages among police officers were off the charts. And police suicides were documented as three times the national average. The total devotion to duty and the isolation from past relationships with family and friends was an ideal breeding ground for Victor to evolve into an emotional deviant, but he learned quite early that the dew was off the rose. What began as an exciting and altruistic pursuit serving the society soon turned Victor into a victim of the system.

The Guardian List

In his fifth year on the force, he was chosen to work with the K-9 unit in which he partnered with a 120-pound German shepherd named Duke. They immediately bonded and Duke became the social lifeline for Victor with his wife, Svetlana, and their two infant children along with the many acquaintances in the community. Children playing on the streets would stop their games to stare in admiration and respect for the cop with the dog. Duke had become as much a part of Victor's persona as a police officer as was his badge, his uniform or his gun. When Victor was not on duty, he and Duke "hung out." The Vordenko family went to minor league baseball games together in the park where dogs were welcome. They took trips down to the beach where Duke could romp in the water and commune with other dog species. They were family.

Three years after Victor began working with Duke, a new Watch Commander was assigned to the station. For no apparent reason, the Watch Commander got a hair up his ass about Victor and decided to reassign him to duty as a jail officer. It was foreign for Victor to have to grovel before anyone for anything, but in this case he actually pleaded with the Watch Commander to reconsider his decision based on the relationship he and his family had formed with Duke. The Watch Commander turned a deaf ear to Victor's plea and at that moment, Victor became a victim. His love of duty and his respect for his superiors ceased in one fell swoop. The emotional impact of losing his friend and partner, Duke, sent Victor into an emotional tailspin. He became non-communicative with his superior officers. He didn't understand how to deal with his children's and Svetlana's pain at the loss of Duke with whom they had related as a member of the family. Although his annual test results were average, his superiors were unable to give very high grades regarding his devotion to duty and his attitude towards his work ethics. He did his job without any show of enthusiasm and when he was up for promotional review, he was passed over on numerous occasions over the years.

Early on, Victor realized that he had a problem and he consciously made every effort not to lose his cool when in a heated situation. As he grew older, it appeared that Victor's Russian heritage left an indelible impression on his personality that caused him to be quick to anger, which sometimes overrode his powers to reason within the department's guidelines. On numerous occasions he overstepped his bounds and physically reacted when he knew there would be repercussions within the department hierarchy. On one occasion, during a traffic violation, he tasered a driver who became verbally abusive, jumped out of his car, and threatened Victor. When the driver hit the ground, he went into cardiac arrest and it was all Victor could do to get the man the needed medical attention as fast as he could call in the alert. The lawyers for the driver had a field day in court with Victor as a scapegoat. The victim received a handsome settlement from the state and the entire incident went on Victor's record.

There was another time, late one evening, when Victor pulled over a driver who was weaving erratically all over the road. It turned out to be an African-American high school kid who was high on marijuana and beer. When Victor asked for his license, the kid threw open the door, pulled out a toy gun as if threatening to shoot. It was too dark for Victor to ascertain if the gun was real or not. He took a defensive stance and from a crouch position, drew his weapon and fired one shot, hitting the kid in the shoulder, causing him to drop the gun. Had he shot to kill, there would have been very little question as to whether or not Victor had been in the right, but because he spared the kid's life, the legal system played havoc with the rights of the student and accused the arresting officer of over-reacting. The case was played out in the press, the ACLU jumped into the fray, accusing the officer of discrimination against a minority and Victor again found himself defending his actions. Where was his support from his superiors? His attorney, who was supplied by the department to defend his actions, proved to be a lackluster, unimaginative novice who appeared to side with the defendant. Victor was chastised by his superiors, suspended from duty for a month (with pay), and when he returned to duty, he was informed that the court records from the incident would go on his record.

There were three or four more such incidents over the course of his career that were added to his record and whenever it came time for Victor to address the promotion board, it appeared that all his good work within the community was overshadowed by those few incidents. At the end of his twenty-fifth year, according to department policy, he was informed that there was a mandatory retirement rule for any officer that did not move up in the ranks. Despite supports from some of his superiors, and in a formal ceremony, Victor was turned out to pasture in his fifty-fifth year.

Only after his forced retirement was he able to recapture some of his early social demeanor, renewing friendships and openly demonstrating concern for the activities and events within his community. The one basic relationship he was unable to salvage was with his wife of thirty years. During his twenty-five year tour of duty as a police officer, there developed a wall between Victor and Svetlana that he was never able to tear down. It was as if they spoke different languages. He was never abusive towards her, but he couldn't find the words to share with Svetlana the details of his anger and disappointment with his job performance. *She just wouldn't understand*, he rationalized. The workings of the police society and mentality were almost a cult concept. He also had become somewhat estranged from his children whose lives had taken them to the far side of the country where their contact with their parents were limited to occasional phone calls and a short note with a snapshot or two.

The retirement years had not been kind to Victor Vordenko. Finding employment outside of the law enforcement field had not been a problem with his experience and education. He worked as a security coordinator for a city department store, but a few years after his retirement from the NYPD, his health began to deteriorate, first with minor ailments and later with more severe issues. Two heart attacks, cancer of the stomach and colon, and issues with the prostate and diabetes had turned his earlier, carefree life into a living hell. Still, Victor managed to keep his pleasant demeanor and sense of humor under pressure, something he had practiced over the years in lieu of his earlier psychological evaluations. The large Vordenko who took such pride in his earlier physical stature was now reduced to a mere shadow of the man he once was. The bathroom mirror had become his worst enemy and it was all he could do to avoid the sight of his own reflection.

~~~

Each day at the retirement home after spending some time with Svetlana, he walked down to the game room where he and Morris Silverstein had a running game of gin rummy that had been going on for a couple of years. To date, Morris owed Victor over ten thousand dollars, all on paper. Better than the actual game was the pastime they indulged in as Victor verbally spent the money.

"Okay, Morris, tonight we eat at Le Cirque and it's your treat. Deal?"

"Le Cirque? You must be crazy, Victor. That's a whole month's Social Security check. Let's make it the Stage Deli, but you can't order anything over ten dollars."

"You're such a *schnorer*," said Victor using a Yiddish slang word for "cheap." With a smile he laid down his hand. "Gin," he said, gloating.

"Such a cheat. You've got to be cheating," burst out Morris. "How can a man have gin so often? I shouldn't be playing with a *goy* cop," he kidded. He pushed the cards over to Victor for a new shuffle. They played on with Victor winning the next few hands.

"How is she?" asked Morris, peering sheepishly over the top of the cards in his hand.

"The same." He paused before he added, "Sometimes I wish it were over, Morris. You know what I mean?"

"Yeah, I know. It would be a blessing if she would go peacefully. My wife Ruthie just closed her eyes one night and it was over. God was good to us. I don't know where you get the strength…" From his seat Morris noticed a short, squat man enter the game room from the hallway. Morris had seen him before; a friend of Victor's. "I think you got company," he said as Victor turned to see who had come in.

He was indeed Victor's friend. He had visited on numerous occasions where the two men chatted in privacy in the corner by the window. Morris was not invited to join them but he just assumed they were talking family business. He never asked.

Victor laid down his cards and got to his feet. "You mind if we finish this another time, Morris? My friend and I have business to discuss…"

"No, no. We'll do dinner later?"

"Sure. About six. I'll knock on your door." Victor walked across the room to greet his friend, Mr. Brown.

Chapter 12

It was good to be back on patrol duty after two months confined to a desk on the North Station. Marge needed the freedom of the outdoors where she could see the movement of street life and activity. Desk duty was nice; it was safe, but patrol duty was a rush with activity going on all around her. Sometimes on her off duty hours, she wished she was actually working. After the breakup of her marriage she sequestered herself from all personal relationships. She dated a few times, but it seemed that all potential relationships were shallow events that were supposed to end up between the sheets. They were meaningless adventures going nowhere with no rewards. She wanted to have something to show for the time she put into dating and making small talk and meaningless petting. There had to be something better.

She looked over at her partner, Anthony, as he sat behind the wheel, cruising along Charleston north of the 95 on a relatively quiet evening. *He's a gentle soul*, she thought. Tall, good-looking, good sense of humor, and rather bright. Funny, but in all the time they had worked together he had never put a move on her. In a way it was comforting. She could relax with Anthony without fear of being hit on. For all she knew, he could be gay, but she doubted it. She just wasn't his type and as luck would have it, he wasn't hers either. They were a good team and there was no way in hell that either of them would want to create a situation where their personal emotions over-rode their sense of duty. She had seen it happen in other relationships; it never worked.

"I spoke to the Captain yesterday," he said. "I think you're at the top of the list for promotion."

"What makes you say that?" she asked.

"Just a gut feeling. He spoke very highly of you, telling me how lucky I was to be partnered with you. I got the impression he was letting me down easy."

"You're probably over-reacting or taking what he said out of context."

He looked over and gave her a reassuring smile. "I'm not upset. Marge. Jeez, if anyone deserves it, it's you. I just thought you'd like to know what's going down."

"Yeah. Thanks." What could she say? She knew he was disappointed, as much as she would be if the shoe were on the other foot. Her thoughts were broken by the static and then the voice from the dispatcher on the other end of the intercom. "Car 211, Car 211, do you read?"

Marge picked up the mike. "211. Linden here. I read you."

They had responded to four calls already, filled out a plethora of paperwork, accompanied a perp down to the station for booking, and were looking forward to the end of their shift when they could drop into Pete's Bar for a quick tequila shooter before contemplating their separate plans for the evening. Now, the body of an infant child had been found in a dumpster only minutes away and before Marge could sign off, Anthony already had his overhead lights flashing and the siren blaring. Of all the calls, the ones she dreaded most those involved a child. Was it just a feminine thing or did every member of the squad react the same way? It would be another one of those late afternoon investigations that would depress the hell out of her and finally be turned over to the detectives for investigation.

The body of a child, one that showed signs of abuse with scarring and discoloration around the head and torso, the death of innocence, was almost more than she could bear. With pad and pen in hand, taking one side of the street while Anthony took the other, they walked up and down questioning onlookers, anyone who might have seen something...anything. The frustration and disappointment was overwhelming. She consciously fought to hold onto her emotions. *My God, it was only a baby,* she thought. *A tiny, black infant barely a year old. What could someone possibly have been thinking? An act of violence compounded by drug usage? Surely not an act of a responsible, normal human being,* she ruminated. She had to get out of here. The alley was suffocating her and the blank faces of the disenfranchised huddled around outside the yellow tape were a blur of anonymity. Thankfully, the detectives relieved her and Anthony to return to duty. They headed to the station over on Stewart and the Boulevard to file their report.

Tonight it will take more than a single shot of tequila to erase the memory of that dead child, she thought.

Chapter 13

Falk was tired of hanging out. That's what he was hired to do; keep his eyes open, take notes and report in. Into the third week he was able to document a pattern. Hassan Mohammed and Imam Jahl met at the Samir Restaurant on Third Avenue, usually on different days. Once their collaboration had been established, it was easy for Falk to plant a small, sophisticated listening device on the underside of the corner table where they customarily sat when dining together. What was most difficult was the waiting since their meetings were never on the same day and rarely at the same time. Falk just had to be patient — what he was being paid to do.

Finally, on a Thursday, late in the afternoon, the Imam and Hassan met for what appeared to be a social repast. Four other men were in attendance; obviously bodyguards who were strategically positioned. Two were at a table near the entrance and two took a table adjacent to the two principals. The Imam arrived a few minutes after Hassan and after greeting each other in the traditional embrace and kiss, they took their seats at their usual table where they could converse without being overheard.

"I have rather disturbing news, Hassan. The F.B.I. has frozen all assets of the Holy Land Foundation. This is a very sad state of affairs. Our friends in Iraq and Afghanistan depend upon our support to continue with jihad. I sometimes have to wonder about the competence of some of our leaders. The last fundraiser that was secretly videotaped by the F.B.I. was way over the line. It is one thing to believe in a cause and quite another to advertise to the entire world that the death of the infidels is the aim of Islam..."

"I heard that they put on a play where they enacted the killing of an Israeli civilian and the audience went wild with applause."

"We are drawing way too much negative attention in a city where the Jews proliferate. This would never happen in London or Paris. I think it is time to consider another action where we can make the infidels take the side with our intafada and at the same time, we must consider other ways to funnel zakat into Hamas..."

"The destruction of the Jewish Center for Cultural Affairs would make a perfect target and at the same time show the government that we are still determined to act in concert with Hamas. I said before and I repeat; the World Trade Center was a mistake. We should have targeted the Jews, hit them hard in their houses of worship, then world opinion would have sided with us. By taking out the Trade Center, we alienated the entire infidel world that has no allegiance to the murderous Jews and their land-grabbing designs. The American invasion of Iraq never would have happened had we chosen the true enemies of Islam."

They continued to ponder the logistics of how they would proceed with the destruction of the Jewish Center. The Imam had long considered the ramifications of such a bold act. Until this time, Hamas and its supporters in the United States were considered nothing more than an impotent group of Islamists capable of talking a more serious game than they were able to perform. *What a glorious day it would be for the followers of Islam if we could shatter the tranquility of the Western world by destroying the cultural center of the Jews,* he thought.

At the same time, Hassan Mohammed was contemplating how he could monetarily profit from this insane attempt to bring the entire world to the brink of a total conflagration.

~~~

The meeting that Victor and John Brown had previously arranged took place at nine in the evening in Room 731 of the Plaza Hotel. It was the first time Victor had come face to face with the priest.

Before we go ahead, Victor, I think that Father Ignatius has a few things he'd like to run by you," said John Brown as he turned his attention to the priest who sat across from the two men.

"John tells me that you're ready to move on, Victor. Is there any reason why you've decided to take the final step at this time?"

Victor paused to reflect on his response. A gentle smiled crossed his lips. "The wheels appear to be fast coming off the wagon, Father."

The Guardian List

"Have you spoken to your oncologist?"

"Probably two months at the very most. The cancer is spreading faster than the doctors can keep it in check. The meds are taking their toll. I could wait for a few more weeks and then check into a hospice. It's bad enough to have to watch my wife waste away, but I don't want to put it off to where my kids' lives will be disrupted any more than they've been these past few months. It's always the living, those we leave behind, who suffer the most."

"So true."

"I've put everything in order. My attorney has the will; the kids get everything that I've put in trust for them. More than that, what else can I say?"

"I must ask you, Victor. Are you a Catholic?"

"You're going to tell me that what I am planning to do is a sin in the eyes of God, isn't that right?"

"Something like that. I'm not here to try to change your mind. I can offer to hear your confession. I can give you absolution, but one does not give a stone to a drowning man. I want you to know that what you are about to do is, in fact, a very brave act and I'm sure God would understand."

"You did say you were a priest," said Victor through a half smile. "What kind of priest would condone the taking of a life?"

"One who understands the real world, the pain brought about by certain acts if those who use God as an excuse to defile the sanctity of human life. I am only a priest, Victor, not God. If it is any comfort, I understand the action you're about to take and I shall pray for your soul."

"I suggest we not wait too long. I have good days and bad days. I don't want the cancer to debilitate me to where I'm not rational or where I physically can't function effectively."

John held up a hand to get Victor's attention. "It's just a matter of days. Everything is almost in place."

Victor rose and shook hands with the two men. With a smile, he said, "It's nice doing business with you both. For what it's worth, you're doing a good thing." With that he took his leave and quietly closed the door behind him.

The two men sat in silence, neither able to summon up the words to describe the pain they both shared.

~~~

Thurman Falk had been on stakeout from the flat across the street from the Samir Restaurant for the better part of two months. It was a painfully tedious assignment. With the use of high-powered binoculars he was able to watch and document the meetings of Hassan and the Imam. Although the cleaning staff at the restaurant stacked the tables each evening, no one thought to search the underside of the table where Thurman had planted the miniature listening device. Fortunately, the meetings between the two men were conducted in English since Hassan spoke no Arabic. The two men met on different days, sometimes twice a week, sometimes as many as four times. The meetings always concerned large sums of money that Hassan turned over to the Imam, money that Hassan had collected from various businesses in the community. Falk could only imagine how much of the total contributions Hassan had skimmed off the top. Around the fourth week, Falk finally found what he was looking for. By the eighth week his suspicions were confirmed. It was on the Thursday of each week that the two men met at six in the evening, just after the call to prayer. It was a social meeting where they dined. Hassan sipped a bit of arrack, a sweet, liquorish tasting aperitif, while the Imam joined him with strong Turkish coffee as they discussed the current state of affairs from abroad. Otherwise, their meetings were random and happened at any time of the week. Falk mentally congratulated himself. All the waiting was paying off.

~~~

In war it is the innocent who always suffer the most," thought Victor. He hoped he would be able to act in such a way as to avoid hurting any innocent bystanders.

The previous evening he experienced bodily pains the likes of which he never could have imagined. The pain in his lower back seemed to move to a new level. He became nauseous and thinking he was going to throw up, he staggered into the bathroom and leaned over the sink. His head was reeling and he held onto the edge of the basin with all his strength, hoping he wouldn't pass out. It seemed that he held that position for a good twenty minutes, just waiting for the next spasm to take him to the tile floor. Carefully, he forced himself to stand erect, testing when the next wave would hit. The back pain subsided somewhat to where he could stand erect, but the nausea persisted. If only he could vomit, perhaps it would relieve some of the pressure on his lower back.

He opened the cabinet above the sink and removed a small, round, plastic vial from a row of various size vials. The chemotherapy had worked for a while but once it metastasized and the cancer moved from his prostate into his stomach and back, Victor began to experience Grade-4 nausea. Where the medications worked for a while to alleviate the nausea, they soon lost their effectiveness and the pain persisted through the medication. The drug, dexamethasone, was considered the optimum medication for his condition, but he was reluctant to take any further meds because he felt there was no way to hold back the tide of pain that was raging through his body.

Despite his resolve, he felt he had to do something to at least give himself temporary relief. There were only four pills in the vial and carefully he removed one, popped it into his mouth, and chased it with a couple of swallows of cold tap water. He had reached the point where he had to try to keep a clear head. Most of the other medications had made him drowsy and some even carried him into incoherence where he neither remembered where he was nor what was ailing him. *Just a few days,* he thought. *If only I can hold on for just a few more days, everything will work out fine.*

~~~

It began as a light drizzle. Rain was never good for business during the week. The Samir Restaurant was nearly empty when the Imam arrived with his entourage of two. They were followed shortly thereafter by Hassan and his two goons. The "Reserved" sign on the table at the rear of the restaurant insured the two men their privacy even though there were only twelve tables in the entire establishment along with a ten-foot service bar. Two other tables were occupied with couples that greeted the Imam, either as friends or as members of his mosque. They were just finishing their early dinners and were getting ready to pay their bills and depart.

The front door opened and Victor Vordenko came in, shaking the rain from his topcoat. The waiter who greeted him seemed to remember him from previous visits since Victor had taken three previous occasions to visit the restaurant to familiarize himself with the layout and the ambiance. He removed his outer coat, which he laid over one of the chairs and was dressed in a bulky jacket underneath. He sat down and ordered hot tea while he looked over the menu. He nodded to the first couple as they paid their bill and exited. Victor would wait until the second couple departed before he made his way to the rear of the establishment on his way to the restroom. He only hoped that the rain, now upgraded to a severe downpour, would discourage any other patrons from entering. He would not be ordering any food on this occasion. His nausea was again acting up along with the pain in his lower back. After a few minutes, the waiter returned to take his order. He placed an order for humus and pita, explaining to the waiter that he had had a late lunch and was only looking for a light snack. As he noticed the other couple getting ready to depart, Victor got up and headed towards the rear of the restaurant to where the restrooms were located. Time was running out and he would have to make his move. As he came abreast of the reserved table with the Imam and Hassan, he paused as if he remembered something. On the other side of the room, one of the Imam's men noticed Victor and as he moved to rise as if to question Victor's intent, a blinding flash nearly incinerated him as he crashed through what remained of the wall. The explosion was strong enough to blow out the front of the restaurant, killing Hassan's two men seated by the window and setting fire to the entire establishment. The Imam and Hassan were immediately consumed, as was Victor Vordenko. He had found the ultimate cure for his cancer.

The late night news on all the channels had broadcast the attack. It did not take the police long to identify Victor as he carried his police identification and badge that were almost incinerated but enough remained for a positive verification. By the following morning, the police had pretty much established not only the perpetrator, but the ten victims in the establishment as well.

~~~

As Morris Silverstein was having his early morning prunes and oatmeal, he happened to glance up at the screen of the television monitor. There was a full picture of his friend, Victor. He got up from his chair, walked over to the television to better hear what the announcer was saying. He reached up and increased the volume. As he listened to the announcer's description, tears welled up in Morris' eyes. He stayed transfixed to the screen as the story developed and only when Nurse Francine came running down the hall past the dining room and shouting at the top of her voice did he turn his attention away from the screen.

Within moments, Nurse Francine, along with one of the administrators from the office and two other nurses, followed by two police officers, passed the dining room going in the other direction. The coverage of the death of Victor had finished and Morris made his way out of the dining room and followed the nurses and police down the hall. He was not surprised to see them all converged in front of the room of Svetlana Vordenko. Within moments a crowd had formed in the hallway and rumors began to proliferate.

Svetlana had been found dead by Nurse Francine, a pillow covered the old lady's face. It was a simple case of homicide and it didn't take an intensive police investigation to put the pieces together, thought Morris.

"Oh, Victor…such a mitzvah," said Morris to no one in particular. "I'll sit Shiva for you both, my friend. And about the money I owe you, I'll make a charitable donation in Svetlana's name."

Chapter 14

Officers Marge Linden and Anthony Canu both received their promotions to detective on the same day. There were rounds of congratulations from their fellow officers with drinks at Pete's Bar to toast their new assignments. Marge's friend, Patty Walsh, who was responsible for her becoming a police officer some ten years before, was the first person she called with the good news.

"I knew it!" yelled Patty with a cry of joy. "I knew you could do it. That is just the greatest news ever. We're going to have to celebrate. How about I take my vacation and come over to Vegas for a week? You have room for me?"

"Oh Patty, that would be the kicker. I've got some vacation time so give me your schedule and I'll see if I can get the time off. Vegas hasn't been the same without you."

So it was arranged that Patty would drive up the following week and stay with Marge. The best part of her good news was that she and Anthony would still be partnered as detectives.

~~~

That evening the celebration at Pete's Bar went into the early morning hours. Marge knew she had exceeded her limit, but she thought that the high she was feeling was merely the exhilaration from her promotion and not the one-too-many Margaritas. She had the assurance that no matter how smashed she got, she could depend on her buddy and partner, Anthony Canu, to keep her on the straight and narrow. So when she awoke and the bedside clock told her it was almost noon and she realized that she was not only completely nude, but also not alone, panic set in. What in God's name had she done?

She was afraid to look to the other side of the bed; afraid that she had acquired some sleaze while in a drunken stupor, obviously had sex and now faced the music. Holding the sheet as demurely as she could to cover her privates, she sat up and put her feet on the floor. Slowly, she turned her head and in an instant breathed a sigh of relief and then shock. There was her buddy, her partner, out like a light. What the hell had she done? If he was dead, she would be off the hook, but she could hear his heavy breathing and this was going to be very bad...very bad indeed. Aside from department policy about fraternizing, how the hell was she going to handle this situation once they were positioned face to face in the light of day? She had to pee. First things first.

Breakfast was awkward, to say the least. Anthony was not a man to gloat after a night of passion. In fact, he hung his head as if he had committed some cardinal sin and was about to face hell and damnation. He poked at his fried eggs as if the yokes were about to explode in his face. He couldn't look Marge in the eye. She had depended upon him to get her home safely and intact. He had crossed over the line, taken advantage of her lack of sobriety, and quite possibly ruined their working relationship. He was oozing with guilt.

"About last night..." he tried to open the conversation.

"Forget it," she replied, keeping her back to him as she finished her dishwashing chores.

"If it's any comfort, you were wonderful. I mean, you were very...friendly. I never thought we'd ever do anything like that, what with our professional relationship."

"Timing, Anthony. I guess the timing was just right."

"Yeah, timing. I hope you're not angry."

"Hey, I'm a big girl. I'm as responsible as you. Don't beat up on yourself."

"Thanks."

~~~

Patty arrived late one afternoon of the following week. The two women were as close as sisters, so in the course of conversation when Marge told her about her liaison with Anthony, Patty went into hysterics. "Anthony and you? Oh, my God, he's the object of every woman in the entire Metropolitan Police Department, not to mention a few men as well... and you nailed him? Oh, honey, they're going to give you a medal for action over and above the call of duty."

"It's not funny, Patty. What happens if Captain Peterson should ever find out?"

"Anthony's not that kind of person, Marge. He's as tight-lipped as a Buddhist Monk. If anyone's going to let the cat out of the bag, I can only imagine it's gonna be you, so watch who you confide in…and that means policewomen from San Francisco as well."

"You wouldn't!" screeched Marge. "Oh, Patty, you wouldn't."

"I can be bought."

"You stinker! And I thought we were friends…"

They laughed through the day and into the early evening, Patty teasing and Marge blushing over her indiscretion. It was 'girl's night' with the two women rehashing tales of years gone by when they were students and first discovering their sexuality and the boys they tormented. It was the highlight of Marge's achievement and promotion to detective and there was no one on the planet with whom she would rather share her good fortune.

Chapter 15

Adam Wicker had been confined to the Marietta County Jail pending arraignment on charges of assault with a deadly weapon and first-degree murder. The trial, which took place in Atlanta, lasted five months and although four members of the jury sympathized with Adam's actions, the guilty verdict was handed down with a sentence of thirty-five years to life behind bars. Adam was remanded to the State Penitentiary to serve out his sentence.

The prison population of fifteen hundred inmates was segregated with ten percent whites sequestered in the north wing away from the majority of blacks and Hispanics. No sooner had Adam been incarcerated than word of his notoriety spread throughout the prison population. Among his fellow white prisoners was a preponderance of sympathizers that immediately accepted Adam into the fold as something of a hero. He was looked upon as someone who represented the morality of the white population.

On the other side, there were black gangs that had already marked Adam as a dead man. There was a price on his head. This type of gang mentality accounted for the segregated prison environment. It was pretty well ordained that the first opportunity in which blacks and whites came together, which in practical terms, was rarely, Adam Wicker would pay in the way the state had failed.

Adam had been incarcerated in the State Penitentiary for five years when the Guardian List first came into existence. Adding him to the list was not an easy decision. He was serving time in a federal institution and he was inaccessible to anyone on the outside who might be recruited to mete out the punishment many felt Adam deserved. In the final analysis, Adam's name was relegated to the back burner and given "inactive status." He would be monitored on a regular basis pending any change in his situation.

In the five years he was incarcerated, Adam lived for the day he would find a way to break out of the institution. He had watched numerous failed attempts to escape, usually the results of faulty planning or carelessness on the part of the escapee once on the outside. His motivation to get out was the result of his burning desire to make contact with his daughter, Amy, with whom he had been deprived of contact all these years. She was now in her seventeenth year and he could only imagine what a beautiful young woman she must be. His love for his daughter was his only redeeming quality. But Adam was no fool; once he was successfully on the outside, he knew he would be vulnerable for re-capture should he try to make contact with his daughter. He'd have to find a way.

Adam's break finally came in his sixth year of incarceration. For the first two years he was held in solitary, sequestered from all other prisoners, both black and white.

Once released into the white prison population he worked, first in the kitchen and then with the cleaning and garbage detail and finally in the library where he had time to dwell on a plausible plan of escape. In anticipation of the day he was able to bust out, Adam took advantage of his kitchen chores to stock up on black pepper that he saved in an old sock and stored in the air vent of his cell. If ever he broke out of this place he would need a way to discourage the use of dogs to track him down and he had heard that pepper was the one great detractor for escaping from the bloodhounds that could surely pick up his scent, no matter how much of an advantage he might have in the dense undergrowth.

It was in his sixth year that he was reassigned to a road gang outside the prison walls. The daily ride on the bus from the confines of the prison to the freedom outside was exhilarating. Over a period of time he became possessed with the thought that he might one-day figure out how to make a break for freedom. The gang to which he had been assigned consisted of twenty prisoners whose daily job it was to cut back the dense overgrowth of kudzu that proliferated alongside the main road leading from the local town to the penitentiary.

The ride from the prison to where the men worked each day was only a twenty-minute trip with each man cuffed and manacled. When they arrived at the location where they would work for the day, the cuffs were removed but the leg manacles remained in place. Should a prisoner attempt to escape from the chain gang, his efforts would be greatly inhibited by the restrictions of the leg irons. Two prison guards accompanied the small cleaning crew. They were mounted on horseback and carried shotguns, ever on the alert. The guards were relieved every two hours with fresh officers as a precaution against anyone growing lax on his job of watching over the prisoners. Each day, as he traveled from the prison compound to the work station, Adam could not help but fantasize that there was indeed something that he was missing, something that he had not yet conceived that was a key to his breaking away from his internment.

Adam shared an eight by ten foot cell with Virgil Cole, doing life for killing some total stranger in a bar fight. Both men had been drinking beer for most of the evening while hanging out in the bar. As was his habit, Virgil always packed a piece when out on the town, ever since the time he'd been jumped by a couple of good old boys who stole his wallet and damn near killed him. So this night, out of the blue, a fight broke out over some backwoods piece of trash, and not to be outdone, Virgil pulled out the gun and fired one shot that killed the other guy. It was a senseless crime. Neither guy would have given a dime for the woman over whom they'd been arguing, but it was just a simple matter of honor, too much to drink, and the other guy lost. Virgil had just turned eighteen at the time and now, ten years later, doing hard time, his only thought was to someday get the hell out of this place, go over the wall, and never look back. Only problem was, Virgil had about as much smarts as an eighth grader, having dropped out of school when he was thirteen to work in the cotton fields just south of Augusta. He knew there was a way to break out of this place, but for the life of him he couldn't put it together.

"You ever think of breaking out of here?" he asked Adam a few weeks after they had first been bunked together. He spoke in a whisper a few minutes after lights out when both men were in their bunks.

"Sometimes," answered Adam.

Virgil propped himself up on his elbow. "You got a plan?"

"If'n I did, I wouldn't be talkin' about it. You ever heard the expression, the walls have ears?"

"Damn, Adam. I'm going crazy in here. That's all I think about day and night."

"You know of anyone who ever made it?"

"Yeah, I knew of a couple of black guys who made it out about five years ago."

"They ever get caught?"

"Not exactly. They was both run down and killed by the Sheriff's posse within a few hours. I guess that don't count, does it?"

"Guess not." One thing was certain; if Adam did finally put a plan together, Virgil would not be included. As he dozed off, his last thoughts were of Amy. She and her mother had moved from Marietta after the trial, their whereabouts unknown. She had lived in fear that someday Adam would get out of prison and try to make contact with his daughter. He assumed they had gone into some sort of protection program and changed their names, just in case there was ever a chance that Adam would ever get out of the penitentiary and try to locate them.

~~~

Father Ignatius had tendered his resignation from the church shortly after the shooting at St. Ann's. It was not unusual for a seventy-year old priest to step down from his ministry so there was no question as to the underlying reasons for his decision to retire.

Father Lucius Moreno was in his mid-thirties when he assumed the duties as administrator and took over from Father Ignatius. His one request was that Father Ignatius would stay on in the parish to assist with various duties on a part-time basis. Father Ignatius' one stipulation was that he would not be required to give sermons or take confessions; rather he would serve as an advisor to the young priest on issues of policy and church doctrine. For the five years since his retirement he still bore ill feelings in his heart towards Adam Wicker and secretly he harbored the desire to see Adam outside the confines of the penal institution. There was most definitely a score to settle and each day of his life he prayed to his God that he would live long enough. Now, in his eightieth year, he felt that God had not been listening to his prayers. His work with John Brown was actually the one saving grace in his life. He felt that he was serving some purpose and that, although his duties as a priest were minimal, he was still doing something constructive within the greater scheme of things.

He felt that there was really very little to live for other than his work on The Guardian List.

~~~

It was during the twenty-minute ride on the bus out to where they were cutting back the kudzu from the highway that got Adam's imagination working in high gear. The manacles on his legs were almost the same as the cuffs on his wrists except they were a larger model to accommodate the size of his ankles. He could see that the cuffs were made of two curved pieces of metal that interlocked when the single rail was inserted into the double rail and the teeth of the single rail engaged and locked into the end of the double rail. They were held together by a single rivet on which the two pieces pivoted. On careful examination, Adam surmised that if he could find something to wedge into the double rail, he could possibly twist it and snap the rivet holding the two rails together. But what could he use that would be strong enough to snap the rivet and release the cuffs? The leg irons were much heavier than the cuffs so it would have to be something on the order of a screwdriver that he could jam into the double rail and twist it with enough force to snap the rivet. There was no way in hell he could get his hands on a tool that would give enough leverage to accomplish the job. What if he could break free of his cuffs and manacles? What then? How the hell could he get from the work area, past the guards, and into the thick growth by the side of the road where the kudzu would offer him cover from detection? And then there were the dogs...they

The Guardian List

could smell out a possum and run it down within a mile. Would the pepper be enough to throw them off the scent? It was a crazy idea that had less than a slight chance of success, but he couldn't get it out of his mind. There had to be a way.

The fall weather had turned unusually cool and the green kudzu had begun to turn a yellowish-brown as it dried for lack of seasonal rains. By spring it would rejuvenate itself and cover everything in its wake like a green ocean of waves. But for now, the fall colors were a pleasure to behold as winter lay just ahead.

It was five in the morning when the sirens began to blare and the guards, walking along the parapets with their nightsticks beating out a steady rhythm against the iron grates of the cells, yelling "Everyone up. Roll it out!" Only in times of emergency or some disaster did the prison staff rout out the men at this hour. "Road crew, fall out in the staging area!" yelled the Sergeant in charge.

The twenty regulars staggered down the iron steps to the staging area where roll call was taken. Then without so much as a cup of coffee and a sweet roll, they were marched to the bus and ordered to board.

"What's up?" asked one of the prisoners. This was not usual procedure.

"Fire broke out a few miles from here and we need to form a defense line to hold it until the army can move in with their heavy equipment."

It was unusual for fire to break out in this area with greenery engulfing every inch of the landscape, but it wasn't impossible. If enough kudzu turned brown and dried out, fire could envelope the whole area for miles around and that included the surrounding towns and the prison. Aside from the twenty members of the road crew, the prison was not equipped to use more prisoners outside the confines of the prison walls. There would be no problem in recruiting a sizeable work force, but with only a limited numbers of guards due to cutbacks in the economy, it would not be practical to have a large number of prisoners without a complementary number of guards. The prisoners would be putting their lives on the line fighting a fire with only shovels until they could be relieved by the army working its way over from the local base.

What the prison authorities thought was just a matter of a small fire contained within a few acres of land adjacent to the prison road turned out to be a raging inferno. The bus could not get within five hundred yards of where the fire was consuming everything in its path and the men had to heft their shovels up to the staging area where the local Sheriff was deploying fire fighters. Although the fall air had turned cool, the heat from the blazing inferno could be felt a hundred yards from their destination as they approached along the road. The guards left their mounts at the prison compound and walked alongside the prisoners. When they arrived at the fire line, it was apparent that any attempt to hold the fire would be fruitless, but the guards had their orders and the prisoners set to work digging a trench to try to starve the advancing flames.

Food had been brought up to the work area from the prison and the men took fifteen minutes to grab some sustenance before again tackling the advancing flames. At the end of the day, after fourteen hours on the fire line and still the army had not arrived with help, the men were ordered to return to the bus for the trip back to the prison. The exhaustion was evident as the men were barely able to make it back to the rendezvous area. They would sleep like babies, thought Adam as the guards herded the men back on board the bus for the return trip. In the midst of all the confusion, Adam had devised a plan.

The following day on the fire line a busload of soldiers from the local army base finally arrived to help fight the fire. Confusion prevailed and it was all that the two guards could do to keep an eye on their prisoners as their ranks were penetrated by the well-intentioned soldiers that made it difficult to determine who was doing what and where. Only the evidence of the manacles determined who was a prisoner and who was military. The Sheriff tried to keep the soldiers from penetrating the line of prisoners, but as the fire raged on it was necessary for the soldiers to break through the line to attack where needed.

Adam's plan revolved around a seat belt, the simple mechanism that each prisoner was required to wear once seated on the bus. There were two parts connected to the webbing − the male and the female where the slide was inserted. He needed to obtain the male part of the belt that could be used to insert in between the two rails of the leg manacle. Some time ago, Adam had removed a teaspoon from the dining hall. Later, while working in the woodshop, he ground down the spoon to a sharp edge that he could use as a knife or weapon should an occasion call for it. Most of the prisoners he knew availed themselves of some kind of makeshift weapon in the event that they were put upon by some crazed, delusional prisoner or one with sexual designs while in the shower when the guard's attention was distracted by some diversion. The spoon had been stashed in the metal frame of his cot and had not been detected during the month since he devised it. Now he could use the sharpened edge of the spoon to cut through the webbing of the seatbelt on the bus.

Under the cover of the activity of fighting the fire, there was a good chance he could make his way into the undergrowth of the kudzu on the opposite side of the road from where the flames were devouring the forest. Using the sharpened spoon, he carefully scraped away the material at the bottom of his workpants until he was able to draw a few strands of thread. These he would use to hold the manacle together once he was able to snap the rivets. Then, when he saw his opportunity, he could cut the thread and once free of the manacles, he would be into the cover of the undergrowth. The timing would have to be perfect, but desperate men are inclined to take desperate measures and no one was more desperate than Adam Wicker.

The Guardian List

Chapter 16

The phone rang six times before Roy Patterson could ascertain that it was not some part of his erotic dream tempered with one too many beers from the night before. He reached out with the one hand, threw back the blanket with the other so the cold night air would help to restore his senses.

"Yeah," he mumbled into the phone.

"Hey, Roy, it's Barney…"

"What time is it?"

"Three."

"Are you nuts? What the hell's so damn important it can't wait till morning?"

"I gotta see ya!"

"When?"

"Now." There was a pause as Roy tried to fathom what in the hell was so urgent that Barney had to see him at this ungodly hour. "I got a friend says he's gotta see ya."

Roy's eyes suddenly sprang open as if he'd been slapped hard across the face. He sat up and wavered, trying to navigate his feet to find the floor. "Don't say nothin'," he ordered. Barney knew that Roy was no longer the horn holder so why the hell would he be calling at this hour of the morning? But ever since the word got out that Adam

Wicker had busted out of prison and was on the run, the FBI had moved into Marietta on the outside chance that Adam would try to make contact with some of the members of the Aryan Knights of White Supremacy. It was a natural assumption, but it had been three weeks since his escape and neither anyone in law enforcement nor his contacts in the Marietta area had seen or heard from him. *Adam's no fool*, thought Roy. That boy could survive on stream water and air if he had to.

"Twenty minutes," was all Roy said and then slammed down the phone into the cradle.

"Who was that?" asked his wife, still in a half sleep.

"G'wan back to sleep," he said as he staggered from the bed to the bathroom where he splashed his face with cold water. His head cleared as he saw his reflection in the mirror gazing back at him through glazed, bloodshot eyes. *This is not good,* he thought. *Not good at all.*

~~~

Barney hadn't moved from the one room studio apartment he'd been living in for the past ten years. It was one of a hundred low income flats on the outskirts of Atlanta on the road to Marietta and during the days when they attended meetings together, it was often convenient for Adam to crash at Barney's place to avoid having a face-off with his wife or be seen by his daughter when he had gotten shit-faced at one of the bars after their meeting. Adam had staked out the flat for some twenty-four hours before he knocked on the door and Barney greeted him as if he had been expecting him at any moment. He had heard about the escape on the television and instinctively knew that Adam would show up. The feds could cover just so many places where Adam might materialize and after a week or two, they moved on, leaving a smattering of surveillance to the local police.

When Roy arrived, the two men greeted each other with a warm hug. It had been almost six years since Adam had been sent away and in that time, Roy had stepped down as horn holder of the local Aryan Knights into the lesser role of treasurer. Times were changing and those years when it was fashionable in the South to harass blacks were coming to an end. Integration was becoming acceptable and those who still hung to their old convictions were way out of touch and greatly in the minority. The membership in the Knights had dwindled down to a mere handful of diehards. But despite Roy's cooling regarding segregation, he had always considered Adam as a friend and as such he greeted him warmly.

"How the hell have you managed to elude the cops?" asked Roy in disbelief. He and his fellow Klansmen had been under scrutiny by the feds since word got out that Adam had escaped.

"Weren't easy," said Adam. He was chewing on half a Kentucky Fried Chicken leg that Barney had been meaning to throw out for over a week. It was on the verge of going bad but to Adam it tasted like a Thanksgiving feast. He'd been eating off the land, stealing fruit from various orchards and dumpster diving late at night to avoid detection. After the small talk was over, Adam got down to business. "Where is she, Roy?"

"I don't know, Adam. Couple of days after the trial she disappeared with the kid and no one's seen or heard hide nor hair from either of 'em. Word has it they're up North somewhere, but that's about as much as I know." He looked into Adam's eyes and could see the same determination he had been known for in the old days. Adam now sported a three-week growth of beard but the eyes; they were still piercing and determined. "Wherever she is, Adam, you can bet your last dollar that the feds have her under surveillance and unless you plan on going back to prison, you'd best keep away from them."

"I hear you," was all he replied. "I need to get my hands on some money. Can you help me out? I'll pay you back just as soon as I can find work and get settled."

"You're not planning on staying around here, are you?"

"Hell, no. Maybe Philadelphia or New York where I can get lost in the crowd."

Roy shot a glance over at Barney looking for some sign that what he was about to do was the right thing. Nothing. "There's some money in the treasury I can dig into. Let me see what's available. I'm sure the membership would want to help out."

"You're a good friend, Roy. I'll get out of here just as soon as I can. I don't want to bring any heat down on you and Barney…"

Roy mentally breathed a sigh of relief. The sooner Adam was out of the county or the state, the better it would be for all of them.

~~~

The news of Adam Wicker's escape from the federal penitentiary was both disturbing and welcome to Father Ignatius. His patience was paying off and God was obviously listening to his prayers after all. *Six years was a long time to wait*, he thought as he stared out the window into the darkness of the night. He could only imagine how Mother Terese would have admonished him for what he was contemplating, but it was no longer just a personal issue but one of man's duty to respond to God's wish. Father Ignatius had learned to live with the knowledge that Adam Wicker would spend the rest of his life rotting away in a cell, cut off from his wife and child, as retribution for his heinous act, but in truth, it was not enough. The sore that festered in the mind of the priest continued to grow on a daily basis and it would never be healed until Adam Wicker had paid the ultimate price. He wanted to be there on the scene when it happened. He wanted to be a witness to Adam's blood washing away the hate that festered in his own mind and body. Only then would he once again be able sleep in the comfort and serenity of God's mercy and love.

Father Ignatius knew that he alone possessed the key to Adam's predestination. He and he alone had laid the groundwork some six years previously when he began to pray for a day of reckoning. After the incident at St. Ann's and the incarceration of Adam, it appeared that the community had all but forgotten that there were other victims of the fatal incident, victims that would never have closure as long as there was a remote possibility that Adam might find a way to freedom. His obsession with his daughter, Amy, and his strange and distorted feelings towards Diane, his wife, would eventually drive him to seek contact with them to satiate his perverted sense of caring. Once he was removed from the public safety, it was now time for the remnants of the Wicker family to try to find some peace in the devastation that was once their lives. Diane had been under psychiatric care. She had withdrawn from family and friends, unable to sleep or eat until she was admitted to Emory University Hospital on the verge of a total breakdown. Amy had been remanded to foster care until that time when her mother could once again resume her care. It was during this period when Father Ignatius tried to give spiritual counsel to Diane that he realized that she and her daughter would have to move away from Marietta where the scars of that fateful event would forever be embedded in their minds. They needed to wash the slate clean, to find a world where they could once again be forever disassociated with their lives in Georgia. Only then would the healing begin. And so it was that Father Ignatius took it upon himself to help Diane and Amy begin their new lives with new identities and new surroundings. He turned to a fellow member of the cloth, Father Peter Dugan, who was pastor of a small congregation in Knoxville, Tennessee. Having gone to the trouble of procuring new identities for Diane and Amy, of instructing them both that their safety depended upon their ability to completely submerge themselves into their new personas, he paid for their rail passage and late one night, he saw them off from the Atlanta Station. As far as he could determine, he was the only person who knew their whereabouts and the new identities of the two women. Other than explaining to Father Dugan that the two women were in need of the protection of the church, he did not go into details and Father Dugan accepted them into the small Catholic community and respected their privacy. From the day they departed Marietta they were known as Victoria and Elizabeth Sullivan.

~~~

Falk entered the Burbank, California apartment as quietly as possible without waking Cathy, but no sooner had he closed the front door and set his overnight bag down on the hall chair than the ringing phone shattered the late night tranquility. He made a silent dash for the extension on the bar before it disturbed her sleep, but she had already responded to the phone on the night table and he heard her say, "I think he just got in, Mr. Brown." She called out in the semi-dark, "You there, Thurman?"

"Yeah, honey, I got it." He waited until he heard her disconnect before he acknowledged the caller.

"Can you speak?" asked John Brown.

"Within limitations."

"You've heard?"

"Yeah."

"When can you get on it?"

"Give me a few hours sleep and I'll catch the first available flight."

"Do you know where the wife is?"

"I've heard rumors. I'll have to check 'em out."

"We'll need an exact location."

"Right."

The phone went dead as Mr. Brown hung up without so much as a "thank you" or "goodbye." Falk could always tell when Mr. Brown was agitated by the way he terminated a call. Also, his greetings were terse, no social amenities; right to the point. Falk knew that his association with Mr. Brown constituted some serious, illegal shit. The money was good and from what he could ascertain from the results of the information he was able to gather, he didn't lose any sleep over how it was used. The less he knew, the better.

Falk knew how to count his blessings. His two-year marriage to Cathy was the best thing that ever happened to him. She knew he worked as a private investigator, she knew it necessitated his spending an inordinate amount of time on the road, and she knew better than to question his erratic hours and time away from home. She was a very special woman and Falk felt blessed for having found her and when they were together, he showered her with affection and his undivided attention. As his conversation with Mr. Brown terminated, the light in the kitchen came on and he could hear Cathy puttering. As he entered, she was pulling things out of the refrigerator and setting them on the island.

"You know what time it is?" he asked.

"Time for you to get some food in you. When was the last time you ate?"

"Chicago."

"Five hours ago?"

"Something like that."

"Sit," she commanded and sit he did. She prepared a dish in the microwave and placed it on the table in front of him along with a glass of his favorite wine. "Tough trip?"

"Not too bad. Just a lot of hours staring into empty space. Goes with the territory."

"After you finish eating I want you to shower and I'll give you a rubdown."

"You my mama?"

"Your mama gave you rubdowns?"

"She bossed me around."

"Get used to it," she said as she glided out of the kitchen on her way to the bedroom.

~~~

John Brown had dispatched Thurman Falk to Marietta to try to get a location for the Wicker family. Once their whereabouts could be determined and leaked to Adam Wicker, it would be just a matter of time until he emerged from hiding and became fair game. But however they managed it, the Wicker family had disappeared without a trace. Falk had hit a dead end as he made his way through the Marietta community trying to get a lead on the two women. It was as if they had just gone up in smoke. As a last resort, Falk tried to pull some strings with the Atlanta Police Department and a few contacts with the FBI, but again, he hit a blank wall. Tracing persons of interest had been Falk's expertise, but in this case he was completely baffled by the way his quarry had simply dropped off the face of the earth. After three weeks of turning over every stone imaginable, he reported back to John Brown that his efforts had proven fruitless. John's only consolation was that if Falk couldn't find them, chances were that Adam Wicker wouldn't be able to find them either. For the time being, the Wicker women were safe, but John's objective was to take Adam Wicker down and he would stop at nothing to achieve his objective.

Chapter 17

Although Father Ignatius prided himself on his good health and the fact that genetically he came from a long line of forebearers that lived until they were almost a hundred, the events leading up to Adam Wicker's violent acts and ultimately his escape from prison left the good Father with a feeling of futility and a lack of desire to go on. There were some twenty names on the Guardian List and much work for Father Ignatius to do, but his heart just didn't seem to be in it. It appeared that he was fixated on how he was going to personally avenge the death of his friend, Mother Therese, and the other innocents.

He was aware that by now Mr. Brown and his network was attempting to track Adam Wicker. Father Ignatius knew that he held the key that could bring Adam out into the open. Should he share his knowledge with Mr. Brown and let him set the wheels in motion to hunt down Adam or was his personal desire for revenge a stronger motive to keep the information to himself? *And, am I equipped to ultimately take matters into my own hands?* he asked himself. The concept was contrary to everything he had believed in for his entire adult life. The teachings of his devout parents, his ties to the church, his faith in the Supreme Power...how was it possible that in one instant in time his whole belief system could fracture and deteriorate, crumble and fade as if it never existed? In the extreme, he had to question his own sanity. Was he mentally regressing into some animalistic, nihilistic state wherein his mind shut the door to the most basic principles of humanity? Why didn't he feel revulsion at his own actions, his participation in what he intellectually knew to be anti-social, anti-Catholic, and illegal behavior? Yes, he most definitely needed help. Perhaps he should seek some relief, some solace in the confessional, he told himself.

Divesting himself of his clerical attire and wearing lay clothes, he boarded a train traveling from Atlanta to Knoxville. As the train traveled though the countryside he could find momentary relief in the colors of the trees and foliage as summer gave way to fall and the yellows and reds burst the skyline like an artist's rendition of the creation. He was at peace as the click-clack of the wheels on the tracks lulled him into a hypnotic state of wellbeing. He tried to pray, to ask God for forgiveness, but his thought that God might understand, might forgive him, appeared false and empty. He had traveled a long road from his theology to his lust for revenge and in his heart, he knew there was no turning back. He was lonely with no God to turn to and no Mother Therese to share his intimate thoughts. He knew that only in the death of Adam Wicker could he find some relief, some inner satisfaction that might eventually return him to his spirituality.

~~~

Over the past six years, the Sullivans had reinvented their lives, put the thought of Adam out of their minds, and moved forward with the help of their faith and newly formed friendships. Diane's major concern was the wellbeing of her daughter who was now on the brink of womanhood and who had learned that in changing her name from Amy to Elizabeth, she had in a sense been reborn. At first, it was almost impossible for a day to go by without dwelling on Adam and the events at St. Ann's, but with their new identities, slowly, slowly, Adam's persona began to fade into the past and in their current lives, there was no longer an Adam Wicker. But that illusion was shattered the morning when Victoria picked up the local paper and read that Adam had escaped from prison and was yet to be apprehended.

All her fears and anxieties returned and all the confusion and guilt of the past overwhelmed her. It had been her choice to bed down with Adam Wicker those many years ago and it was her getting pregnant and producing a love child that was to bring all the imagined joys of living with the man of her choice to fruition. But as her dream slowly dissolved into Adam's alcoholic binges and physical abuse, Victoria turned inward and accepted the responsibility that everything that had gone wrong was her fault and her fault alone. She needed to speak to Father Ignatius. He would be able to give her the confidence she sorely needed in this time of confusion and anxiety. What would she do if Adam found them, if he tried to see Elizabeth or harm her in any way? What could she do? The phone rang and as if he was reading her mind, it was Father Ignatius.

"I'm in town for a few days and I thought it would be pleasant if we could dine together, you and Elizabeth."

"We need to talk, Father."

"I know. That's why I'm here, Victoria."

~~~

Adam was still hiding out at Barney's place while he tried to formulate some plan that would ultimately reunite him with his wife and daughter. He refused to accept the fact that in the eyes of the law, Diane was no longer his wife, the divorce having become final the year after his incarceration. He had convinced himself that what had transpired in the past between him and his wife was merely an unfortunate incident and their estrangement was temporary, nothing that he couldn't set right once he could meet with her face to face. He had not had a drink in six years, thanks to the state that forced him to kick the habit, but he was delusional in thinking that it was only his drinking that was responsible for their marital problems. Over the past six years he had convinced himself that given the opportunity, he could set things right.

The beard and mustache along with his shaved head had altered Adam's appearance enough to where he could appear in public without detection. Among their friends and associates, Barney was never considered the brightest bulb on the tree, but periodically he had flashes of brilliance that were unexplainable. While taking care of some errands over by St. Ann's Parish, he happened to

The Guardian List

notice the new priest, Father Moreno, standing on a ladder changing the marquee with the quote of the week and an announcement of the day's hours and activities. Barney had seen the priest on various occasions and knew him by reputation, but he no longer attended mass since some time before the Adam Wicker incident. As a gesture of friendliness, Barney stopped to chat.

"Anything I can help you with, Father?" he asked.

Father Moreno looked down from the ladder but did not recognize the speaker. "That's very kind of you but I think I've got a handle on it."

"You're the new priest, aren't you?"

The priest smiled. "I guess that's relative. I've been in this parish for six years. You're not a member, are you?"

"Oh, no, sir. I used to attend regularly with my parents…when Father Ignatius was pastor."

"Unfortunately he only recently decided to leave us. Don't know what St. Ann's will do without him."

"Is he no longer serving? In the church, I mean."

"Oh, you know how it is with us priests. We can retire, but we continue to be involved one way or another in some parish or church project. Father Ignatius has moved up north to work in another parish, I believe."

"Really? And where might that be?" asked Barney.

"Were you a friend of Father Ignatius?"

"He baptized me and he gave last rites to both my parents. I guess you could say we were friends."

"Yes, I guess so." Finished with the sign, the priest alighted from the ladder and wiping his hands on a work cloth, he extended his hand in greeting. "With whom do I have the pleasure?"

Barney shook the hand and mumbled his name almost incoherently as the priest beamed. *He's a friendly guy*, thought Barney. "About Father Iggy," said Barney, using the priest's nickname that only his closest associates dared to use.

"He moved up north to a small community outside of Knoxville. Didn't say much about it but I think he's got some distant family up there."

"Would you happen to have the name of the parish?"

"C'mon into the office. I'm sure the secretary must have it."

~~~

It was the first plausible lead as to the whereabouts of his wife and daughter. "Follow the priest," joked Barney. He was proud of himself and even if the whereabouts of Father Ignatius proved to be a dead end, at least it would get Adam out of his apartment. Barney had the impression that Adam was destined to stay entrenched in his pad indefinitely with no way to get him to move on. If it happened that the local police or the FBI ever got wind that Adam was taking refuge in Barney's pad, he could be indicted for aiding and abetting a known felon which could mean a long haul in prison. The day that Adam announced that he was leaving was the day that Barney and Roy breathed a collective sigh of relief.

~~~

Father Ignatius settled in to helping Father Dugan with administrative chores. The younger priest appreciated clerical help from his guest, but Father Ignatius declined the offer to serve mass or hear confession. He claimed that his health was not up to the rigors of administering the sacrament. He was still fighting his personal demons and his mind was elsewhere.

Had I left enough bait in the trap? he asked himself. *Will Adam bite?*

~~~

Thurman Falk was tenacious when he set his sights on a task. He had turned over every possible stone trying to find where Adam could conceivably be hiding. He was convinced, without a doubt, that the road to Adam's whereabouts was tied to the location of his ex-wife and daughter. Their disappearance was much too neat, too perfect. Falk's instincts kept bringing him back to the one theory that kept eluding him: Adam's wife had been a devout member of the church and whenever Falk was able to interview one of the congregants, the name of Father Ignatius always seemed to come up. Since the escape of Adam Wicker, Falk had interviewed the priest on two occasions. If Father Ignatius knew of the whereabouts of the Wicker women, he did not give Falk the impression that he was a party to their disappearance. Why shouldn't Falk take his word? Wasn't the priest an associate of John Brown? But Falk needed to reassure himself that Father Ignatius was not holding back information. He had to speak to the priest one more time before he closed the door and moved on.

Father Moreno was now at a loss for what to do in light of the fact that all of a sudden the whereabouts of Father Ignatius was a question of concern to more than one source. When Falk learned that Father Ignatius was no longer associated with St. Ann's, he considered the outside chance that the good Father could easily be the key to locating the Wicker women. Father Ignatius had not appeared to be secretive in revealing his destination to Father Moreno. If he preferred that Father Moreno not reveal his destination, he had only to say the word. Such was not the case and Father Moreno had already told the other gentleman where Father Ignatius could be found. Now this officious, private detective was intimating that Father Ignatius' safety could be compromised. He could only surmise that the proper thing to do would be to share whatever information he had with the detective.

~~~

It was not difficult to locate the Priest who was now residing in a small cottage on Robinwood Lane in a cozy, middle-class section of Knoxville. After some investigation that revealed that the cottage was rented to one Victoria Sullivan, Falk was able to put the pieces together and the full picture evolved. His duty was to report back to John Brown who had hired him and was paying his expenses. But Falk concluded that there was something going on with the priest that was out of character. If the priest knew where the Wicker women were living, why hadn't he reported it back to John Brown? Where were the Wicker women now? No one had seen or heard from them in almost a week. Victoria had taken an extended leave of absence from the real estate office where she was employed as an office manager and Elizabeth had dropped out of school the same day her mother disappeared from the house on Robinwood Lane. It didn't take a brain surgeon to conclude that the two women were on the run, but what could possibly be going on in the mind of Father Ignatius?

It had been over a week since the priest had helped the Sullivans board a bus to New York City where he had arranged for them to take temporary refuge in the Marymount Convent in the Bronx where only the Mother Superior had an inkling of their situation. On the word of her longtime friend, Father Ignatius, she accepted the two women into the safety of the church. *But have I outsmarted myself?* thought the priest. Did Adam Wicker take the bait and at this very moment, was he trying to locate his whereabouts? Or had he miscalculated Adam Wicker's craving to make contact with the daughter he had not seen for some six years? With each passing day, the priest was losing confidence in his plan. The one thing he had not counted on finally came to pass.

The ringing of the front doorbell aroused him from a restless sleep. The clock on the nightstand read 2:10 in the morning. This was it, what he had been waiting for these past nine days. He slipped into his robe and opening his overnight bag, he removed a small revolver, a P32 like the one he had seen government assassins use in the movies. He drew back the slide releasing a round into the chamber and then placed the compact weapon in his robe pocket. He was amazed at how calm he felt, how clear was his head with his determination to carry out this act. Placing his hand around the grip of the revolver, he cracked the door a few inches without removing the safety chain. It was too dark outside to ascertain who might be visiting at this ungodly hour but in his mind there could be no doubt. He stepped back from the door expecting the caller to make a move to kick in the door. The voice from outside was calm and friendly.

"Sorry about the hour, Father. Can we talk?"

Father Ignatius released his grip on the weapon, closed the door and released the chain. He flipped on the wall switch that illuminated the room in a soft glow from four table lamps. He opened the door and stepped back as John Brown entered. Without exchanging amenities, he did a cursory glance around the room. It reeked of the feminine touch. As he heard the door close behind him, he turned to confront the priest.

"How did you find me?"

"Isn't that the message you were sending? Not very subtle, Father, and I must say, a bit ill-conceived. May I?" he asked, pointing to the couch. The two men sat facing each other. "I should have anticipated this the moment I learned that Adam had escaped."

"Mr. Falk?"

"Yes. It took him a while to put the pieces together, but in the end he proved worthy of the high esteem in which he's held by the organization." Without changing a beat he removed a small vial of pills from his pocket. "May I trouble you for a glass of water? I've been traveling for the better part of the night."

The priest got up, went into the kitchen where he retrieved a small bottle of purified water from the fridge that he handed to his guest. The priest suddenly felt uncomfortable, like a schoolboy who'd been caught in the act of some childish misadventure.

"You and I, Father; it appears that we're cut from the same mold. Had I been there, at St. Ann's, the night of the massacre, I'd have done exactly what you're planning."

"This is between Wicker and me…"

"You and I, we have a pact."

"This goes beyond our agreement."

"And then what?"

"The clock is ticking."

"There is still much to be accomplished. We *have* made an impact, believe it or not. I implore you, Father, to leave Wicker to the organization."

The priest did not reply and out of respect, John did not press him. He glanced around the room. It was scantily furnished, almost austere. He could only surmise what life must have been like for the two women these past four years, never knowing when they might have to pack up on a moment's notice and head for another place of refuge. Now that time had arrived.

The priest sat stoically lost in his own thoughts. Intellectually he knew that John Brown was right, but in his heart he was consumed with a kind of anger that obscured his power to reason clearly. As he looked over the simple furnishings of the cottage, he questioned his own motives for placing the Wicker women in harm's way, knowing that one day he would use them as bait to lure Adam Wicker. The austere setting was depressing. He had sequestered the two women away like lowly animals convinced that his actions were for their safety, obscuring his own true motives. How often had he told his congregants, "The road to hell is paved with good intentions."

"The women…I assume they're out of danger?"

The priest nodded, not wanting to divulge any more information than necessary.

"Have you considered that what you're planning could very well implicate the women? You've done an admirable job in providing for their safety, but there were other ways you could have provided for them if you'd taken me into your confidence." He looked around the room with a sense of pity. "These women deserved better. I must be honest, Father; you took them from one place in hell and relegated them to another."

As Father Ignatius sat and heard the words of John Brown, he realized that his own actions began to take on a clarity that repulsed him. What had he done to these poor women in the name of his own desire for revenge? In a sense, he had imprisoned them as surely as the state had imprisoned Adam. The sound of John Brown's voice brought him back to the reality of this encounter.

"I beg you, Father, reconsider your intent. The wheels to bring Adam to justice have already been set in motion."

"You know where he is?"

"We know where he'll eventually end up, thanks to you. The question is, 'Do you step aside and let us do what we're best equipped to do or do you still feel that taking matters into your own hands is the way to go? I once walked in your shoes, Father, so I won't try to dissuade you. But I do wish you would reconsider."

Their association over these past few years had created an unusual bond between the two men. They had dealt in the most costly commodity – death. John Brown was the practitioner; Father Ignatius was responsible for the morality and spiritual conscience that absolved their fellow compatriots of the stigma of killing another human being. It was a marriage made in heaven and now its continuation rested solely on the shoulders of the priest.

Chapter 18

Among friends and colleagues, Mason Arnot was referred to as "slicker than owl shit." An insatiable appetite, not only for fame and fortune, but to win at all costs, drove the forty-five year old attorney. An acquaintance once said of him, "He'd defend Adolf Hitler, Charles Manson, and the Devil, if the price was right. Sadly, he'd probably get a verdict of 'not guilty' for all three!" He was that powerful in his courtroom presentation. He could wrap a jury around his little finger as if they owed him money. He depended upon his movie star good looks and his ability to subvert the meaning of the law, leaving the jury confused and unable to conclude "guilt beyond a reasonable doubt" despite the preponderance of evidence for a guilty verdict. It was a gift. Most prosecuting attorneys in the Los Angeles criminal court system dreaded the thought of having to face off with Arnot, even with the weight of evidence against the accused. He could have been successful as an actor had he chosen to take that road early on in life, encouraged by a domineering mother and a successful father who sat on the State Supreme Court, his bent in life was pretty well-plotted out for him at an early age.

While attending UCLA law school, he clerked for one of the leading criminal law firms in the city. Early on he learned that the law, as written, was fraught with errors of omission and ambiguities, hazy, loose, muddy, nebulous, obscure, and unspecific. 'What a goldfield of unclear legalese was there just waiting to be manipulated in the defense of an accused,' he concluded early in his introduction to trial law. He began with the premise that a jury was composed of twelve individuals totally ignorant of jurisprudence. They were best equipped to hand down a verdict, not on the basis of the letter of the law, but on the emotional fervor and ardor the defense attorney was able to elicit. Murder: unless the perpetrator was actually caught in the act, or the DNA somehow matched the victim, or there was an outright confession; all else was ambiguous, hearsay, conjecture, held up to scrutiny wherein the concept of "guilty beyond a reasonable doubt" could be influenced and manipulated by a cleaver defense. Mason Arnot was a perfectionist when it came to the manipulation of evidence. Black could easily be construed as gray, as could white; the preponderance of guilty evidence rested on the side of the prosecution and loomed like a large bull's eye to be targeted by a cleaver practitioner firing off volleys of doubt.

The year was 1999. Liam McNair had gone on a rampage after a heavy night of drinking and drug use. He entered a bar, gun in hand, another stuck into his waistband, and arbitrarily began firing into the crowd of late night revelers. He managed to kill six patrons of the bar along with the bartender and the bouncer. There was no doubt as to his guilt. But Mason Arnot saw a man who was mentally disturbed and obviously not competent to stand trial. The lawyer pleaded out a verdict of not guilty on the grounds of insanity and McNair was remanded to a state facility for the mentally disturbed.

In 2005, upon his release from custody on the grounds that he had paid sufficiently for his crime and was well enough to return to society, McNair got into an argument in his workplace, an upscale restaurant that had a history of hiring ex-cons to help them in their quest to return to society as responsible citizens. He walked out in a huff only to return hours later, gun in hand, shooting everyone in sight. By the time he was taken down by an off-duty police officer, McNair had killed the restaurant owner/manager, two kitchen workers and wounded six others. The front pages of the local newspapers devoted a half page condemnation of the penal system. How could Liam McNair have been paroled back into the society that he had violated only five years previously? Anchor evening news condemned everyone even remotely connected with the action of permitting McNair to return to society.

It appeared to John Brown that no one looked to the real source of McNair's actions upon his release from his incarceration. No one considered for a moment that the attorney who pleaded out insanity for his client knew that he was defending a time bomb, knew that sooner or later McNair would return to society and repeat what he had started. In reviewing the background of Mason Arnot, John Brown found two other cases in which Arnot had defended known killers, twisted the evidence in such a way that in its confusion, the jury handed down not guilty verdicts, only to have the defendants commit almost exactly the same crimes shortly after their trials. *"Doesn't Mason Arnot have any social conscience?"* thought Brown. Sure, the lawyer was doing his job and he was giving the best defense he could possibly give, a trust that he held sacred. But in the final analysis, there were more than fifteen dead in the wake of three murderers and no one held either the court, the jury, or the defense attorney to account. John Brown had debated with himself the pros and cons of including Mason Arnot on The Guardian List. He knew that he was playing God. He knew that he alone was making decisions that most probably could best be handled by a committee. But in the final analysis, the responsibility rested on John Brown's shoulders alone. He could not, in good conscience, expect others to share in the decision of whether or not a fellow human being should or should not live.

Chapter 19

Arnold Hoffman and his younger brother by one year, Sidney, were products of a Jewish family, raised in a middle class neighborhood of Brooklyn, New York. The brothers both attended Erasmus Hall High School and both went on to attend Brooklyn College where they received degrees in Business Administration. Upon graduation, both Hoffmans gravitated to Wall Street and the firm of Dunbar and Watson, a medium-sized brokerage house. Everyone said that the Hoffman boys could have been twins, so close were they in physical appearance and business acumen. But the younger brother, Sidney, was more reserved in his personal demeanor than was his older brother. Sidney was quite conservative in his dealings with his customers as if each investment was a financial responsibility to be taken with the utmost care and fiduciary obligation.

On the other hand, Arnold had a gambler's mentality and in many instances, placed his accounts in high-risk stock situations that often resulted in financial disaster and loss of client confidence. He rationalized that "there were plenty of fish in the sea" and he was right. Arnold not only recklessly played the market with his client's funds, but his own as well and by the fifth year as a broker, he had accumulated debts in excess of quarter of a million dollars.

To offset his personal losses, he made bad judgment calls on behalf of some of his clients in order to generate more commissions. He was caught up on a veritable downward slope, unable to reverse the flow. He borrowed from his younger brother and his father to meet his day-to-day obligations, all the while searching for some scheme to reverse his losing ways. Although conservative in his business relationships, Sidney turned a blind eye to his brother's reckless dealings, never questioning how or when he would be reimbursed. Such was the bond among the Hoffmans.

Although in their middle thirties, they both lived in the home in which they were raised only a few blocks from Prospect Park, a neighborhood in Brooklyn that at one time was fashionable and middle class. However, over the years, the demographics of the area had changed from Jewish working class to ethnic black and Hispanic gang-infested. The community at one time took pride in the clear sixty-acre lake within the park. Parents could rent a rowboat for an outing with the family on a weekend afternoon. That lake was now a cesspool of debris with a foul smell emanating from the algae and rotting garbage. The once beautiful 585-acre park with its rolling hills and carefully tended plants and trees was now a veritable battlefield dominated by gang warfare. The Hoffman boys lived for the day when they could move their parents out of the Brooklyn squalor and into a modest home somewhere on the North Shore of Long Island. Thus motivated, Arnold conceived of an idea that had the potential of solving all of his monetary problems. He patiently recruited his brother who was wary of any financial dealings that Arnold might conceive.

Arnold attempted to explain to his younger brother who was dubious about the whole idea. "Young people pay into the system. The money that has been acquired from year to year gets paid out to help support older people who paid into the system over a prolonged period of time. You could say it's like a pyramid where those people entering the system at the bottom support the guy at the top. As long as the public pays into the system, its solvency is secure just as long as the guy at the top eventually dies."

"I thought pyramiding was illegal."

"It is. That's why they call it Social Security."

Sidney was at first reluctant to use his client accounts for any kind of scheme that might jeopardize their security, but Arnold was a manipulator, a silver-tongued con artist who knew just how to manipulate his younger brother.

Over a two-year period, the Hoffman brothers created the financial fund bearing their family name: The Hoffman Fund. Its investors were promised outlandish interest returns on their investments in the form of shares, which they could redeem yearly or reinvest and over a period of years, their money would compound with unimaginable returns. The Fund used current investments to cover current payouts and the original equity was invested in highly speculative stocks and bonds with great potential that could be realized in a strong bull market with a quick turnover.

The Guardian List

In only five years, The Hoffman Fund had a bank value, on the books, in excess of five billion dollars and had a potential of earning well over ten times that amount *if* the investment market of the latter part of the first decade of the second millennium had not gone belly up. The Hoffman family enjoyed five years of prosperity, the likes of which they never could have predicted. Intent on keeping the family clan close, they moved from the modest home in Brooklyn to a luxurious five-acre estate in Huntington, Long Island.

There were three separate residences on the property. The senior Hoffman and his wife occupied the 2,500 square foot house referred to as "the gardener's cottage." Sidney and his newly acquired wife and their two-year-old son occupied the 3,000 square foot guest cottage. The main house, a 6,000 square foot Georgian manor, was inhabited by Arnold and his betrothed, an exquisitely beautiful New York debutante and successful fashion designer in her own right. All three houses were set back from the shoreline with an expansive, rolling green grass lawn beyond which was an unobstructed view of the Sound and Lloyd Harbor in the distance. Arnold prided himself in the acquisition of the estate for a mere twenty million dollars, a deal he referred to as "a distress sale." To avoid the daily trek into and from the city, for a mere five million dollars, he managed to acquire a fortieth floor penthouse on Central Park South.

The Bernie Madoff debacle of 2008, estimated by government prosecutors to have cost individual and institutional investors over sixty-four billion dollars, was only one of the early indications that The Hoffman Fund was teetering on the brink of disaster. The sudden turnaround in the stock market with some securities plummeting below ten year levels, had investors divesting themselves of their stock positions overnight, causing a run on the market, the likes of which had not been seen since 1929. The viability and success of the Hoffman Fund was dependent upon an influx of fresh capital to support the weight of the payouts to previous investors.

With the majority of government auditors and investigators bogged down in the Madoff scandal, The Hoffman Fund was scrambling to salvage as much capital as they could possibly divert from the Fund, funneling huge amounts of cash into offshore accounts and out of the possible detection of the government. So convoluted was the Pyramid/Ponzi scheme that it would take months for federal investigators to begin to unravel the complex investments of The Hoffman Fund.

As the pressures from the imminent repercussions became clear, the Hoffman family began to come apart at the seams. The patriarch, seventy-year-old Hyman, was overwhelmed by the news that the wheels were coming off the wagon. He had not been actively involved in the sales of the Fund, but on occasion, he may have mentioned to relatives or friends the advantages of investing, thereby feeling responsible for the financial losses of those effected within the family social circle.

The Guardian List

"Don't worry, Abba," assured Arnold. "It's only a temporary setback. Give it a few months and it will right itself." But no matter how hard he tried to convince his father and brother, his words rang hollow.

The Madoff fiasco was now front-page news. The failure of the banking and automobile systems was adding to the weakness in The Hoffman Fund. As clients scrambled to withdraw their money from the Fund, Arnold was attempting his "Houdini maneuver" by taking funds from one investment to firm up the failure of other investments, pulling money from one stock to pay off investors panicking in lieu of media reports that the country was on the verge of a financial depression the likes of which had never before been seen. Day by day the news became more grim, the reports from Wall Street spelling imminent disaster in the financial sector.

Three months after the revelation of a market crash, Hyman Hoffman, in a severe state of depression, committed suicide by hanging himself. Upon learning that their life's savings had gone up in smoke and were worthless, fifteen clients of The Hoffman Fund also committed suicide. There were reports of a dozen heart attacks of elderly clients brought on by the disastrous financial news. Numerous wives and elderly widows were left destitute, facing bankruptcy and unable to afford the most meager of daily needs. Finally, the government turned its attention to The Hoffman Fund after numerous reports that "something was not kosher."

In the confusion and activity of the feds with their acquisitions of files and computers, Sidney had already packed up the family and booked passage to the Bahamas where large sums of money had been deposited into private accounts. As long as he and the family remained on the island and kept a low profile, chances were they could live out their lives quite comfortably. It was Arnold's intentions to join his brother, but his future wife was reticent to just pick up and run off to live a life of a fugitive in lieu of her successful career in the fashion industry. Torn between his love for his fiancée and the need to get out of the country, he momentarily chose the former and before he could make a more practical decision, the feds had swooped down and Arnold was indicted for fraud and racketeering. Under house arrest in his five million dollar, fortieth floor penthouse, he conspired with his attorneys as to how he was going to beat the government in their wild accusations. But the writing was on the wall – the outcome imminent.

In the lavish barbecue pit on the patio, Arnold burned all papers that might incriminate him beyond what the government had already acquired. He had always prided himself in having very few weaknesses with little concern for what others might think about him, but here was a man who chose his personal feelings over his common sense that told him to get out – to run, to seek refuge in some far off place away from extradition or prosecution. Now the love of his life, the one weakness he had allowed himself, had finally seen the reality of what was to come, and in a clandestine move, packed up and was gone from his life.

The ride down from the fortieth floor was both exhilarating and frightening. One moment he was standing at the edge of the patio, contemplating his world and all he had acquired and the next he was airborne.

The police report indicated that there was no evidence of foul play. The remains of Arnold displayed no evidence of him having been pushed or thrown over the edge of the railing and there was very little left of the body that resembled a human form. As the coroner's crew went about cleaning up the remains and cordoning off the area for the investigating team, no one took notice of the lone, black man standing at the rear of the collected crowd. Thurman Falk usually did not take an active interest in the how's and wherefore's of his handiwork, but he needed to be sure that his associate had finished the job without any complications.

After a complete investigation by the police, Arnold's death was listed as "suicide" and the case was closed. What assets the authorities were able to recover from The Hoffman Fund, the lavish estate and condo, the cars and any other assets they could recover, would be liquidated and the proceeds would be distributed among the investors at great loss to their original investments. The death of The Hoffman Fund was relegated to the back page of the financial section of the local papers. News of The Hoffman Fund was swallowed up in the notoriety of the Bernie Madoff trial and by the time he was convicted, bigger fish than Ponzi schemes were now swimming on prime time news. Names like AIG, B of A, GM, and

Citigroup were the big stars in the mammoth production of the nation's failing financial reports.

Chapter 20

Over the past five years, John Brown had kept meticulous records of the fate of those who had been on The Guardian List. The only record of the names was inscribed on a computer disk that was stored in a bank vault under John Brown's name. Also, the information about each and every name was coded and only John Brown could decipher the code, so if by some set of unfortunate circumstances the disk fell into unauthorized hands, the names and the information therein would appear to be nothing more than a garbled mess.

There were 155 names inscribed on the original disk; 155 men whose lives had been cut short and terminated for deeds they had perpetrated against their fellow man in violation of the society's rules. Included on the disk were the names of 155 men who had agreed to forfeit the remainder of their lives for that which they believed was for the good of the society. Twenty-three men who had not perished in the act of taking a life, or who had not died from some terminal illness shortly thereafter, had survived to face the legal system. Of those, seven were brought to trial and sixteen were incarcerated in medical facilities where they lived out the remainder of their lives with the aid of artificial means, including intravenous life support and drugs. The seven who lived to stand trial were subjected to the ordeal of prolonged legal proceedings that cost the states massive amounts of money for defense and legal expenses. Only two of the seven lived to be convicted and sentenced to long terms in prison, but they also died before the state could exact its toll. None of the survivors offered up a reasonable defense in lieu of their crimes and none offered the state any information that could possibly be construed as part of a conspiracy.

John Brown was proud of what he had accomplished in five short years of the List, although there was some degree of disappointment. The present day List could have been doubled had he the manpower to carry out the necessary hits. Unfortunately, the number of candidates on the List had diminished, the present number now stranding at fifty-five names. He was constantly reminded that caution and security were the first considerations and foremost in the basic concept of the operation. Over the years he could have given in to his emotions and spread a reign of terror throughout the society, but his chances of any longevity were very limited. He had protected his people knowing that he had made intelligent and careful choices that left no trails. His was not an easy task. He had chosen carefully, both victim and assailant. He had researched each and every case down to the most minute detail leaving absolutely no trail that could possibly incriminate any of the members of the organization. The twenty elders of the Guardian List were spread throughout the country and rarely, if ever, did they come in contact with their compatriots. It was their jobs to recommend candidates for the List but as to the actual workings of the final determination of a candidate, they were completely removed from the physical workings of the organization. They received more information from the local newspapers than from anyone within the organization. The death of a recommended candidate did, in fact, offer up some sense of accomplishment and pride on the part of the member who had brought the candidate to the attention of the organization. One of the members had once likened the secrecy of the Guardian List to that of the great Masonic tradition that dated back to almost the beginning of civilization. But the secrecy of The Guardian List had far more significant implications over the matter of life and death than did any of the Masonic orders since The Knight Templars. Unlike their Masonic counterparts, the guardians of the List were dedicated to seeing justice served in the final analysis where government had failed in its convoluted and flawed systems.

And yet, there was an actual defect in the basic concept of The Guardian List and John Brown knew that sooner or later he would either have to face up to it or take drastic measures that could very well jeopardize the security of the organization right down to its very core.

~~~

The first crack in the foundation of the organization that was devoted to The Guardian List reared its ugly head in the fifth year of its existence. One of the members, an eighty-three year old retired police officer, George Delaney, had been admitted to the Summerlin Retirement Facility on the north side of Las Vegas. His wife, Edna, of almost sixty years, opted to have her husband admitted after a series of awkward incidents that the doctors attributed to the onset of dementia. Edna, a frail woman near eighty, felt that she could not give her husband the necessary care and attention required at home under the circumstances. Hospice care appeared to be the answer and over a period of six months, George's condition continued to deteriorate. There were numerous occasions when he didn't recognize his wife, had no idea where he was or what was happening to him. But for some bizarre reason, he alluded to the name John Brown and quite often referred to The Guardian List, both out of context. Of course, his thoughts were disjointed and he couldn't explain exactly who John Brown was or what was the implication of the List.

Nurse Brenda entered George Delaney's room and prepared to get him ready for the day's activities. Did we sleep well?" she asked.

George was still half asleep and grunted in response.

"We've got to get you all cleaned and ready for your wife's visit today," she said cheerfully as she pulled back the sheet to get George ready. He had messed the bed and Nurse Brenda recoiled as the smell was overpowering. She reached down and helped the old man to a sitting position as she assessed the situation. She went to the door and pressed a button on the wall that would alert an orderly that a nurse needed assistance.

"Do you know if John called?" he asked.

"John who?"

"My friend…you know. He was here the other day…"

"I didn't know you had a visitor the other day other than your wife."

"My wife is dead, Gladys."

"I'm Brenda, Mr. Delaney. Remember me, Brenda?"

"Where's Gladys?"

The orderly, a young Hispanic man, entered the room and immediately assessed the situation. He helped George to the bathroom where he assisted him in removing his pajamas that were covered with feces and urine.

"I knew you'd come today, John," he said to the orderly whose name was Jose. "Are we having a meeting today?"

The orderly went about his task without responding to George's questions. He was accustomed to conversations that were usually one-sided and disjointed.

Meanwhile, Brenda stripped the bed, rolled the sheets into a ball and put them into the cart that the orderly had placed outside the room in the hallway. She could hear the shower running in the bathroom and knew that Jose had the situation under control.

Edna usually arrived at ten in the morning and stayed with George until four in the afternoon. It had become a ritual although on most occasions he could barely remember her. She entered the room tentatively and placed her things on the guest chair. She never knew what to expect from her husband. Would he know her? Would he think she was someone else? The door to the bathroom opened and George, dressed in a terrycloth robe, was lead into the room by Jose.

"Did you bring Maggie?" he asked Edna. "You promised to bring her," he said, somewhat chagrined. Maggie was their pet cat that they had put down some twenty years earlier. It was all Edna could do to refrain from falling apart but she somehow found the strength to stay the course in the hopes that a miracle would bring her loving husband back to her one of these days.

George had remained very active in all sorts of projects until he was taken down with dementia. He had been an active member of the Fraternal Order of Retired Police Officers. He had been an active member of his church, volunteering for all sorts of chores whenever he could help out. He was one of the few members of the organization that had periodically met to add names to the Guardian List and to learn of updates. It had been George's plan to exit his life by his own hand when the time came for him to serve. But over the five years, it had been decided by John Brown that George's frailty prevented him from taking an active role in any assassinations. His input was invaluable and respected and George lived in the hopes that one day he would be called upon to take an active role in removing a name from the List.

The Guardian List

When it came to the attention of John Brown that George Delaney was infirm, he made a point to visit the home where George was in hospice care. No matter how carefully he had planned, there was always something that changed the course of his strategy. He was usually prepared to make last minute changes if and when the opportunity called for it. That was part of the success of the organization. What wasn't foreseeable was the eventuality that one of the members might inadvertently, in a state of dementia, begin to talk about the organization or mention names.

John Brown entered the room only to be greeted by Edna Delaney who was sitting bedside as her husband napped. John introduced himself.

"I'm so pleased to meet you, Mr. Brown. George has spoken of you so often," she said with no small amount of pride.

The hackles stood up on the back of John's neck. His stomach tightened as he tried to keep a pleasant demeanor. "I hope he hasn't bored you with a lot of dull tales."

"He spoke most glowingly about you, Mr. Brown. I'm only sorry that you couldn't take the time away from your business to visit our home."

"Yes, my work does consume much of my time. I travel a lot, you know."

"George told me…"

"Really? And what else did George tell you about me? I mean, about my work and all."

"Only that you're in…what in the world did he call it? The extermination business, I think. I hope I didn't get it all mixed up, Mr. Brown," she said sweetly.

"That was pretty accurate," thought John.

"We've had considerable problems over the years with pest control so I can imagine how your work keeps you so busy. A couple of years ago, when we had an outrageous infestation of roaches and spiders, I asked George if we just might be able to call on you for your expertise but he explained that you were more into the industrial end of the business."

"Right…right," said John with some amount of relief. He suddenly felt very uncomfortable, as if his collar size had just shrunk down a size or two. It was obvious that George would sleep right on through and John was prepared to make some excuse to be on his way when the door opened and Nurse Brenda came into the room, all cheery at the sight of Mrs. Delaney. They exchanged greetings and Edna introduced John Brown to the nurse.

"Oh, of course," said Nurse Brenda. "The Guardian man," she announced with pride. John Brown could feel his knees buckle. He sucked in his breath as if the wind had been taken out of his sails. He could feel the blood rushing from his head and he reached for the railing at the bottom of the bed.

"I beg your pardon?" he asked, as if the name meant absolutely nothing to him.

"Oh, you know…that Guardian thing he's always ranting about. I just assumed he had an interest in Greek

The Guardian List

mythology. I could never figure out what he was talking about half of the time."

John could tell that the mention of Guardian had been taken out of context and he began to breathe a bit more freely. If the nurse didn't have a clue what Guardian alluded to, he wasn't going to pursue it any further but he could see how very fragile the secrecy was of the whole organization.

~~~

The two men sat across from each other with nary a word about their clandestine activities. Theirs was a meeting of friends come to pass the time of day and to savor the delicacies of the good life. The Revere Restaurant sat high on a hill overlooking a golf course and beyond, an unobstructed view of the entire city of Las Vegas with its lights appearing like jewels of a precious necklace trailing off into the foothills of the mountains on all sides. It was an unusually quiet evening at the Revere with only three tables occupied. John Brown and Father Ignatius enjoyed their wine and dinner as they were seated at a table set apart and some distance from the other patrons. It was difficult not to continually glance out over the landscape and appreciate the beauty of the panorama below. There was camaraderie that had grown between the two men who had spent the past five years dedicated to serving their fellow man in an exceptional way. During their association they could boast that neither had ever personally found it necessary to take a life in the service of their cause. They had, in turn, given purpose and reason to those men who had served their cause and were now ready to pass on to another dimension. It was actually a very simple calling when one considered how necessary it was to break the chain of social imbalance and thus serve justice where the system had failed. But as John Brown looked out over the beauty of the scene in the distance, his mind kept repeating one simple phrase: tempest fugit. He had given the past five years of his life to a cause in which he believed. He began at sixty-eight and now he was turning the pages of the book and was staring into his seventy-third year. It seemed like only yesterday when first he conceived of the idea of The Guardian List. It seemed like a lesser time when his wife of over forty years had departed this earth. He held up his glass and observed the lights of the city as they played through the aromatic liquid.

"We've come to something of an impasse," he said as if speaking to no one in particular.

The Priest took a sip from his glass and placed it carefully on the table. "I can tell that there is something bothering you, my friend. I have never pried into your business but if there is something you would care to share with me."

"Do you want to hear my confession, Father?"

The priest smiled. "How about something more in the line of friend to friend? I sometimes wonder what it must be like to walk in your shoes, John. Personally, I don't think I could handle the burden, to be quite honest. I must say that you have done an exceptional job in your devotion to every detail. I don't believe there is another person on the planet, man or woman, who could have successfully accomplished what you have."

John listened to his words and glowed in the praise bestowed upon him by the priest. He knew he had chosen wisely in bringing the clergyman into the organization. "I take that as a compliment, Father. But at the same time I feel we are serving a higher need. I see the clock ticking and I ask myself if our work stops with us or is there some way we can perpetuate the work we've begun. My heart is heavy with the thought that it might all stop when we are forced, either by reasons of health or age, to cease being effective. I paid a visit to the bedside of George Delaney."

"I heard he was not doing well. I meant to go by the hospital, but I wouldn't want to presume to take his confession what with the weight of our venture hanging over my head. I may not be defrocked, but I know that I shall have much to answer for come the day of reckoning."

It saddened John Brown to hear the priest speak in terms of his failure to serve his God according to the doctrines of his church. If God couldn't speak for the priest, surely John Brown would be only too glad to put in a good word.

"Father, I believe the time has come for us to think about what will happen to the List should our time run out. I just presumed that I would live forever and suddenly I realize that such is not the case. The idea of choosing men whose time is about to expire was a brilliant concept back when. Now, it doesn't seem to be as clever as I gave myself credit for. I concentrated all the decisions in myself, which at the time seemed to work best. Now, as I look around and realize that you and I are standing on the brink of our own mortality, I fear that what I have so carefully conceived and executed just might all be for nothing."

"I share your dilemma, John, and the thought has crossed my mind on numerous occasions. I don't know why we hadn't discussed it before. Perhaps our egos came into play. We executed the list exactly according to your plan. What could possibly go wrong? Internally, it was a perfect plan. Whoever gave a moment's thought to the idea that one day we would no longer be here to serve? Have you made any decisions?"

John Brown smiled. "I am loaded with questions and totally devoid of any answers. I thought that the two of us might come up with an equitable solution that could work. Let me suggest that we take some time to collectively think about the problem and over the next few months, perhaps we can come up with something."

And so it was agreed upon by the two men, precariously balanced on the edge of their lives, that in order for the List to prevail and successfully function, they would have to implement a viable plan. It wasn't as if they could put an ad in the local paper: "Wanted; assassins to serve God and country."

BOOK TWO

Chapter 21

The fog rolled in across the bay hugging the shoreline and wrapping itself like a blanket over the Presidio and the adjourning neighborhoods. It was a normal occurrence at this time of the year when the warm ocean currents met with the cool air announcing that spring was about to make its mark upon the land. The early morning sight of athletic men and women running with no particular destination or obvious goal dotted the landscape along Buena Vista Park heading over towards the Marina District and the Golden Gate National Recreation Area.

Attired in her Reebok sweats and hi-tech sneakers, Patty Walsh reached up to the overcast heaven as if to stretch the lethargy from her sleep-deprived body. Six in the morning and already the world was racing by on its way to the fantasy that exercise made for a happier and healthier journey through life's deteriorating saga. Standing on the top step in front of the brownstone building where she rented an upscale, one bedroom pad for the past ten years, Patty stretched, first to one side, then to the other, waiting for that moment when her body would tell her that it was time to begin her morning run through foggy San Francisco. As she applied those last few stretches, she berated herself for that late night tête-à-tête with Marge, a ritual that dated back to when both women were high school classmates. Now the two were separated by professional dictates: Patty a member of the San Francisco Police Department and Marge, a police detective in Las Vegas. Although the geographical distance between them was a mere 575 miles, they shared the events of their daily lives no less than bi-weekly, either by phone or through the Internet. All too often, their conversations went on into the wee hours of the morning leaving both of them exhausted when their alarms announced that it was time to rise and face their civic duties.

Today, Patty would answer a subpoena to testify at ten in the morning in the criminal court case of State of California v. Warren Price, a recidivist child molester whose arrests numbered no less than half a dozen. But in each indictment the parents of the children in question would or could not testify, either because the legality of their residency was questionable and they feared the repercussions from the immigration authorities, or because Warren Price was a professional who knew how to circumvent the letter of the law. The heir to a sizeable

The Guardian List

family fortune, he could afford to hire the best that the legal system had to offer. A sexual pervert for the better part of his forty-five years, Price had learned the legal ramifications of answering to the state's charges. Therefore, he accosted children of families in the barrios, aware that in the event he should be apprehended, there was very little chance that charges brought by illegals would hold up in a court of law.

For the better part of her tenure with the S.F.P.D. Patty Walsh had followed the book on Warren Price, often consumed with the frustration of not being able to bring an indictment to fruition. Price was something of a cocky bastard who took to smiling at the police officer with whom he was on nodding acquaintance over the years. His very attitude left a bitter taste in Patty's mouth. Here was an individual she could wantonly empty her service revolver into without the slightest sense of remorse. He was grossly overweight and slovenly dressed, a picture of everything Patty detested in a man. *Just one shot,* she thought. *Just one well placed shot into the temple of this bloated piece of excrement.*

But Warren Price was neither the first nor the last of the criminals that passed through the San Francisco legal system that Patty personally detested. She was a fanatical critic of the system that gave refuge to the criminal element with less regard to the plight of the victim. It was a shortcoming built into the entire system. Over the years with the San Francisco Police Department, Patty Walsh had mentally created a list of people who had circumvented the law in one way or another. It was not a list that she intended to use in any way to take personal revenge, but a list the likes of which most police officers likewise collected in the course of their tour of duty. Sometimes over a drink or a snack, the names on the list would be shared with other officers, along with the events that led up to the arrest and trial of the perp. Little did Patty realize that over the course of years, more than one of the names on her list had been included on The Guardian List.

By the time she had run her five miles, returned to her flat, showered and dressed, she was ready for the inevitable. There was no doubt in her mind that Warren Price would once again beat the rap. Here was a situation where a ten year-old boy had been sexually molested, but his testimony was less than credible because he was mentally retarded. This was Price's "M.O." He sexually preyed on youngsters whose testimony was almost useless. In all probability, by the end of a week of legal calisthenics and despite the testimony of Officer Walsh who served as the arresting officer, the court would have to dismiss the charges for lack of credible testimony. As Patty exited the courtroom at the end of the session, she could feel her blood boiling and it was all she could do to mentally prevent herself from exacting justice on her own terms. At the end of a day in court, she sometimes needed to stop off at a local bar with one or two of her fellow officers to recap the events of the trial and clear her mind of the mental anguish that dominated her personal thoughts. She hated herself for her negativity regarding the system and everything that repulsed her about her work. It was like an open sore; the more she thought about it, the more it festered. She had spoken to Marge about it on numerous occasions. It was not foreign to Marge who experienced much the same dilemma.

"You need to get some help," suggested Marge. "You can apply for psychiatric counseling from the department, you know."

"Yeah, but it goes right on your record and when it's time for consideration for promotion, you're dead in the water."

"How about someone in the area who you can turn to for counseling? Surely you must know any number of psychiatrists or therapists with whom you can talk. Someone who you can turn to off the record. What you're going through isn't healthy, Patty."

"Is that what you do?" asked Patty.

"Just between us, I've been in therapy for over two years. The frustration got so severe that it got to the point where I thought I was going to explode. When you begin to think that every person on the street is a potential criminal, you become a liability to both the department and yourself. Sooner or later you're going to make a mistake…"

"How's that?"

"When you have to make a decision between right and wrong, and your eyes are clouded with all the crap that you've experienced in the past, there's a good chance that you could make a terrible mistake…maybe something fatal, if you know what I mean. I was there, Patty."

"My God, you never told me."

"It was a kid, sixteen years old. I pulled her over for erratic driving one Saturday night up on the north side of town. She was obviously on something because she had to hold on as she got out of the vehicle. She was a large kid, overweight and dressed in jeans two sizes too small. She looked like something out of a circus. I told her to step away from her car and I could see her shaking her head as if trying to figure out what she was going to do. Then she turned, as if to reach back into the car for something and again I yelled for her to step away from the vehicle. All of a sudden I was overwhelmed with apprehension about what could possibly happen. I mean, was she reaching for a weapon? She obviously wasn't about to do as I told her. I drew my service revolver, took my stance ready for the worst. I was a hair's breath away from dropping her when my back-up pulled up alongside, lights flashing, and siren blaring. He yelled through his bullhorn for the kid to back away from the vehicle and from there on it was his collar. The kid obeyed but as I watched the scene taking place, I realized that I was shaking all over. I'd come that close to shooting a kid because I was in fear of having to make a decision of life and death. As it turned out, the kid was suffering from a breathing disorder because of her weight and she had been reaching back in her car for an oxygen canister. Is this making any sense, Patty?"

She's making plenty of sense, thought Patty.

~~~

The final day of the trial, Patty took a seat at the rear of the courtroom. She didn't have very high expectations for a guilty verdict. As the jury returned to the box she tried to read the foreman, but there was nothing. The twelve members of the jury took their seats as the judge entered from his chambers.

"Has the jury reached a verdict?" he addressed the foreman.

The foreman got to his feet. "We have your honor."

"What say you?"

"We, the jury, in the case of the State vs. Warren Price, find the defendant…guilty as charged."

There was a sudden flurry of activity in the court as members of the press headed for the door. The judge rapped his gavel to restore order. Patty could feel a rush of relief and satisfaction. *Now it was only a matter of a sentence to make the system work*, she thought. But sentencing would not be for another week and Patty would have to refrain from celebrating until that time. A long sentence would be reason to rejoice. It would absolve the system for its failure to defend and protect.

CHAPTER 22

It was the night after the final day of the trial and Patty couldn't wait to call Marge with the good news. She left a message on her machine and with a sizeable shot of Tequila, she settled down on the couch to view on old film she hadn't seen before. Her cat of eleven years, Smokey, cuddled up beside her as Patty gently stroked his favorite spots, under his chin and behind his ears. She had rescued Smokey from the local shelter shortly after her arrival in San Francisco. She had a few acquaintances but no friends in the new surroundings and adopting an animal was Marge's idea; that or hop into the sack with the first good-looking cop and hold on for dear life. Patty opted for the cat. She'd had enough one-night stands, she told herself. If there wasn't a serious relationship in her future, so be it. She was a very attractive woman; not *Glamour Magazine* cover good-looking, but surely attractive enough to stand out in a crowd. She stood about five-four, with short red hair and a trim figure from working out regularly. She had rather cute features with a turned-up nose and brown eyes. If anything, it was her rather brisk personality that drove potential suitors away and attracted undesirable men. She'd been hit upon any number of times by fellow officers (both men and women) but there wasn't anything that felt right...no chemistry. Nothing she felt comfortable in pursuing and to accept an invite with the expectation of ending up in bed in a short-term relationship. Well, the dew was off the rose. A good book, her cat, her vibrator, and the television would serve just fine until Mr. Right came along.

Knowing that she had a problem, Patty spent endless evenings availing herself of printed material that exposed many of the problems within the ranks of a working police officer. It seemed that almost everything mentioned in the material applied to her. Depression, lack of support from her superiors, being thwarted by the department, society, and the courts, and the list went on. Many times she thought about leaving law enforcement, perhaps finishing law school, something she started over a dozen years ago and abandoned for her desire to be a policewoman. During her time in the Academy she had been warned by superiors and old timers about the obstacles she would have to face once she was out on the streets. She laughed. After all, she was young and full of piss and vinegar. there wasn't very much she couldn't handle. She never had to stand up in a courtroom, take an oath to "tell the truth and nothing but the truth" and have some wily attorney rip her a new asshole as if she were the perp. All this was the downside; there were still many positive aspects of working in law enforcement even if they got clouded over from time to time with the negative sides. Early on she learned that she would have to develop a hardened mind-set wherein she could handle anything that came her way. The part that really hurt, the part that was difficult to take was when her own superiors, the people upon whom she depended most for support, turned their backs and chastised her for an action she had taken, all the while believing that she was doing the right thing. It took her the longest time to accept the fact that she was not singled out because she was a woman, a scenario that most female officers entertained at one time or another. She was definitely a minority within the man's world and her actions and attitudes were constantly being held up to scrutiny by the male establishment. So over the years she learned to walk softly, not express her opinions publicly and accept criticism from almost every source. That was the plight of a female police officer if she wanted to survive her tenure until retirement. It sucked.

Two weeks after the last day of the trial of Warren Price, she took a seat at the rear of the courtroom to hear the sentencing. She didn't have to be there. Her job was finished after her testimony was completed, but there was something special about this case, something that grated on her about a man who would knowingly molest a child. She wanted to be there when justice was meted out just to know that there was an iota of virtue in the law. As Price was led into the courtroom by a deputy, he still retained that cocky attitude Patty had observed for as long as she had known him. Here he was, facing incarceration for God knows how long and he approached the defendant's table as if he were preparing for a romp in the park. This was the first case on the blotter and Patty was relieved that she would not have to spend the entire afternoon tied up in court. It was her one free day off and there were other things she'd rather be doing.

As the judge entered, the court was called to order and everyone was seated. From where she was seated she could see the Ramirez family seated in the first row behind the prosecuting attorney. Juanito Ramirez was not in attendance. It was not necessary to put the mentally retarded ten year-old through more than he had already suffered.

Again the bailiff read the indictment and instructed the defendant to rise. The judge peered down from his bench, cleared his throat and selected a page from a file folder. "Having been found guilty by a jury of your peers, it is my duty to remand you to the State Prison at San Quentin for a period of not less than two years…"

The entire trial had turned out to be nothing more than a sham. Warren Price had again beaten the system. He would be put into a rehab program. He would do the time and in two short years he would be back out on the street, ready to commit the same acts that he had done repeatedly over the years. Patty was on her feet and out the door before the Deputy had cleared the courtroom with his prisoner. Her legs felt rubbery as she made her way to the elevator. Her throat had constricted and there were tears in her eyes as she impatiently waited to get out of the building and onto the street where she could breathe. All she could think about was little Juanito Ramirez and his family and how the system had failed them and all the youngsters

Warren Price had molested over the years. In the back of her mind she swore that one day Warren Price would pay. Of this she was sure, but at this very moment in time, she hadn't a clue how that would come to pass.

~~~

Thurman Falk felt uncomfortable about the pending meeting with Mr. Brown. Most of their communications had been by phone and rarely did they meet face to face in a public place like a restaurant. Strings Restaurant was a small family-style bistro located just off of Eastern Avenue and a stone's throw from the Las Vegas strip. The specialty of the house was Italian, but "their salad is to die for" assured Mr. Brown. The lighting was subdued and the sound fairly muffled. Their conversation would be private as their table was tucked away in the far corner out of earshot of any of the patrons of the establishment. They ordered wine and talked about political issues and the state of the economy; nothing that related to the business for which Mr. Brown had called the meeting. They were well into their main course before he broached the subject.

"What I am going to ask is a bit out of the usual course of our business, but if you'll be patient, I think you'll understand where I'm heading," he said. "It's time for the association to either think of finding someone to take over the reins of leadership or to disband the entire concept of the List. You've been an invaluable asset over these past few years and I've grown to trust you like no one else. So you will understand that unless there is someone who is trustworthy enough and with the same social philosophy, the List will not continue beyond my tenure."

Falk listened attentively. Was Mr. Brown about to ask him to assume the leadership? Of course it would be out of the question. He was merely a hired hand, an investigator. He knew he lacked the wherewithal to assume the role or make the decisions that Mr. Brown had these past five years.

"I don't mean to be personal, Mr. Brown, but are you...how can I put this? Are you ill?"

"No, just old, Mr. Falk, and getting older. I'd hate to think that when the day comes that I can't rationally make the necessary decisions to carry on our work that it will all have been for nothing." He reached over for the wine decanter and poured a fresh round. After savoring the excellent vintage he continued, weighing his words carefully. "I would like you to do a search, Mr. Falk. I would like you to find someone trustworthy, dedicated, and philosophically attuned to what we are attempting to accomplish."

Falk realized what a tall order it would be to find a replacement for Brown. "I would need some parameters within which to work, Mr. Brown. Age, sex, educational background, employment record...I mean, there's a multitude of requirements, besides which there's the most important one of all — once I find a likely candidate, would that person be willing to step up to the plate, put his or her life and possibly their career on the line so to speak."

"I realize that, Mr. Falk. That's why I've asked you here. First of all, you would be compensated for your time as in the past. I don't have to tell you how sensitive such an endeavor will be. I am turning to you because the thought of the dissolution of the List saddens me to think that my demise would be the end of a mission that we've put so much effort into."

"I assumed that Father Ignatius would be the most likely candidate to carry on your work."

Mr. Brown smiled. "This is difficult to comprehend, but the good Father has not been totally supportive of our activities. Although he offers spiritual counseling, taking the life of another human being is an anathema to him. His theology, his struggle with the whole concept is constantly tearing at him, but intellectually he is attuned to what we are about. It appears that his devotion to his God still stands in the way of how we balance the scale of social incompetence."

"And the other members of the organization? Is there no one who can assume the leadership?"

"It's one thing to be a soldier devoted to the cause and another thing to ask someone to take the role of leadership. Besides, after careful consideration, I think we should be looking for someone not so…shall we say 'elderly?' Anyone addressing the final chapter of their life would present the same problem in a short period of time that we're faced with now. I've often wondered how I'll respond when it's time for me to move on, to move up to the firing line and assume the role of avenger. I don't know if I'll have the wherewithal, but sooner or later I'll have to find out. It's a tenuous situation, Mr. Falk. I've never tried to impose my philosophy on those other members of the organization. I've presented our objectives and the final decision was either shared or rejected. To lay down one's life for a cause is the highest form of religiosity. You either believe or you don't. You either accept that you are going to go out performing an act in the interest of those whom the society has failed to protect or you will quietly close your eyes and pass on to the next level without a whimper. It's not an easy choice, Mr. Falk."

"I understand, Mr. Brown, but I don't know if I can guarantee that I can come up with that one person who will be able to assume your responsible position. After all, this whole concept of the List is contrary to a society that prides itself on Christian values and morals. 'Thou shalt not kill' is embedded in the minds of almost every member of the society from earliest childhood until the grave. To be perfectly honest, if I had to make a decision whether or not I could assassinate another person, no matter how heinous a crime that person committed, I don't know if I could step up and assume the role of equalizer. Don't get me wrong, Mr. Brown...I'm not criticizing what you've accomplished. I stand as guilty as anyone in the organization, just by virtue of my knowledge of the objectives of the List. Were you to ask me to give my life to avenge another person's guilty act, I don't think I could personally assume that responsibility."

It was this honesty and intelligence that Brown could expect from Thurman Falk that made him so invaluable to the organization. "I understand where you're coming from. You're a healthy, vibrant man in the prime of life. No one could expect that you would give up your life for a cause unless you were some kind of religious fanatic. But let us assume that one day you had to face imminent death through disease or just old age. Would not the thought appeal to you of meting out justice to some criminal element that had, through some loophole in the system, managed to avoid a legal penalty? I'm not looking for an answer, Mr. Falk; I'm only throwing out a hypothesis for you to weigh. Obviously, you cannot put yourself in the shoes of someone whose days are numbered. To be perfectly honest, I am having trouble dealing with the concept myself." Again Mr. Brown filled the glasses from the wine decanter. "I would like you to take some time to think about what we've discussed. You can give me your answer in your own time. For the moment, I'm not planning to step down but I would like to be instrumental in passing on my knowledge to the person who will eventually replace me..."

CHAPTER 23

Often in a person's life, a meaningful relationship, though not easy to come by, just rears its head without fanfare and catches the participant off guard. Patty Walsh could count on one hand the number of "meaningful relationships" she'd had endured in her thirty-six years. They had all begun on positive notes, all with visions of lasting, serious relationships destined to develop into matrimony, but Patty's work with the department deprived her of any sort of normal routine in which she could commit to a reciprocal experience. In each case, the demands made upon her in terms of the simplest expectations were beyond her ability to meet her suitor at least halfway. So in each case, over a period of months and in one case two years, the rift was inevitable. Over a period of time she became jaded and wore her negativity like a badge of honor so that no matter how potentially available a candidate was, in a matter of one or two dates, he was out the door. There were just too many available dating candidates on the open market. Slip into any bar at ten in the evening and it was like a cattle drive and the perfume of preference was testosterone.

Patty had drawn the late night shift patrolling the Potrero District just west of the Third Street Causeway. She had responded to a call to help a homeless person find refuge in one of the shelters on the bitterly cold night. After that she slowly patrolled the warehouse district where drug deals proliferated, but on this night there wasn't any action that she could ascertain. In fact, over on the east side, the usual contingency of street hookers preferred to call it a night finding more comfortable pickings in the local bars. *Four more hours to go*, she thought. All she had to do was keep her eyes open, stay alert and avoid an accident. She checked her watch for the fifth time in the last hour. She needed a stimulant, something to keep her awake for the remainder of her watch. There was an IHOP a few blocks over. She pulled a left onto Vallejo and found a convenient spot in front of the door to the almost deserted establishment. She called in, announced that she was taking a break, put her portable phone on her belt and entered. The late night waitress was seated behind the register, magazine in hand, also trying to survive her shift.

"What can I do for you, Patty?" Beth, the waitress, immediately recognized the officer from years on the same night shift. She automatically reached for the coffee pot and drew a cup. "Slow night?" she asked as she placed the cup on the counter in front of Patty.

"Murder," said Patty. "Haven't seen it this slow in here in years. I heard there's more activity going on down at the morgue."

"No one comes down to the district on a cold night. It'll pick up in a couple of hours when the warehouse crews come in." She reached down behind the counter, produced a late addition of the local paper and placed it on the bar in front of Patty. It appeared to be part of the ritual. It wasn't five minutes into the front page before she heard the crackle of her portable phone. "Ten-23, do you read? Over."

"Walsh here. I read you."

"We've got a 10-54 over by 20th and Illinois. A warehouse alley behind the Illinois entrance. Do you read?"

"10-4. I'm on my way…" Patty got to her feet and reached for some loose bills in her pocket.

"Forget it," said Beth. "I needed the company." She smiled as Patty threw her a wave and was out the door.

It didn't take three minutes from the IHOP to 20th and Illinois. There was already an ambulance on the scene with an unmarked detective car and a tall man in his early forties walking over the scene, obviously plain clothes homicide. As Patty drove up and exited the car, he turned and approached her. "You Officer Walsh?" he asked.

"Yeah," she replied without any formality. "You out of Central?"

"Homicide. Sergeant Decker. The dispatcher told me you were on your way." He stood about six feet tall with a slightly receding hairline. *"A sign of superior intelligence,"* thought Patty.

"What have we got?"

Decker read from his notepad. "White male in his fifties. No I.D. One shot to the head, execution style. Coroner's on the way. You mind taping?"

Patty went to her vehicle and took out a roll of yellow tape. Without any fanfare she began to tape off the alley to make sure no one would contaminate the crime scene. *Kind of ironic,* she thought. Beside the two attendants in the ambulance and the detective, there wasn't a soul in sight. When she finished, she returned to her car and dropped the tape onto the passenger seat. The detective was still making notes in his pad as she approached.

"Anything?"

"Nope. Looks like he was shot and then dumped in this alley. Very little blood, no evidence, no witnesses. Cut and dried."

Together they ducked under the tape and walked over to the body lying on the ground. The victim was neatly dressed wearing a suit over which he wore a fashionable topcoat. His hat was on the ground a few feet away. With flashlights the two officers scanned the scene trying to determine if they had missed anything. The detective was right. Other than the victim, there wasn't anything out of the ordinary that would give a clue as to his identity or who might have wasted him. Once the coroner got his fingerprints, homicide could take it from there.

By the time the coroner's van pulled up, the area was buzzing with activity. Two more patrol cars with police officers had been dispatched to the scene to assist with crowd control. *That's a laugh,* thought Patty. Within an hour the victim had been photographed from every imaginable angle, loaded onto a stretcher and placed in the wagon. As quickly as the scene had come to life, it was suddenly

The Guardian List

deserted. Sergeant Decker walked Patty to her vehicle as if she needed protection. She liked that.

"Guess I'll see you at the inquest," he said as he held the door for her to get in.

"Guess so. Does Sergeant Decker have a first name?" she asked with a smile.

"Oh, yeah," as if he forgot. "Michael...but most everyone calls me Mike."

Patty didn't have to introduce herself as her name was clearly printed on the brass nameplate fastened to her jacket above the pocket.

"Well, it's been nice working with you, Officer Patty Walsh. Maybe we'll do it again sometime." He smiled and she noticed what a warm and friendly smile it was.

"I was on my break when I got the call. Just having a cup of coffee over at the IHOP. Guess I'll call in and see if I can finish that coffee. My shift is almost over."

"Sounds reasonable. Care for company?"

"Sure. You know where it is?"

There was that smile again. "I think I'll be able to find it," he said as he closed the door and waited until her vehicle had cleared the area.

~~~

Thurman Falk had pondered the assignment that Mr. Brown had presented to him and concluded that it was all but an impossible task. Even if he were able to find the perfect candidate, even if that candidate filled all the requisites necessary to take over the List, even if that candidate were standing in front of him with open arms;

how the hell could he endure, without putting his head on the chopping block by saying, "I'm a nut who is authorized to offer you the opportunity to head up a group of vigilantes. You interested?" What if that candidate was ex-law enforcement? Would he take it as a joke or would he pass it on to the legal authorities? Falk could face arrest for soliciting a police officer to commit an illegal act. No matter how he sliced it, his ass would be grass. Suppose it was a potential candidate who filled all the qualifications, but who had not been connected to law enforcement? What was to prevent that candidate from getting power-hungry and begin to arbitrarily use the List as some kind of social vendetta without carefully investigating the full background of the perpetrator? The ramifications for abuse were endless.

On the other hand, here was an impossible undertaking that no one had the credentials to fulfill…no one on this planet other than possibly Thurman Falk, he rationalized. After all, he'd been with the organization since the beginning. He had set up more hits than he could count. He had investigated and bird-dogged most of the animals that deserved what they ultimately got…and in the process he had gotten…rich. Not just comfortable but outright rich. Much of the money he'd received from Mr. Brown's organization had been squirreled away in an offshore account in the Bahamas where he and his wife spent three lavish, two-week vacations over the past five years. Unfortunately, he couldn't use any of the money from the organization, all in cash, to improve his middle-class lifestyle to purchase a condo or a home in some upscale community. There was no way to account to the IRS where the money was coming from to rationalize any change in his lifestyle. So Falk was able to declare a modest income from other investigating jobs not connected to the organization and on which he paid yearly taxes without raising a red flag. The entire process was carefully thought out and executed with the assistance of Mr. Brown and Falk would be a damn fool to change the rules.

~~~

Within a two-week period, the organization had witnessed no less than five names removed from the List. The cities in which the miscreants had been executed were New York, Los Angeles, Las Vegas, Miami, and New Orleans. Only the Miami assassin survived to be arrested for the crime. All the others perished either at the scene or within a short period of time thereafter from natural causes. All of the killers had at one time been members of law enforcement within their respective communities.

Only Carlos Ortega, the seventy-eight year old retired Police Sergeant who was convinced that he would go down in an all-out shoot-out with three drug dealers, happened to survive with multiple wounds. As he lay in his bed in Miami General, tubes connected to almost every orifice of his body, he cursed his bad luck in having to endure the degrading inquisition from people who had been sucking on their mother's tits when he was actively fighting the criminal element in the greater Miami area decades before. For almost a month he slipped in and out of a mini-coma, having to endure the disappointment on the faces of his three grown children who were raised in the belief that their father walked on water.

The two men and one woman that Ortega had taken down in an all-out shootout had been suspected of activities in the drug trade, but local authorities had not yet been able to build a sufficient case to warrant arrests. "How was Ortega privy to the information in an ongoing investigation?" was the question on everyone's mind. If he survived his injuries (and everyone within the law enforcement community prayed he would not), heads would roll from the cop on the beat to the highest-ranking members of the department. "Something was rotten in Denmark," quoted one of the more well-read officers in the ranks. But within weeks the department collectively breathed a sigh of relief when Carlos Ortega quietly died in his sleep without incriminating anyone connected with the department.

~~~

The investigation of the death of the body found in the alley failed to produce an identity. The case to which Mike Decker had been assigned seemed to go nowhere. It was as if his John Doe just materialized without leaving any pertinent information as to his identity. Mike found it convenient to use the lack of any forward momentum in the case to call Patty on two occasions to bring her up to date on the investigation. "It isn't possible that someone reaches maturity without leaving so much as a scratch in the hourglass of time," he told her. He could only surmise that John Doe was possibly a foreign national, in which case, he would turn over the file to Interpol to see if they had any better luck. The body in the alley had all the earmarks of a drug deal gone sour, but without an identity. Decker closed the file and hoped that something would turn up later. On the positive side, John Doe's demise served as the door that brought Patty Walsh into Mike's life.

It wasn't a date in the true sense of the word. They were just two cops that got off duty at the same time and agreed to have breakfast together to discuss the logistics of a case in which they had both been involved and that was all but closed. There were no formal words like "Would you like to have breakfast with me?" or "I've got tickets to the ballgame…" It was awkward at first. Patty had to admit that she was physically attracted to Detective Michael Decker. What was not to like? She could only describe him as "a hunk" that appeared to take good physical care of himself. His voice was rich and full with no trace of a regional accent and he had a habit of looking right into a person's eyes as if he was attempting to read their mind. Patty found it a bit unnerving. She wished he would divert his look, read the menu or look around at some of the activities in the restaurant, but no, he was staring into her soul and it was disconcerting.

"Are you married, Detective?" she asked him before she could stop the words from cascading out. Not "where are you from?" or "how long have you been with the department?" *Why didn't I just ask if he wants to get laid? Get right to the point*, she thought.

He smiled at the suddenness of her inquiry as if he was a perp and she was in the process of interrogating him. He didn't mind her directness. "I was married a while back. It didn't work out. She taught school and I worked odd hours as a patrol officer and before long…well, you get the picture."

"Oh, yeah," she concurred. "How many times I've heard the same story from almost every cop I know who's in a relationship…"

"And you?" he asked, picking up the cue from her direct approach. "Obviously a woman as beautiful as you must have tried it at least once."

"Nope. Not unless married to the department counts. I don't know how some of the guys who marry and raise a family are able to do it. I guess it take a certain kind of person, someone who's willing to work at marriage as much as he's devoted to his career."

"Well, when you figure out the answer, I hope you'll let me know."

The time had escaped both of them and before they realized where it had gone, it was almost nine in the morning. Patty had to get home, feed the cat and get ready for her morning run. As charming as he was, he didn't take precedence over her daily routine. He insisted on picking up the check and walking her to her car. He gently held her by her elbow and that made her think perhaps he thought she was an elderly aunt or invalid. She smiled. This whole thing was ridiculous. What made her think that two members of the same police department could make it work any more than a police officer married to a school teacher?

"You on graveyard much longer?" he asked.

"For another two weeks."

"If you're not tied up, we could have dinner one evening before you have to check in."

That appealed to her. There would be no excuses why she couldn't invite him over to her place for a late night repast. Dinner would be just that without the usual wrestling match. "I think I'd like that. I'm free tomorrow night."

She removed one of her cards from her jacket pocket, wrote her address and home phone number on the back and handed to him.

"About seven?"

"Great." She got into her car and he offered her his hand, which she shook. She started the engine and threw him a wave as she exited the parking lot. She felt like a schoolgirl who was about to have her first date, all giddy and flustered.

~~~

In the three months since Thurman Falk had the initial meeting with Mr. Brown with the purpose of finding someone to replace him, Falk had reviewed no less than four-dozen candidates, ultimately rejecting all of them. It was a time-consuming process with no end in sight. Just when it appeared that a candidate might possibly be the one, a glitch in their profile in which they either had political or religious issues took them out of the running. The likely candidate had to be intelligent, squeaky clean with absolutely no police record, preferably single, although being married was not grounds for exclusion, not over the age of fifty, in good physical condition, a background in law enforcement would be a positive, and the requirements went on for what seemed ad infinitum. The two men met on a weekly basis to discuss Falk's progress. Mr. Brown never once criticized Falk's attempt to find the right candidate. He was neither discouraged nor pushy. He accepted Falk's efforts with a great amount of understanding and patience. "You'll know it when you've found the right person," he said supportively.

~~~

There were times when Patty Walsh had to question her own sanity. Over the period of three months that they had been dating, she realized that this was turning into something much more than a passing attraction. She knew he had been on the force for some twenty years, was divorced from his wife of five years, no children, and no family. His father had suffered a massive heart attack when Mike was a senior in high school and a member of the football squad that his father coached. On a bitter Saturday afternoon in winter, the team had beaten a rival team for the first time in fifteen years of competition. Mike and another member of the team took the ice chest and poured it over Coach Decker's head in celebration of the long-awaited win. It was a practice done on most winning teams, but this time it had very unexpected consequences. Coach Decker laughed as the freezing icy water cascaded down over his head and into the protection of his parker. But to the horror of the entire squad, the coach suddenly slumped down to the ground holding his chest. He died before help could arrive.

It took years of therapy for Mike to accept the fact that his participation in this harmless prank had nothing to do with his father's demise. It was just one of those horrible, unfathomable tricks of fate. Two years later, his mother died of cancer and Mike had no doubt that her passing had been brought on by the early death of his father. It was a cross he carried through most of his adulthood.

It had taken three months for all the pieces of Mike's life to fit into the puzzle and each time they met, another piece found its way into the overall picture. Mike's schedule was much more flexible than Patty's so when she was no longer on night duty, he arranged his schedule to coincide with hers. Before long, they were an item. They took pleasure in each other's company and unless Patty read their relationship wrong, it was blossoming into something much more than just a casual fling on his part. It had taken them almost two months to consummate their liaison. He had been patient with her, realizing that she had come to the table with baggage and from past experience he knew that rushing into anything would only lead to a major disappointment for them both. But when it finally came to fruition, it was like the Fourth of July, New Year's Eve and the end of World War Two all rolled into one as they explored each other's sexuality. It was just meant to be and they both accepted the fact with a philosophical *élan vital*.

It was on the evening of her thirty-seventh birthday, July 10th, when he proposed marriage and she tearfully accepted. They didn't set a wedding date. He presented her with his late mother's engagement ring, an antique that had been handed down in his family for generations. Together they made plans to find a place that would be large enough for both of them. There were adjustments to be made and it would take time. They had both spent the better part of their adult lives in their own private worlds and now they were on the brink of giving up their solitude and privacy to share it with each other. They spent many hours airing their apprehensions and doubts as to whether they were equipped to make such a major life adjustment. But at the end of their long periods of examination and self-analysis, the only conclusion was that they were meant to be together and they were prepared to move ahead with their commitment to each other.

Patty was never happier and when she called Marge to give her the good news, the two of them screamed like two kids in the final stages of adolescence recounting the events of their first sexual experiences.

In the twenty years Mike had served as a police officer he had become a pragmatist out of necessity. Prior to his promotion to Detective Sergeant ten years before he was shot in the line of duty. But for the fact that he was wearing his chest protector, he would not have survived.

For weeks thereafter he suffered severe chest pains and some minor complications. He had been in a number of vehicular incidents in which he had come close to death. While answering a call of a bank robbery in progress, as he turned the corner to make his approach, he could see an officer on the ground and the robbers attempting to make their getaway. Per procedure, he should have done a one-eighty in pursuit, but decided to make the most expedient maneuver. He stomped on the gas pedal and crashed headlong into the oncoming getaway car, thereby foiling the robbery. The three robbers died at the scene and Mike spent three weeks in intensive care before learning that he could expect a full recovery. It was three months before he returned to active duty and instead of receiving plaudits and commendations from his superiors, he was severely reprimanded for his actions that cost the department a police cruiser and jeopardized the lives of a number of pedestrians at the scene.

    Now that he was about to take on the responsibility of a wife and possibly a family, he had to ask himself if he'd take the same action again? Would he be as effective and as efficient as he'd been in the past or would he stop and take into consideration the ramifications upon Patty should anything happen to him? He had to admit that it was definitely a dilemma with which he would have to deal.

Chapter 24

The white, wood-framed, three-story house that had been built just after World War II, was something of a landmark on Piedmont Street in the Haight-Ashbury district of San Francisco. During the "Hippies" invasion of the Sixties, no less than four of the most famous rock bands and personalities of that era occupied the premises: Jimi Hendrix, Janis Joplin, Sly and the Family Stone, and the Grateful Dead. More amazing was that with all the drugs and unusual behavior of the times, the house on Piedmont Street managed to maintain its charm and with the exception of a few minor acts of vandalism, there was very little structural damage during those ten years of occupation. In the latter part of the Seventies, the property was purchased by a well-to-do, black physician who had moved his family from Raleigh, North Carolina to take up residency at San Francisco General.

Dr. David Wilcox and his wife, Mattie, raised three handsome children in that house —two sons and a daughter. Devon Wilcox, the eldest of the three, set up residency in the house with his family when his brother and sister decided to return to Raleigh with their parents. It was the doctor's established plan of years before that he would return to his roots when he decided to retire from practice.

Devon Wilcox was a successful computer technician with a business that afforded him, his wife, and their teenage son, Vernon, a very comfortable lifestyle. One could only imagine that the Wilcox family had found a small piece of heaven here on earth in their corner of the colorful City by the Bay.

At sixteen, Vernon Wilcox was not only bright for his age, but he had great aspirations to follow in his grandfather's footsteps and pursue a career in medicine. His family nurtured his ambitions and barring any unforeseen events, Vernon would graduate high school at seventeen and move onto the next step towards his life's goal.

Vernon smoked his first joint when he was just fifteen. He and two friends, Denzel Parker and Carmelo Diaz, were what might be considered, peripheral members of a neighborhood street gang called The Skulls. It was not one of those street gangs that vied for geographical supremacy, but rather a bunch of teenagers who got together to commit small acts of vandalism and petty thefts. Just a bunch of kids crossing over into young adulthood, a rite of passage, so to speak. Then there were those few initiation gatherings where the drug of choice was crystal meth and a smattering of heroin. In a matter of months, Vernon's grades in school had dropped precipitously, but with parents who were riding high on their own successful endeavors, Vernon's slide went unnoticed.

The Wilcox house was situated a short three blocks from a very fashionable and unique Victorian manor house on Clifford Terrace known as The Feldman Estates. It occupied half an acre of prime San Francisco property and dated back to the turn of the century when the family patriarch, who arrived in this country at the turn of the Twentieth Century from Germany, established a retail clothing empire that stretched from Seattle to San Diego. The main house had eight bedrooms and full baths with a great hall that could accommodate a hundred guests for sit-down dinners. Some thirty yards from the main house was the carriage house, originally built with stalls for eight horses and two carriages. It had since been converted into a garage to accommodate six cars, a workshop and an upstairs one-bedroom apartment. The Feldman family rarely used the estate, having their main residence on the east side of Manhattan in New York, but the San Francisco estate was used both as a corporate headquarters for the Feldman family when on the West Coast for business and when associates were summoned for business meetings. Otherwise, the house was rarely used and was surrounded with a security gate to keep out intruders and tourists.

Mike Decker had been renting the carriage house for the better part of twenty years. It was his own private comfort zone where he could retreat from the rigors of his duties with the SFPD. The rent was nominal, well within his means, and in return, the Feldman family only asked that Mike "keep an eye on things." There was a security company that patrolled the estate a number of times each day and the house had been secured with a very high tech burglar alarm system complete with cameras strategically placed on the grounds and inside the mansion. Unfortunately, although the carriage house apartment was of sufficient size to accommodate one person, it was definitely not large enough for two grown adults to live in with any comfort or privacy. Mike would have to make other plans for the day when he and Patty tied the knot. He had considered asking the Feldmans if he might turn one of the wings of the main house into a private living quarter but after some thought on the subject, he could anticipate the Feldman's reluctance to make such an arrangement. After all, it would necessitate hiring a staff to clean and maintain the house, were it lived in on a full-time basis. He had already looked at a number of very comfortable condos in the area that were available and waiting for Patty to make a final decision. Mike lamented that he would miss the unique living arrangement he had on the Feldman estate, but his anticipation of his impending marriage to Patty would surely compensate.

It was Friday night when Mike returned home to the estate after an eighteen-hour shift in which he was the chief investigator in a murder case. Four members of a working class family had been shot and killed in a dispute over supremacy in a drug cartel in which the family had been involved for a decade. It had finally come to a head when the elder son, high on heroin and having been chastised by his father for jeopardizing the family interest with his reckless behavior, retaliated by turning a gun on both his parents and his two younger brothers. The son had been apprehended within hours after the killing wandering aimlessly through the streets in a drug-induced fog. Mike had been working the case for almost a week and as the arraignment date drew near, his schedule was suffocating. He and Patty had barely a moment to spend together and although they spoke by phone a number of times each day, she understood the nature of his job and that work took precedence.

He arrived home at eleven, stripped off his clothes that began to smell putrid from the long workday and stepped into the shower for a much-anticipated cleansing. He needed a few hours of sleep before he returned to the office and as he was getting into a fresh pair of shorts, he thought he heard the sound of someone or something outside the apartment. Through the window he could see the compound that was bathed in light each evening after sundown. Nothing. *Probably my imagination,* he thought. *Plays tricks on me when I'm tired.* He slipped into a terrycloth robe, turned off the overhead light, and threw himself down on the bed. In a matter of minutes he could feel himself slipping into another dimension as sleep began to overtake him. Just as he was on the edge, there it was again. It was a noise coming from the main house as if glass was breaking. It wasn't his imagination. He was sure there was someone on the property. He went to the window and pulled back the curtain, but again there was nothing he could see. This time he was sure he'd heard something from across the compound. Quickly he slipped into a pair of pants, threw

The Guardian List

on a shirt and a pair of slippers, and headed for the interior door leading down to the garage.

Using the two-way radio in his car, he called in "a burglary in progress" and asked for a back up. *Better safe than sorry*, he reminded himself. He slipped into his protective vest, removed a service revolver and flashlight from the glove compartment, and eased out the side door of the garage. As he made his way towards the main house, he could ascertain the movement of a light through one of the downstairs windows of the library. Cautiously he made his way up onto the porch and looked in the window. He could make out two men as they ransacked the desk drawers. Whatever they were looking for was obviously not found as they threw papers and desk objects helter-skelter about the room. *"Was it an act of robbery or merely vandalism?"* he asked himself. He had two options: he could surprise the perps and affect an arrest on his own or he could wait for his backup, which would be the expedient thing to do. But as he was weighing his options, the two burglars moved from the library, exiting into the main hallway of the great house. As Mike was making his way around the side of the building towards the front of the house, the door opened and two youngsters carrying a number of items from their search, stepped out cautiously into the light that bathed the compound. From where he stood, Mike could ascertain that they were merely kids in their teens. He didn't want to act in an imprudent manner as to jeopardize the lives of a couple of kids if they were merely vandals.

Mike pointed his weapon at the two suspects as they neared the porch steps. "Halt!" he called. "This is the police…"

He never heard the third suspect come up behind him and the last thing he heard was the report of a weapon being fired as the bullet entered his brain, killing him instantly.

Photos of the three killers were lifted from the video of the security cameras and within hours, the three teenagers were apprehended and placed under arrest for murder.

~~~

Patty was just signing out of the station when Captain Craig stopped her at the front desk. He was a large, slightly overweight officer who had always been known for dealing with his subordinates at arm's length in order to command respect, so it was most unusual for him to reach out and gently but firmly take Patty by the arm and lead her into his office. He closed the door behind them.

"I think you'd better sit down, Officer," he said with no small amount of authority.

"What is it?" she asked, holding onto the back of a chair.

The Captain appeared to be at a loss for words. He was one of those officers who lived by the book and when he had first learned that Patty and Mike Decker were contemplating marriage, he frowned at the thought that they had fraternized against departmental rules. But upper echelon authority extended just so far and two members of the department choosing to enter into a serious relationship was outside his venue.

Had she done something wrong? Was some irate denizen she may have offended in the line of duty bringing her up on charges? Her mind raced over the previous evening's activities but nothing stood out as unusual.

"Oh, my God," said the Captain, as he took a step towards Patty and looked into her face. In that moment, she knew. She could read it in his eyes.

"Oh, no, not Mike…" was the last thing she remembered as blackness overwhelmed her and the Captain reached out to catch her as she fell.

Chapter 25

Falk had been working on the List project in San Francisco for the past three weeks which made it easy for him to get home to Burbank on weekends. He and Cathy cherished the time they spent together. When the weather permitted, they took advantage of their proximity to the beach and savored the time they could revel in the California sun. Sometimes they spent a day at the zoo since both of them loved animals and planned for the day when they would have a home where they could have at least two dogs and two cats. Their apartment lease prohibited pets, which was the one drawback to renting. At least once a month they drove down to Anaheim for an outing with friends at Disneyland, followed by an early evening of dining out. When time permitted, they splurged on a room at the Disneyland Hotel to complete a perfect weekend. But Thurman knew that sooner or later, Cathy was destined to rock the boat.

"It's getting close to that time," she announced as if it didn't happen at least once a month.

"I know. Are you sure this is what you want? I mean, we could wait for a few months until I finish the case I'm working on and then head on down to Nassau and look for a home to buy. I thought we were both on the same wave length on this."

"Suppose you don't finish the job in a few months? If you're serious about raising a family, Thurman, there's no better time to start than now. Neither of us is getting any younger, you know. If I get pregnant, you'll still have the better part of the year to finish your current case. Isn't that enough time?"

"I guess." He wanted to start a family as much as Cathy, but the current assignment for Mr. Brown was consuming his every waking hour. Sooner or later, what with a family to consider, there was a good chance he would have to resign from the organization. On the positive side, he was convinced that he had a very viable candidate under investigation that would serve the organization well. It would be just a matter of weeks before he could make the final determination and then plan a strategy. It all had to be presented to Mr. Brown, but Thurman was sure he was onto something realistic. "And school? Once you get pregnant you can't continue teaching. Do you feel that now is the time to give that up?"

"Oh, Thurman, it's not as if we need the money from my job, is it? I mean, if that's the case, then raising a family is certainly out of the question."

"God, no," he said, reassuringly. "We're fine. I guess I was thinking that we'd have to tie up some loose ends before we got into the family thing, but if that's what you want and now is the time, hey, I'm willing to let you ravish me for my sperm."

She loved the way he was able to make light of the subject. She couldn't wait to get him up to the hotel room to get started on their new family.

~~~

The sex was awesome and as they lay in each other's arms, Thurman could think of nothing in this world that would make him happier than to impregnate Cathy. They lovingly touched and whispered words of endearment to each other and explored. If ever she got pregnant it would be on just such a night as this when their passions were beyond their greatest expectations. They dozed, only to awaken to a gentle touch or the purring sound of the other. By eleven at night, they were both wide-awake, but physically spent, so Thurman asked if he could turn on the evening news. It wasn't five minutes into the broadcast when the story flashed on the screen. At first, the murder of a police officer by three teenage vandals did not cause Thurman very much concern, but as the story developed and the location became clear, his mind suddenly began to defog and his eyes widened in astonishment. Slowly he rose to a sitting position in order to better ascertain whether what he was seeing was true.

"Sergeant Michael Decker of the San Francisco Police Department was shot and killed today by three teenage vandals in the Haight-Ashbury district of that city…"

As quickly as the story registered, Thurman was on his feet and dressing. Cathy couldn't understand what could cause the most beautiful night of her life to suddenly come to an abrupt halt.

"I'm sorry, babe. I've got to go," he said as he gently bent down and kissed her tenderly on the lips.

"The story…on the news?"

"Yeah. I'm so sorry…"

"I understand."

"I'll leave the car with the garage attendant so you can get back to town. I'll catch a cab to the airport." He was out the door and gone.

Cathy kept watching the story of the dead police officer as it developed on the TV, but she couldn't fathom how it had anything to do with her husband. In truth, she really didn't want to know.

~~~

As soon as she heard, Marge asked Captain Peterson for a leave of absence and caught the first plane from Vegas to San Francisco. She had to be with Patty. Their calls had been less frequent since Patty had gotten engaged to Michael, but they still managed to keep in touch two or three times each week. Marge had no idea what she could say or do to help, she just knew she had to be there for her. A young, female officer in uniform answered the door.

"Are you family?" asked Officer Denise Posner. She appeared to be a rookie, judging by her age and the sparkle of her uniform as if it had just come out of the wrapper.

"Marge Linden," she said as she flashed her badge. "Patty and I were classmates together in high school. We go way back."

"C'mon in. I'm sure she could use a friend right now. My Captain has me standing by, he didn't want her to be alone. I don't know her all that well but from what I've heard, she's a good officer."

Marge placed her overnight bag on the floor by the doorway. "That was very thoughtful of your Captain. I can take it from here if you'd like to head back to your station."

"Let me check with the Captain." She went over to the phone on the table. "There's a Las Vegas police officer just arrived. Name of Marge Linden. Says she's a friend of Patty's and that she's offered to stay with her. What do you want me to do?" Pause. "Right. Yes, sir." She hung up the phone. "Did you know her fiancé?"

"Never had the pleasure, but Patty and I spoke quite often and I felt as if I knew him."

"I saw him a number of times. Good-looking man. Older, but good looking."

Marge had to smile. Officer Posner couldn't have been more than twenty-two or three, at most. "I'll be here if you want to check back later."

The young officer picked up her hat and exited the apartment. Marge looked around at the rather austere surrounding. Nothing had changed since the last time she had visited. She could only imagine how elated Patty must have been knowing that soon she would be moving on to a larger and warmer dwelling that she was going to share with someone she loved. *It's not fair,* she thought. *It's just not fucking fair!*

The shades in the bedroom were drawn and the room was almost in darkness as Marge entered. She stood in the doorway, not wanting to disturb Patty if she was sleeping. She heard Patty call out.

"Is that you, Denise?"

"No, honey, it's me, Marge…"

She walked over and sat on the edge of the bed. The two women embraced and the tears flowed. They may have been police officers, but they were both caring women who were sharing a bitter life experience. They held onto each other until the tears finally dried up with nothing left in the well. Patty extricated herself from her friend's embrace and laid back down on her pillow. "I must look like hell." She tried to sound jovial.

"I've seen you under better circumstances." She held Patty's hand not really knowing what to say next. "I'm so sorry, Patty. Oh, my God, I'm so very sorry," she sobbed.

Suddenly it seemed as if their roles were reversed. It was Patty who was comforting Marge as she patted her hand. "I knew you'd come," was all she said.

When it appeared that the conversation had reached a stalemate, Marge rose from the edge of the bed. "Patty, I don't expect you to rise up from your mourning bed and make with the wisecrack jokes like we used to, but would you mind if I raise the shades and get some light in here? We should talk."

Patty merely nodded and Marge went to the window and drew the shades to let in the midday light. She went to the kitchen to heat a kettle of water for tea, and then returned to the bedroom. She went into the bathroom where she turned on the hot water in the bathtub.

"C'mon," she said to Patty when she returned bedside. She held out her hand and Patty took it and raised herself to a standing position. "Get out of that nightshirt, soak for a while, and I'll make us something for lunch." She watched as Patty tentatively made her way into the bathroom. Marge retreated to the kitchen where she checked out the fridge and set to work preparing something for them to eat. Of one thing Marge was sure; there was no way in hell Patty was going to be able to recover from this tragedy unless she kept up her strength. Not all the talking in the world would help if Patty let her defenses down. Marge felt she was on a mission and she would expect no less from Patty were their positions reversed.

Lunch consisted of canned chicken soup, fried eggs, bacon, and buttered toast. Not a word was spoken for the better part of the meal. They silently drank their tea, each waiting for the other to break the ice. Finally, Marge couldn't take it any longer. "Wanna talk?" No response. "How do you feel?"

Patty's attention was fixed on her teacup as if it was a crystal ball. She didn't raise her eyes. "Angry. Miserable and angry."

"I know."

"They were just kids, Marge, sixteen year-old kids looking to make a score so they could buy some dope and for that Mike paid with his life. They stole from me as well and I'm angry. All I can think of is…revenge. I want to…" Her words failed her and trailed off. She didn't have to say anything more. As they sat in silence with their own thoughts, the doorbell rang.

"I'll get it," said Marge. She crossed the room and opened the door only to be greeted by a Police Captain in full dress. He carried a bouquet of flowers and respectfully removed his hat.

"May I see her?" he asked.

"Who is it?" she heard Patty call.

"Come in," said Marge as she stepped to one side.

Captain Craig entered the apartment and placed his hat on the hall table. He was a large man and despite his rank, it was obvious that he was out of his element and most uncomfortable. He saw Patty at the dining room table and crossed to her, extending the flowers as an offering of condolence. "I was just in the neighborhood," he lied.

"That's very kind of you, Captain. Have you met my friend, Marge Linden? She's come in from Vegas to stay with me for a few days."

The Captain nodded to Marge who took the flowers from him. She found a vase in the kitchen cabinet and made an arrangement. "Patty, I'll leave you two to talk. I'd like to freshen up," she said, retrieving her bag and heading for the bedroom.

"May I offer you something to drink, Captain? Tea? Coffee?"

"No thanks. I'm fine. I don't mean to intrude."

"Not at all. Please, sit down."

"I know you have company so I won't stay long. I'd like you to take all the time you need to put this behind you. You're covered down at the Precinct, so you've nothing to worry about."

"Thank you, Captain. I'm glad you came by. I think there's something I should tell you."

He could anticipate what she was about to say. "If it's something to do with your place down at the Precinct, it can wait."

"I've been thinking, Captain. Maybe I should tender my resignation."

"Can we discuss this another time, Patty? I understand what you're experiencing and I don't want you to make any decisions in haste. Take all the time you need and when you feel up to it, we can talk. Meanwhile, I didn't hear anything you said about resigning so nothing has changed as far as the department is concerned. If there's anything you need, call me. I'll check in on you later."

Out of respect for her privacy, the Captain rose and turned for the door.

"When will they be arraigned?" she asked.

"In a couple of days. I'll let you know exactly when. I know you'll want to be there."

"Yes, most definitely. And thanks for everything, Captain."

Without another word he retrieved his hat and closed the front door behind him. Patty sat alone for a moment collecting her thoughts. She wanted to cry, but she was drained. She was sad and lonely. She found solace in the fact that Marge had come to stay with her. She put her hands on the edge of the table, straightened her back, got to her feet and began to clear the dishes.

Chapter 26

The funeral procession through the streets of San Francisco drew over two thousand spectators. Had Patty and Mike tied the knot before his demise, she would have been granted all the amenities as a member of the family, but since she was considered merely a friend, a comrade in arms, she was relegated to the role of one of more than two hundred fellow officers that followed the hearse carrying Mike's cremated remains. There was no family since Mike was the last of the Deckers. Marge walked alongside Patty, as did Captain Craig. It was a fitting tribute to a fallen comrade, but with every step it was all Patty could do to control her ever-increasing rage. She had run the gamut of emotions from sadness to anger to the desire to see justice meted out to the kids who had performed this senseless, devastating act.

As the funeral procession passed, Thuman Falk removed his hat and respectfully lowered his head. Michael Decker had been the most viable of candidates on his list to step up to assume the role of leader of the organization. Falk had spent hundreds of hours researching his background — everything from his family, to his military record, to his record as a police officer, to his personal relationships, his high school transcripts, his college transcripts, his medical records. Falk knew Mike Decker better than anyone else who had ever come in contact with him, including his current fiancée, Patty Walsh.

Falk had been minutes away from announcing to Mr. Brown that he had indeed found the perfect candidate to take over the supervision of the Guardian List. Now, all his investigative work was for naught, cancelled with one bullet to the head. He didn't have to be present, to stand with the citizens of the city and watch the procession of the fallen officer, but Falk was drawn to the curbside as if he had experience the loss of a dear friend. It was crazy. He had never formally met the man, although on a couple of occasions Falk had undertaken to be present when Decker was testifying in a case. It was part of Falk's M.O. to cover every angle in his investigation. There was no detail that was not completely covered. So well did Falk know Mike Decker, he would have bet his life that had the offer been made, Decker would have accepted. The one questionable element in the selection of Decker was the Sergeant's current plans to take a wife, but his other qualifications so completely overshadowed the one questionable act that it did not hold any weight in the final selection. *Back to the drawing board,* thought Thurman Falk as the funeral procession passed and disappeared from sight.

~~~

Vernon Wilcox, Denzel Parker, and Carmelo Diaz were led into the courtroom and seated at the defendant's table along with their attorney, Max Schoenfeld. Seated behind them were the members of the Wilcox, Parker, and

Diaz families, as well as a member of the ACLU, three church leaders from the African-American community, and a number of local political leaders. The press occupied most of the other seats with very little room for spectators. Patty and Marge were seated behind the prosecution table where they could observe the demeanor of the three juveniles.

It appeared that the three defendants were having a pleasurable outing as if the whole proceeding was some kind of adolescent joke. They interacted with each other in whispers, smiling and throwing furtive glances behind them to their families that were obviously diametrically stricken with grief over the severity of the proceedings. In a pre-trial meeting, it had been determined by counsel and the families that the three should stand trial together, all with the same lawyer. In that way, there would be no chance that one or the other might turn state's evidence against the other two to save his own skin. The state had petitioned the court that the three defendants be tried as adults due to the severity of the charges, but a black judge had denied that petition. All through the morning's proceedings, Patty got the impression that this was a stacked trial and that although the weight of evidence clearly spelled out "guilty" in the end, the three defendants would be remanded into juvenile detention to serve a limited term. There was testimony to the effect that the three were acting under diminished capacity due to their use of drugs, that they knew not what they were doing when they committed the act, and that they all three pleaded "not guilty" to premeditated murder. The video that the prosecution entered as Exhibit A, clearly showed Vernon Wilcox as the perp who actually pulled the trigger. Their act of burglary which led up to the killing of the police officer (who, the defense pointed out, "was not in uniform at the time he confronted the juveniles") was unpremeditated — an act of involuntary manslaughter.

The trial lasted two months. Marge had long since returned to her duty station in Las Vegas where she called Patty at the end of each day. Patty attended the proceedings of the trial religiously. As Thurman Falk was also in attendance in the courtroom on a daily basis, he had a sudden revelation.

~~~

"I'd like to request a leave of absence," said Patty as she stood, hat in hand, in front of Captain Craig's desk.

It had been two months since Mike Decker's death and the Captain had hoped that the passage of time would have helped to heal the wound in Patty's heart. He had grown fond of her, empathized with her pain and tried to encourage her to stay the course, but it appeared that the wound was deeper than anticipated and although he hated to lose her services, it seemed the expedient thing was to grant her request. "Is this in anticipation of a permanent move, Officer?" he asked.

"I'm not sure, Captain. I need some time to work things out. Everyone has been so supportive and I feel I'm letting my fellow officers down, but I'm still having nightmares and I'm easily distracted and that's not me. I don't know if this makes much sense, Captain."

"Have you spoken to our chaplain?"

"I've preferred to see the Department psychiatrist, Doctor Lake. He's helped quite a bit but there are still issues only I can resolve. I need some time."

"I understand," he said as sympathetically as he could. "How about a month?" He got up from his chair and walked around the desk. "Take a month, Officer. After that, we'll talk. I'd hate to lose you, Patty." He held out his hand in a fatherly gesture and she took it.

What difference would a month make? she asked herself. She wished he hadn't been so damn understanding, it would have been so much easier. "Thank you, Captain. I'll clear out my things." She turned and exited his office thinking that this could very well be the last time they would meet.

Patty had mentally prepared herself to undertake the winding trip from San Francisco to Vegas. When driving in the city in a police cruiser, she never had time or the inclination to enjoy her surroundings. Being on an extended trip, the driving was exhilarating; sort of like therapy. The sound of the tires on the road created a semi-hypnotic, out-of-body experience in which her mind traveled over the highway of her life where she could stop and dwell on one event or travel on to another if the experience was not to her liking.

In the background she could entertain the classical selection from her CD and the occasional meow from

Smokey, who occupied the passenger seat in his Pet Taxi that was secured in placed with a seat belt. Smokey was usually not a good traveler. A trip in the car often meant a visit to the veterinarian's office where he would be probed or stuck with a needle. After an hour of letting his dissent be known, he settled down to a catnap. Actually, he was perfect company for the long trip; his presence was known but he kept his thoughts to himself. Occasionally Patty would verbally address him as if he were a passenger that was sharing an adventure. "How about that Barry Manilow? And of course, Bette Midler...if we can get tickets. You'll love the Disney show, *The Lion King* and I heard that 'Jersey Boys' is a must..."

It was fun having someone with whom she could share her thoughts as they crossed over the winding road through Yosemite National Park and into Nevada where she picked up I-95 down to Vegas. Patty had packed a small thermos and cooler with sandwiches so she wouldn't have to make any extended stops. She didn't relish the thought of leaving Smokey alone in the car for any prolonged period of time except for an occasional pit stop where she could use the people-kitty-litter-box and walked Smokey for a few minutes on his leash. She could never figure out why the cat didn't do his business when she took him for a walk on the grass, preferring to do his business in the litter box in the laundry room and then scatter sand all over the floor. While on the road, she'd placed the litter box on the rear seat for his convenience. What the hell, it was a small price to pay for his exceptional company and she was forever grateful that Marge insisted she bring Smokey along rather than commit him to the kennel for as long as she would be away. With all the trauma of the past few months, Patty found it comforting that there was a very warm place in her heart for her relationship with Marge. Had they been twins, they couldn't have been closer. For this she was grateful.

The phone tap on Patty's line was all Thurman Falk needed to plan his next move.

~~~

The meeting of the organization had lessened to six members from the original count of twenty going back to its inception six years before. Some of the members had passed on from natural causes; others had taken contracts in lieu of their impending demise from illness. The suite at the Hilton had been scanned for bugs and taps and came up clean. The order of the day was addressed to accepting new applications that were nominated by the remaining members. Nothing was committed to writing and the petitioners presented each applicant's qualifications orally. By the end of the two-day meeting, six new applicants had been accepted for membership.

It was John Brown's intent not to divulge to the membership his plans to abdicate his position as leader of the List. When the time was propitious and a serious candidate had passed the scrutiny of the committee, he would make a motion to introduce the prospective nominee. *No need to rock the boat,* he thought. After the final meeting adjourned until the next get-together, the members disbursed back to their original points of origin. His next order of business was to meet with Thurman Falk to assess progress in his headhunting assignment. *Poor Thurman*, he thought. *What a miserable task I've assigned to him. I wouldn't be the least bit dismayed if he wasn't able to find a viable candidate."*

The two men dined at the Benihana Village, a restaurant whose Japanese cuisine was equal to or finer than any in the city. As was their usual preference, they chose a booth at the rear of the great room sequestered away from most of the other patrons. Falk carried a small laptop computer that he set on the seat between the two of them and out of sight of the waiter or any other casual passersby. They dined on sashimi, teriyaki chicken and rice, and warm sake. Not a word passed between them regarding the basis for their meeting. After refreshing his hot tea and without further small talk, Falk flipped open the lid of his laptop. He hit the enter key and the screen came to life.

As Mr. Brown glanced down at the screen, he could ascertain what appeared to be an extensive resume. It took him only a few seconds to realize that the party in question was an active female officer with the San Francisco Police Department. He looked over at Falk who had a Cheshire cat grin on his face.

"You're joking," said Mr. Brown.

"Hardly."

"It's a woman."

"I know."

"We didn't discuss the possibility of bringing a woman into the organization."

"We discussed me finding someone with all the right credentials who could take your place when the time came for you to step down. I think she is that person," said Falk with sincere conviction.

Mr. Brown scrolled down. There was a photo of a rather attractive young woman dressed in her dark blue police uniform. "She's an active police officer?" he asked.

"She's on administrative leave at the moment, pending her resignation."

Falk had put together a rather lengthy summary of Patty Walsh's career and personal life, which included her relationship with Mike Decker that ended in tragedy. It was not a presentation that one could absorb in a few short minutes. "May I have some time to go over this in depth?"

"Of course. This is not carved in stone, Mr. Brown, but of all the candidates I considered, she is by far the most qualified."

"And what makes you think she would want to associate herself with the organization?"

"Intuition. I have a feeling she's ready to move on…"

The Guardian List

Chapter 27

Marge was on a full time schedule; twelve hours a day, four days a week. On her three days off, she and Patty took advantage of the warm spring weather and enjoyed their days shopping and casual walks through Sunset Park. One day they drove up the I-95 heading towards Reno to the Cold Creek turnoff. There they hung a left and traveled for about five miles along a deserted asphalt road heading towards the mountains. Marge slowed the vehicle and stopped when they suddenly encountered a small herd of wild horses grazing alongside the road. Without letting on about the horses, Marge had brought a small bag of carrots and as Patty exited the car, one of the horses broke from the herd and sauntered over to her in anticipation of a treat. Marge handed her a carrot and Patty held it out to the impressive stallion. He accepted the carrot, then bobbed his head as if to thank her and fixed her with his big, brown eyes. She reached up and gently patted his nose, then his flank.

"My God, he's like an overgrown puppy," she said.

By now, three other horses surrounded Marge as she offered up the carrots. "This is how I get away from the daily routine of chasing the crazies in Vegas. It's how I keep my sanity."

They stayed with the herd until all the carrots were consumed. Tearing themselves away, they got into the car and headed back to the city.

It was good therapy to get away from the everyday routine of police work and Marge could see how Patty was reverting back to her old self. On the days that Marge was on duty, Patty took a book and a blanket and spent her free time in the park just hanging out. It was a luxury she rarely had time to contemplate in San Francisco what with a full work schedule and the infrequent days when the weather rarely cooperated, but in Las Vegas, she considered it "a sun culture" where people appreciated the outdoors even when the temperatures soared into the hundreds. *What in the world ever possessed me to leave?* she asked herself. It seemed like so long ago. Now, most of her friends and acquaintances had moved on but she and Marge seemed destined to be a part of each other's lives ad infinitum.

She had been in Vegas just over a week and been enjoying the same daily routine. She had plenty of time to contemplate whether or not she would be returning to San Francisco and the department. She could reapply in Vegas and probably have no difficulty getting back on with Metro, but was that where she wanted to be, what she wanted to do? She felt confident that she could return to school and probably take the bar in a matter of a couple of years. But on careful consideration and what with her association with the lawyers she knew from her courtroom appearances, she surely could not imagine herself defending some of the trash she had encountered in her line of work. Of course, there were other fields in which she could specialize other than Criminal Law, but how long could she see herself working in real estate, or corporate, or medical malpractice? There had been a time, before being a cop and before contemplating the law, when she thought she might like to be a teacher. That was a long time ago when she was in high school, when she had her head in the clouds and thought of all the good things she was destined to do working with kids and opening some of the avenues available to them in the real world. *Where did all that selflessness go?"* she asked herself. As she contemplated those years gone by, she could feel herself sliding back into that old melancholy brought on by her lack of accomplishment in her chosen field. And then she would think of Mike and all the plans they had made and how his death had created a void in her the likes of which she never could have imagined. She checked her watch and realized that Marge would be home from work in an hour and they had plans to see a show that evening on the Strip. As she gathered up her blanket and book, she happened to notice an elderly gentleman seated on a bench on the path leading back to where she had parked her car. He looked very familiar but then she realized that she had seen him on a couple of other occasions when she came to the park. As she passed, he glanced up from his paper and nodded as if in a greeting. She smiled and continued on her way, never giving it a second thought.

    As Patty passed on down the path and into the parking lot where she retrieved her car and drove off,

Father Ignatius, dressed in lay clothes, folded his paper and prepared to call it a day. This was the third time he had made himself known to Patty, but this was the first time she'd acknowledged his presence. It was all part of the plan.

~~~

Starbuck's Coffee Shop was located in The District on the street that the two women traveled when running their morning route. At the two-mile mark, they stopped for a latte before the final leg of their run. Patty admitted that it was not a very healthy practice, loading up on carbs while pretending to engage in a healthy exercise regime. *What the hell, that's why they called it "vacation."* They found a table outside on the promenade and settled down to watch the people-parade. It was still early before the heat of the day became too oppressive for outdoor activities and from the number of runners passing by, it was gratifying to realize that they were not the only crazy people in Las Vegas.

Patty's attention was drawn to a tall, rather good-looking black man, another jogger perhaps in his late thirties or early forties, who occupied a table four or five tables removed from where they were sitting. She couldn't help but notice that he had a striking resemblance to that movie star…whatsisname? Morgan Freeman, that's the one. Obviously it wasn't the actor because this man must have been half his age, but they both had that tall, angular look with a gentle face. *Perhaps they could be related,* she thought.

"See that gentleman over there, over your right shoulder. Who does he remind you of?"

Marge turned to look over to her right. "Oh, yeah, I know who you mean. I can't think of his name but there is a striking resemblance."

"Morgan Freeman. Remember we saw him in that prison film a few years back…something about a redemption?"

"*The Shawshank Redemption.* Oh, my God, what a great flick."

As if on cue, the Morgan Freeman double got up and joined the passing joggers, getting swallowed up in the moving crowd. He had established a pattern, the route that Patty traveled either alone or with her friend, Marge. When the time was propitious, someone from the organization would make the first move. Falk knew they had to act soon should Patty suddenly decide to leave Vegas and head back home to the Bay area. Nothing on the recordings of the tap of Marge's phone indicated that Patty was contemplating leaving town in the immediate future.

Timing is everything in life, thought Father Ignatius as he glanced at the article almost hidden away in the third section of the *Review-Journal.* "After having passed the Prison Review Board, the state recommended that Warren Price be released from custody, having served twenty months of his sentence and that he be returned to society with the following restrictions…" And the article went on to list a number of restrictions, including registering as a sex offender and reporting periodically to his parole officer.

This could very well be the bait Mr. Brown had been hoping for in order to make a presentation to the candidate.

In a most unusual meeting in which the three principals all came together at the same time, John Brown, Father Ignatius, and Thurman Falk met at a suite at the Rio Hotel a few blocks from the Strip. It was a critical meeting to ascertain just how they might enlist the chosen candidate to step up to the leadership role.

"I've gone over the dossier of the candidate you submitted, Mr. Falk. I must admit that at first I was dubious about considering a woman, but after careful contemplation, I'm pleased to concur with you that this might very well be the perfect solution to our problem."

Falk was suddenly filled with a sense of accomplishment as he heard Mr. Brown's references to the positive results of his endless hours of legwork and research. If Patty Walsh was indeed the candidate of choice, Falk could anticipate his plan to move on from his association with the organization. It was never his intention to make this a lifetime occupation and what with the financial security he had built up, he could visualize a life with Cathy in some remote part of Nassau in early retirement. Perhaps, though, if the situation called for it, he might take on an assignment on a temporary basis. Full time retirement had its drawbacks and Falk could not picture himself as master of the mansion, growing old and fat in his prime of life.

"How do you suggest we proceed, Mr. Falk?"

"I think that Father Ignatius should be our lead man. He's already made contact and the sooner he arranges a meeting, the sooner we'll know if we're on the right track."

Both men looked to Father Ignatius. "The first day Officer Linden returns to duty I'll take it from there when Mr. Falk lets me know…"

~~~

With latte in hand, Patty took a small table on the promenade in front of the coffee shop. From her fanny pack she removed a small notepad and a pen and began to scribble some notes to herself. So preoccupied was she with her writing that she didn't notice the tall man approach her table until he blocked out the light as his shadow ran across the page on which she was writing. As she looked up, there was a momentary flicker of recognition, but when she saw the clerical collar, she thought she had been mistaken.

"Is this seat taken?" asked the tall priest.

"I beg your pardon, Father. Do we know each other?"

"From Sunset Park…the other day."

There was a sudden light come on as Patty realized where it was she had seen this person before. But in the park he did not wear clerical vestige and for a moment she was disoriented.

"You're Officer Walsh, aren't you?"

Now Patty was really confused. This elderly priest was addressing her by name but the other day, in the park, he merely nodded to her. She immediately went on the defensive with this unusual approach from a perfect stranger. A nervous smiled appeared on her face as if this was the opening of some kind of joke. "Do we know each other?" she asked again.

"You might say we had a friend in common." He motioned towards the empty chair. "May I?"

She nodded and the priest sat across from her. He placed the copy of the *Review-Journal* on the table between them, but didn't allude to the article. "I'm Father Ignatius. I was a friend of Captain Henning."

That immediately got Patty's attention. The Captain had been her commanding officer when first she joined the force some twelve years before in Las Vegas, but shortly thereafter he retired. She remembered the incident in which the Captain had shot a killer in a convenience store robbery a couple of years ago, but she had already moved on to San Francisco. She remembered that Marge had befriended the Captain up until the time of his death.

"Are you with a local parish?" she asked.

"Retired. You might say that I'm in Vegas ministering to a long-time friend and parishioner. I live on the East Coast…"

An awkward silence ensued, neither taking the initiative. Finally, Patty said, "Is it a coincidence that we've run into each other three times in as many days or is it just my imagination running wild?"

"I was hoping we'd meet again. I heard from reliable sources that you might be leaving the force in San Francisco."

Patty could not refrain from a short, uncomfortable laugh that emanated from her throat. "Reliable source? My word, Father, how in the world would you be privy to such information when I'm not sure what my plans are from one day to the next?" There was a cutting edge to the sound of her voice as if she was annoyed that someone would presume to know what was in her mind. She changed her demeanor from casual interest to annoyance. "May I ask if you have some identification, Father?"

The priest took out his wallet and removed an identification card that he handed to Patty. He was indeed a priest according to his ID. She returned the card. "This is very unsettling, you approaching me in this manner."

"I didn't mean to upset you, Miss Walsh. I had heard of your recent loss and thought I might be able to offer you some comforting words. I, too, have experienced an untimely personal loss and I know how deeply it hurts to the core. I meant no disrespect."

"No, no, I didn't mean it that way, Father. You coming over to me out of the blue is a bit bizarre, to say the least. As for my personal loss, I'm dealing with it as best I can. It's caused me to re-evaluate some of my own goals and personal beliefs, but to be perfectly honest, I've not sought solace in the church." She was still shaken by the information to which the priest was privy. "May I ask where you got your information about me leaving the department?"

"Rumors. You taking an unscheduled leave of absence…just a normal conclusion under the circumstances."

"Tell me, Father, are you privy to private police scheduling in the San Francisco Police Department? Why do I have the feeling you're not leveling with me?"

"I understand your suspicion, but let me turn back a page." He took a long pull from his latte as if trying to carefully chose the right phrasing for what he was about to say. "Did you know that Michael Decker was contemplating leaving the department before he was killed?"

Patty stared at the priest in disbelief. "I don't believe it. Michael would have told me if he was contemplating such a move."

"What I'm going to share with you is just between the two of us, Miss Walsh." Just the tone of his voice was almost hypnotic as he stared deeply into her eyes. Deliberately he unfolded the newspaper to the article about the release of Warren Price. As she read through the article, Father Ignatius said, "I have reason to believe that there is someone out there who wants to see Warren Price dead."

What a naïve thing to say, she thought. *Anyone with one iota of social consciousness that detests child molesters would certainly want to see Warren Price get what's coming to him.* "Is this something you've heard in the confessional, Father?"

"I can't reveal my source."

"Have you reported what you know to the police?"

"I was hoping you might have the time to advise me on the subject."

"What the hell is going on here?" she asked herself. Was this some kind of setup? Was this priest for real? Was he wearing a wire? There was no way in hell she would promise him immunity from prosecution if he revealed something that violated the law. She wasn't about to stick her neck out for someone who just walked up to her table out of the clear blue without any references or referral. Yet he did mention that bit about Mike, about him planning to leave the department. That stuck in her throat. How could she learn more about Mike's intentions without compromising her position as a cop? She could promise him that anything he said would be off the record and then, if what he told her was either illegal or reeked of some violation of the law, she could always deny anything she promised him. Damn, what a dilemma!

"I'd like to know more about Mike Decker's intentions to leave law enforcement. After all, I had a vested interest in his future and now you're telling me that he was making plans and didn't take me into his confidence. That's really upsetting."

"He was offered a high-paying corporate position with a private company that deals with law enforcement. That's about all I can divulge right now. I do know the people who made him the initial offer and I could arrange a meeting if you'd like to learn more."

"When and where?" she asked.

She was hooked. Now all he had to do was reel her in and set up the meeting.

~~~

Although she hadn't discussed it with Marge, she had planned to head on back to San Francisco in a couple of days, tender her resignation, close up the apartment and return to Las Vegas, perhaps within the month. Beyond that, she was still up in the air as to what came next. Now, she was faced with this meeting that Father Ignatius was going to set up and she had promised she would not repeat anything they had discussed. What was she getting into? Should she tell Marge about her meeting with the priest? Should she mention that she was going to have a meeting with someone who professed to having offered Mike a security position that he'd been considering? There was a knot the size of a golf ball in the pit of her stomach and she could feel a throbbing in her head. Her skin was crawling and she was going through mental anguish with uncertainty. She contemplated a good stiff shot of tequila, but settled for a beer to try to settle her stomach. She heard the key in the door as Marge entered, still dressed in her uniform.

"God, I'm beat," she announced as she threw her bag on the couch and headed to the cabinet, took down a bottle of Johnny Walker and poured out three fingers over some ice.

"Tough day?"

"Hell, I can handle the murders and the drugs and the hookers, but the paperwork is going to kill me. I've decided that when I'm Commissioner, every cop is going to have a private secretary to take care of all the paperwork. That will free us up to fight crime and become candidates for the role of the Caped Crusader. I think I'm getting arthritis in my hand from all the writing."

Patty could sympathize with her. Every cop from California to New York had the same grievance. "You have plans this evening with Anthony?"

"He's got special duty tonight with the Mayor's office. Why, you have anything special you wanna do?"

"I thought we'd send out for Chinese, maybe watch a flick…talk."

"You know, girl, if I wasn't so involved with Anthony I'd make you an offer you couldn't refuse. We're so much alike we could be clones. A movie, Chinese; it's me all over. You call in our order while I grab a quick shower and freshen up."

Two hours later, they were watching a Mel Gibson feature in which he was performing some impossible feats with a police cruiser and shooting up the entire city without breaking a sweat. Patty looked over to see if Marge was not enjoying it as much as she and from the expression on her face, Marge was about to drop off. "You mind if we kill it?" she asked.

"Please, before I barf. Does anyone really enjoy all this crap?" She got up to get some ice and another finger of scotch. "Another brew?"

"No thanks." She'd already decided that there was no way in hell that she was going to attend some clandestine meeting without some kind of a back-up. Marge plopped down in the overstuffed chair opposite the couch where Patty was seated.

"What's on your mind?" she asked.

"What d'ya mean?"

"You know what I mean. I'm sitting here all evening waiting for you to tell me what the hell is bothering you, so don't give me 'what d'ya mean?' You've got that look on your face as if your world is crashing down around your ears. Talk, girl or I'll slap it out of you."

Patty laughed. "That obvious, huh? That's why I gave up wanting to be an actress."

"Don't bullshit me, Patty. You never for a moment wanted to be an actress."

After a few moments, she broke the ice. "I met a guy."

All of a sudden, Marge was on the edge of her seat leaning forward so as not to miss a single word. "A guy-guy?"

"A priest."

"Oh, jeez," Marge exploded as if Patty had burst her bubble.

"He said he knew Mike and that before he was killed, he was contemplating leaving the department."

"Mike ever say anything about it to you?"

"Never. This priest, Father Ignatius, says that Mike was offered a job in the private sector and was seriously considering it when all this happened. Marge, I'm not supposed to discuss this with anyone, but I don't know what I'm getting into and I need a back-up just in case there's more to this than meets the eye. I've got an appointment to meet the principals that were dealing with Mike."

"When?"

"Tomorrow evening at South Point. Obviously you can't go with me, but I'd like you to be close if I need you. I'll wear a wire so you'll know exactly where I am every minute of the meeting. I can understand if you don't want to get involved."

"Don't be an ass. Of course I'll be there."

"I'm curious about what these people were offering Mike that was so secretive that he couldn't share it with me."

Chapter 28

Patty took a seat in the Sport's Book of the South Point Casino where she could observe a dozen screens of sporting events: horse racing, baseball games, soccer, football. She placed her bag on the seat next to her signifying that the seat was taken. At seven in the evening the casino was crowded with a variety of fans dressed in Western attire. The South Point facility entertained a large, indoor arena for rodeo events that drew contestants and fans from the four corners of the country. This weekend was one of the largest rodeo events of the season on the West Coast and boots, Levi's and Stetsons were the dress code of the day. Patty felt out of place in her fashionable Sear's suit, a rip-off of Armani. Inside her jacket, tucked into her bra was a small, digital mike whose signal was being monitored by Marge, stationed in the parking lot of the Hotel-Casino in a Dodge van that she requisitioned from the motor pool. Before leaving Marge's apartment, they tested the equipment that appeared to be in perfect working order.

Patty ordered a glass of white zinfandel from the roving waitress and as instructed by Marge as a sign, she placed it on the table to her right without drinking any. She wanted a clear head for what was about to take place and wine made her sleepy.

"This place is a madhouse," she said into the mike, hoping that Marge was receiving a clear signal over all the extraneous noise. She was watching the last furlong of a race being run at Hollywood Park when she realized that someone had taken a seat next to her. As she glanced over, she immediately recognized the runner she had seen at the District the day she and Marge had stopped for coffee, the one who resembled Morgan Freeman.

"Do you like the trotters?" he asked.

"I prefer the flats myself," she responded.

"Whenever you're done with your drink, we can leave. They're waiting for us."

"Do we have far to go?" she asked.

"Right here in the hotel," he said as they both stood to leave. As he reached his arm across her body to direct her towards the elevators, the electronic scanner on his left wrist sent out a signal that immediately scrambled the electronic signal of the mike hidden in her bra. The last thing Marge heard was "right here in the hotel..." before static took over her receiver. There was a moment of panic when she realized that she was out of communication with Patty. She scrambled from the van and ran into the Casino in hopes of catching a glimpse of the two before they were swallowed up in the surging crowd. There was no way in hell she could find them as she ran back and forth through the Casino cursing her luck. After a few minutes of futile attempts to locate them, she returned to the van and headed back home in the hopes that Patty would contact her first chance she got. Short of alerting the entire police force that Officer Patty Walsh was in imminent danger of harm, there was nothing else she could think of that was in keeping with Patty's instructions.

Falk knocked on the door to Room 428 that was immediately opened by Father Ignatius who greeted her warmly.

"Officer Walsh, I see you've already met Mr. Falk." He stepped aside as Patty entered. Waiting for her in front of the window of the suite was a short, frumpy, elderly man who immediately crossed to greet her with an extended hand.

"My name is John Brown," he announced and waited for the usual response. As she raised one eyebrow, he laughed. "No, really. It's my name. You can ask the good Father."

"At this point you could tell me that you were the Virgin Queen and I'd take your word. I'm still trying to figure out what I'm doing here."

"All in good time, Officer Walsh. Would you mind if I call you Patty? I'd prefer if you called me John."

"All right," she agreed.

"Please…" He motioned to the seating area and the four settled in for their meeting. After she declined something to drink, John Brown took the lead. "Mr. Falk is a licensed private investigator that works for my organization."

"And what organization is that?" she inquired.

"All in good time, Patty. Father Ignatius tells me that Mike Decker didn't share with you his plans to join our organization. First, let me extend our sincere condolences. Needless to say, we held him in the highest regard. Permit me to shed some light on his reluctance to announce this sudden move. We were still in the negotiating stages at the time of his untimely death, but I have no doubt that given a bit more time, he would have shared with you everything we'd planned. May I inquire, are you contemplating tendering your resignation from the department?"

"Did I miss something? It appears that what was merely a passing, personal thought seems to have ended up on the front page of the daily paper."

"For the sake of conversation, let me take that as a 'yes'." This was the sticky part, thought John Brown. From here on out there was no turning back. "Tell me, Patty, have you ever heard of an organization that keeps a compilation of names called The Guardian List?"

"It doesn't ring a bell."

"I can tell you that the name of Warren Price is on the List."

"I don't understand."

"Let me go back about six years…"

BOOK THREE

Chapter 29

It had been almost five hours since Marge had lost contact with Patty. What the hell to do? Did Patty have any inclination that they had lost contact and that she was out there on her own? What if the whole meeting was bogus? What if the priest was just some felon masquerading as a clergyman and was in some way connected with some criminal element that Patty had been responsible for putting away. Her train of thought was clearly about to run off the track when the phone rang. Marge almost jumped out of her skin.

"Where the hell are you?" she yelled without even asking who it was.

"You know where I am. I repeated the room number and was wired for the entire conversation. I've been walking all over hell and back trying to find the van."

"The wire went dead just after you made contact. Something tells me they did something to short it out because all I got was static. I ran all over the hotel trying to find you and when I realized that we'd lost contact, I came back here. Are you still at the hotel?"

"You want me to catch a cab?"

The Guardian List

"I'll pick you up in front in fifteen minutes…"

~~~

The van pulled up to the waiting island in front of the hotel and Marge jumped out. The two women embraced as if they hadn't seen each other in months.

"You scared the shit out of me," said Marge.

"Oh, honey, I'm so sorry. I had no idea you weren't listening in on the whole meeting…" In truth, Patty breathed a sigh of relief when she realized that Marge didn't hear the first part of the conversation. She was wondering how she was going to explain some of the information the three men discussed with her. In fact, once she got the gist of the meeting, she excused herself, went to the bathroom and purposely disconnected the mike from the battery. Her head was spinning like a top as she tried to put all the pieces together.

"So, what happened?" asked Marge.

"That's what's so funny. Nothing happened. It was like a job interview. From what I can gather, Mike had been a candidate to run the security for a consortium of law firms throughout the country. I guess he didn't want to say anything until he was sure everything was on the up and up so as not to disappoint me."

"That's it?"

"Yeah, other than the fact that they asked if I'd be interested in heading up the security division of the consortium."

"You're kidding. Are you thinking of taking it?"

"I might. I had planned to tender my resignation from SFPD. I thought of going back to school, but this just came out of nowhere, as if it was meant to be. Know what I mean?" Patty was lying through her teeth, but the more she talked, the more it was beginning to make sense, to sound as if she was speaking the gospel. She felt guilty about lying to her best friend but there was no way in hell she could take a chance of implicating Marge in anything that could be construed as being outside the law.

Patty still wasn't totally convinced that taking on the responsibility of administering The Guardian List was the answer to her malcontent. Mr. Brown had divulged information that was incriminating should Patty consider blowing the lid off the entire organization. But her mind kept coming back to Mike, to the fact that he had considered taking over the leadership and should she consider blowing the whistle, his name would be dragged through the mud as sure as if he had been one of the assassins with the organization. But she had to admit, the whole idea was titillating and the more she thought about it, the more she could see the justification for such a venture. She would sleep on it, but she knew that if it took her a day, week, year, or ten years to make up her mind, there would not be a moment's sleep or a moment of peace until she had made a final decision.

~~~

The transition from the SFPD to the organization was a timely process with numerous meetings involving the principals with whom she would be working. As she

The Guardian List

referred to her notes in the little pad she carried with her, Mr. Brown reminded her that "nothing should be in writing that might refer back to the organization unless it was in code that only she could decipher." That made sense. Over the period of a month, she and Mr. Brown had met on numerous occasions in various locations in the Vegas area and never at the same place twice. In between, she had returned to San Francisco and tendered her resignation from the police department, arranged for her mail to be forwarded to a P.O. box in Vegas, (she had decided to temporarily keep the San Francisco apartment) and gone by the cemetery to say her last farewell to Mike. As she stood graveside, she mentally asked Mike to help her decide if what she was doing would meet with his approval. Was she carrying out his wishes? After all, there was no way to know if, in the final analysis, he would have decided to make the move to take over the organization. She had to rely solely on the word of the three principals and with all the information they had revealed to her, there was nothing in her mind that made her dubious about what they said. Standing graveside, she made a vow that she would return whenever she was in San Francisco. She was filled with emotion as she placed a small bouquet of flowers on the headstone and left the cemetery.

How in the world had the organization managed to function without detection for over six years? she asked herself. She immediately realized that some of the names on the List were those of criminals with whom she had come in contact or whose trials she had followed over the years.

The incident in Marietta, Georgia, was one that she followed in the press. She vaguely remembered the news photos of the distraught priest holding the dead nun who had been shot in that senseless killing. The name of Adam Wicker was right at the top of The Guardian List as one that had yet to be resolved. Of course she remembered Arthur Bienvenides who had been assassinated by Captain Henning. He had been her commanding officer when she first joined the force. And who could forget the killing of Hassan Mohammed and Imam Jahl, suspected terrorists under federal investigation, in the New York restaurant, killed by the explosion set off by the retired police officer, Victor Vordenko, who sacrificed his own life? My God, never in a million years could she have been able to tie those killings together as something cleverly conceived and executed by a covert organization. And then there was the "suicide" death of Arnold Hoffman. No one ever imagined that his plunge to his death was an act of murder in retaliation for the innumerable lives he had ruined through his self-indulgence and avarice.

By the end of the second month, Patty had spent untold hours with John Brown learning about the history of the organization, who were the candidates on The List, who were the potential assassins, and how she would be responsible for recruiting new members into the organization and the addition of new candidates to be placed on The List. Fortunately, she would not be expected to step right in and fill John Brown's shoes. He would remain on indefinitely until age or ill health demanded he give up the reigns of leadership. His demeanor with Patty was akin to a father taking a daughter under his wing as he walked her through the machinations of the organization. There were also other logistics to be worked out, such as how she was to be paid. She would have to establish a legitimate source of income to cover her expenses and which she would have to report to the IRS each year. The organization was capable of meeting the salary she drew as a police officer, but there were issues to be addressed such as health plan, retirement, car and travel allowances. John Brown had arranged for a dummy corporation, Supreme Security, to be set up with enough assets to cover all of Patty Walsh's needs. He was quite an expert in creating delusion in the real world.

Patty spent hours in meetings with Father Ignatius, as well as Thurman Falk. Their knowledge of the logistics of the organization was invaluable and whatever Mr. Brown did not cover, the two associates did. Patty's head was soon bursting with questions, but she refrained from appearing too eager. She didn't want to give the impression that she might be a mole looking to upset the organization. It would take time for them to accept her and much of the information, names and places, were not divulged.

~~~

Upon arriving in Las Vegas, it was convenient for Patty to share the apartment with Marge because there was usually someone home to tend to Smokey and his needs, and because it cut expenses in half where there was really no need for separate accommodations. Despite the fact that Marge wasn't home all that much, what with her flourishing romance with Anthony, to say nothing of her erratic work schedule, it soon became apparent that the one bedroom apartment was closing in on their personal space. So Patty found a small house over in the Green Valley area that served her needs. From all accounts it was apparent that she would be spending an inordinate amount of time traveling so Marge agreed to care for the cat when Patty was on the road. At first, Marge had a plethora of questions about Patty's new job with Supreme Security, but with Mr. Brown's tutelage, Patty was able to explain in detail her responsibilities with the bogus firm. A one-room office as a front for Supreme Security was rented on the premises of Enterprise Realty, a thriving company near the airport, complete with telephone and secretarial services. From time to time, one of the members of the organization from another part of the country was instructed to call the office of Supreme Security and leave a message for Patty Walsh. That added credibility to Patty's cover as a representative of the company.

Three months into her association with Supreme, Mr. Brown decided that it was time for Patty to be present at the next meeting of the organization. It was a risky idea to introduce her to the men who nominated candidates to The Guardian List but they would have to get accustomed to the idea that a woman was being brought on board to organize and implement the work that had been exclusively the responsibility of Mr. Brown. The meeting was scheduled to take place at the Trump Towers in New York with ten members in attendance, along with Mr. Brown, Father Ignatius, and Patty Walsh. As the members arrived at the appointed hotel suite, there was an atmosphere of puzzlement at the sight of a woman in their presence. This was most definitely a first for those who had been with the organization since its origin.

As a police officer, Patty had been under the impression that there was a "good ol' boy club" mentality within the department that pre-dated women on the force. She had spent much of her association with other officers trying to prove that she was worthy of the role of a police person. Now, as she looked around the room, noticing that there was not one retired police officer in attendance under the age of seventy, she would have to work her ass off to gain their approval and respect. *Back to square one,* she thought.

Not without a bit of apprehension, Mr. Brown called the meeting to order after most of those in attendance availed themselves of refreshments from the bar.

"I am pleased to see so many healthy, happy faces…" he began. That usually got a smiling reaction from the aged and infirmed membership, but on this occasion their collective attention was drawn to the woman in their midst. Trying to keep it light, he continued, "I thought it would brighten up our usually dull meetings by having a bit of diversity within our ranks. I'd like to introduce you to Officer Patty Walsh."

Not a smile. Not a break in the sober demeanor of the group. Patty offered a feeble wave in the hopes of breaking down the wall of suspicion. After all, every one of these men was part and parcel of an organization that operated outside the laws of the society, the very laws that they defended for the better part of their professional careers. Not once since its inception had the notion of having a woman in their membership been brought up for consideration and not only a woman, but one who clearly was barely half the age of its youngest member.

Brown continued, "I will turn seventy-four this year and like most of you, I am beginning to feel the pangs of old age slowly creeping into this ancient temple of a body. There will come a time, hopefully not within the foreseeable future, when I shall have to consider moving on and relinquishing my role as director of our organization. In order to perpetuate the work we have started, I would be remiss to wait until the last minute to make a decision as to who would be a worthy candidate as my successor." A blink here, a clearing of a throat there, an awkward adjustment of uncrossing of legs. "For the past six months we have conducted an extensive search for possible candidates, someone with the necessary requirements, to come into the organization on a provisional basis. We boiled down the application list to a chosen few and after careful consideration, our final choice has come down to the young lady you see sitting before you."

There was a sudden sound of activity as the members exchanged glances, moved restlessly in their seats, and some shared hushed observations with those within earshot. One of the members, a retired officer of seventy-eight years, nervously raised his hand. Mr. Brown nodded in recognition. "How far have we gone in the recruitment process with this candidate, Mr. Brown?" he asked.

Brown could see where this was heading. "She's been indoctrinated into the past, present, and future activities of the organization…with reservations. Once you have had a chance to meet her, we will leave it up to you to determine if you want to divulge your identities to her. I know this is a very melodramatic picture until we…all of us are comfortable that she is the heir apparent to my position in the organization. I could have called for this meeting without her appearance, in absentia so to speak, but we have put in countless hours investigating her background and I feel confident we have made a wise and prudent choice."

"May I ask how old you are, Miss Walsh?" asked the examiner.

Patty glanced over at Mr. Brown for his approval to respond. He nodded. "I'm thirty-six and I've served twelve years as a police officer in Las Vegas and San Francisco. I have half a dozen commendations for my work in the line of duty. Recently I decided to leave the service for personal reasons."

And thus began the inquisition of Patty Walsh…

Chapter 30

Patty's inclusion into the organization was a towering success. Every man present greeted her warmly and with a commitment for his full cooperation. But she was emotionally torn between gratitude and sadness knowing that every person present was on the downhill side of their lives and it was just a matter of time until they moved on. Retired police officers were a breed apart from other retirees in that they had all stood on the precipice of the worst that the society had to offer and they had been tested as to their courage as well as their compassion. Patty felt humbled in their presence and vowed that she would serve them with the same due diligence as did both John Brown and Father Ignatius.

~~~

The Lowe's Building Supply Store on Route 107 in Beth Page out on Long Island was set back from Hicksville Road with a parking lot in front about the size of a football field. In weather both clear and inclement, anyone looking to hire a handyman to do odd jobs was sure to find no less than a dozen dark-skinned men huddled in groups of two's or three's, standing curbside in the hopes of picking up a day's wages. Some of the laborers were illegals and from time to time the local authorities harassed them, picking up those without green cards. But in truth, the meager wages they demanded for doing backbreaking work was actually a benefit to the community that would just as soon take a chance of breaking the law by hiring someone off the street than having to pay the outrageous cost of hiring a union laborer to do the same menial job. Most of the day laborers were hard workers and well worth their weight when it came to gardening or hauling cinder blocks to build an illegal wall without a permit. The language of preference was Spanish, but most of the workers spoke a smattering of English, just enough to tell a prospective employer how much they get an hour and *"Yes, I speak good 'hinglish."*

A few yards away from where the group congregated a lone worker stood. He was built like a fire hydrant with a shaved head, a Zapata mustache, dark-skinned from long hours working in the sun, but obviously not Mexican. His contempt for the other workers was apparent in his desire to stand apart from the other men and they, in turn, didn't appear to want anything to do with this surly, physically muscular recluse. An outsider represented one more worker competing for the very few jobs that were offered at this particular station. This outsider was more hirable than were most of the Mexicans since he spoke perfect English, was physically larger than his Mexican counterparts, and worked for a competitive daily wage.

It took a certain animal prowess to be able to evade the law for over two years, but that's what Adam Wicker had done. His escape from a Georgia chain gang, his search for his wife and daughter in Marietta, his tenacious search on up to Knoxville which proved fruitless, and his ability to survive from day to day in a hostile world, had only proved him to be a superior, cunning killer. Before his fateful killing spree seven years earlier, his experience as a heavy equipment operator and other jobs in the construction field had physically prepared him to survive as a hunted animal.

Months before, while hitchhiking from Knoxville and heading up the East Coast into New York, he stopped at a diner to get a late night snack just a few miles south of the big city. There were only a handful of patrons in the eatery, but Adam's attention was drawn to a fellow diner sitting alone who could have passed as his clone or at least a close relative. Patiently, Adam waited until the look-alike patron got up to leave. Adam followed him into the parking lot and as the driver was about to get into his car, Adam came up behind him, knocking him unconscious with a blow to the side of his head with a revolver Adam carried in his belt. He stripped the unconscious driver of his wallet and a few dollars from his pocket and then dragged him into a clump of bushes bordering the parking lot. He returned to the car and with keys in hand, perfected his getaway. Within an hour and fortuitously before anyone detected the unconscious driver, Adam drove into New York City where he abandoned the car to begin his new life as Irving Walston, his new identity.

~~~

It had been almost seven years since the Adam Wicker trial and his incarceration and two years since his escape from prison. Although his name remained at the top of The Guardian List, no one could figure out how he managed to elude capture by the police or the investigation of Thurman Falk. Almost every lead had been exhausted by the time Patty Walsh had come on board and once her memory was refreshed that Father Ignatius had been the pastor of St. Ann's Church where Adam Wicker had committed the murders, she became obsessed with the desire to see Adam Wicker pay for his crimes.

Sonny Brissette had been a member of the organization since its inception some years before, but John Brown considered him "something of a strange bird...a loose cannon" that rebelled at the thought of waiting for the gray reaper to track him down. He felt it was his calling to continue investigating the Wicker case without authorization from the police or any private agency. Unknown to Falk and the organization, Brissette had taken it upon himself to devote an inordinate amount of time to tracking Wicker. Using his own resources, he had traced Adam from Georgia to Knoxville, where the trail virtually went cold. But there had been sightings in towns and cities along the way and on a hunch Brissette was convinced that one day Wicker would turn up in New York. The seventy-five year-old retired policeman who compared himself to "an old race horse" could not let go of the Adam Wicker case and every chance he had, he doggedly spent an innumerable amount of hours down at the 67th Precinct where he perused untold numbers of photos and documents in his search. It was one of those compulsive things that some retired policemen go through after leaving active duty.

In going over the Adam Wicker profile, Brissette's attention was drawn to the fact that Wicker had been in the construction trade before his run-in with the law. He concluded that there was an outside chance that Wicker might be working in the city for one of the many construction firms in the area. What the hell, with nothing better to do, he began to make the rounds of the various construction sites in the city. It was a tedious pursuit that had futility written all over it. He circulated flyers of Wicker in the hopes that the photo reproduction in some way still resembled the escapee, but after many months of unsuccessful investigation, Brissette was losing heart. He could feel it in his gut that he was on the right track but not a single response to his queries turned up.

One afternoon when he was killing time down at the precinct, there were half a dozen Mexicans sitting in the lock-up area of the station. He had seen this kind of arrest before when things were slow and a patrol had nothing better to do, they would team up with a couple of cops from Immigration and perform a "round-up" at a number of supply stores where day workers congregated. As Brissette was passing through, he noticed that one of the Mexicans in the cage was standing in front of the bulletin board on which was affixed a number of WANTED photos, including one of Adam Wicker that Brissette had posted months before. The Mexican seemed transfixed in front of the Wicker photo. Brissette flashed his badge and the Desk Sergeant buzzed him into the holding area. He approached the Mexican.

"You know that man?" he asked.

The Mexican was apprehensive and reluctant to respond since he was virtually under arrest and facing deportation.

"You see this man before?" Brissette asked again.

"I don't know," said the Mexican and sat down on the bench.

"I can help you," Brissette said in a very confidential tone as he sidled up next to the Mexican. "What's your name?"

"Miguel. Miguel Montero."

"Listen, Miguel Montero, if you know that man I can help you with the immigration people. You understand?"

"How you help me?"

"I know people…very important people who can help you. I know a lawyer who can help you, but you have to help me."

Miguel Montero lowered his eyes as if there was an answer written on the floor between his feet. "I no sure…"

"You're not sure you've seen him or you're not sure he's the right man?"

"The man I see no have hair…and have *bigote*…how you say…mostacho."

"So what makes you think you've seen this man?" Brissette asked, pointing to the photo of Adam Wicker.

"The eyes. I think I see in the eyes…and big face is like in the fotografia."

Brissette was on his feet and rattling the cage to get the Desk Sergeant's attention. He had to get out of the precinct to where he could use his cell phone.

He tried to reach John Brown when he learned that there was a possible sighting of Adam Wicker. When his attempts to reach the therapist were unsuccessful, he resorted to his second choice. His only contact was with Patty Walsh at the Supreme Security office where he left an urgent message. In a matter of minutes his call was returned and in a meeting of Patty and Brissette a plan was set in motion to apprehend Adam Wicker.

~~~

Using a Ford van without any markings, Thurman Falk parked some ten rows from the street in the parking lot of Lowe's Hardware. From the rear window of the van he could observe the workers congregated along the curbside awaiting anyone who was looking to hire day laborers. On this day, the available number of workers had been reduced to five after the recent roundup by Immigration. Some distance from the pack stood a lone worker, tool belt slung over his shoulder and a small gym bag in hand. Falk had trouble reconciling the photo he had of Adam Wicker with that of the man standing curbside, but as he took a number of telephoto shots and held them up alongside the hard copy, it was apparent the two men were one and the same.

The Chevy pickup pulled a hard right into the parking lot in front of Lowe's and stopped a few yards from where the workers congregated. The driver was a woman dressed in jeans with a headscarf to hold her hair back from her face and no makeup. She appeared to be a rather dowdy homemaker looking to hire a day worker. She no sooner cut the engine than the five Mexicans crowded around the driver's side of the cab, pushing each other to get her attention. The burly man who stood apart had now approached from the rear of the group. He stood out like a sore thumb as he towered over the Hispanic men.

Patty rolled down the window and gave the group the once over. Each of the Mexicans was waving his green card in front of her face to get her attention and assure her that they were legal. The mustached man at the back of the group held up a driver's license. As the men were all talking at the same time trying to convince her that one was more qualified than the other, Patty pointed to the man in back.

"You do drywall?" she yelled.

"Yeah. Drywall, plastering, painting. I do it all."

"How much?"

"How many hours?"

"Probably two, maybe three days."

"Ten an hour…"

"I do it for eight!" yelled one of the Mexicans.

"Seven-fifty!" called out another.

Adam Wicker began to back away from the rear of the group. He wasn't about to get into a pissing contest with these guys.

"Hey, you!" she yelled out. Adam turned as she waved him towards the pickup. "It's heavy work. If you think you can handle it, get in."

The group of Mexicans stepped back from the pickup as Adam moved around to the passenger side, opened the door, threw his bag and tool belt on the back seat, and climbed in beside Patty. As she drove away from the group of disgruntled Mexicans she took a card out of her pocket and handed it to Adam. The calling card identified Patty Walsh as a Real Estate Salesperson working for Enterprise Realty.

"You have a name?" she asked her passenger.

"Irving."

"Just Irving?" she smiled.

"Walston."

"All right, Mr. Walston. I've got a place over in Huntington that needs some work. It's about ten minutes from here so relax and enjoy the scenery."

~~~

The house on the Hoffman estate in Huntington had been vacant for two years since the "suicide death" of Arnold Hoffman. In a depressed real estate market, investors were reticent to step up and purchase a twenty million-dollar piece of property. It was obvious to prospective buyers that the three houses on the property were in a state of neglect and in need of repairs.

Patty parked the van in front of the main house bypassing the garage. She and Adam got out, he collected his tool belt and gym bag from the rear seat, and together they ascended the steps to the front door. Adam could not help but notice that aside from the shabby way she dressed, the lady was not half bad looking. The six years he had spent in custody tended to cool his sexual desires but subsequently, after his escape, he managed to find sexual gratification with women he picked up in out-of-the-way bars and food joints. In a few instances, he had resorted to rape after which he had to make a hasty retreat to get out of the area before the act was reported and he was apprehended.

As Patty reached over to insert the key into the lock, Adam wondered what it would be like to… *Naw*, he thought. *That would be stupid.* If he played it straight he could pick up a few bucks to carry him over until he moved onto another store in another town. In order to keep one step ahead of the law, he had to constantly move from one location to another. Just as long as he kept moving he knew he would be safe.

As they entered the large, main hallway, Adam could not help but be impressed with the luxurious interior. "You live here, Miss Walsh?" he asked.

"I'm the realtor. I have the listing on this place. Hopefully, once we get it in shape one of my prospective buyers will make an offer to the bank that holds the mortgage."

"Just out of curiosity, how much are they asking?"

"You in the market, Mr. Walston?"

Adam smiled. "Yeah, sure. In a pig's butt," he replied.

As she led the way through the empty house, their footsteps resounded off the vacant walls and floors. They passed through the great hall and stopped at the door to the library. Patty opened the door and stepped aside for Adam to enter. He took three steps into the empty library lined with empty floor to ceiling shelves. Then he noticed someone standing in front of one of the large, picture windows, his back to the room. Adam stopped, sensing that something was amiss. Swinging his gym bag from his shoulder in an attempt to get his gun, he suddenly froze in place as Patty stepped up behind him and placed the business end of her revolver up to his neck.

"Just drop the bag, Adam."

He immediately obeyed.

"Against the wall and assume the position," she ordered as she kicked his bag halfway across the room beyond his reach.

Adam did as he was told. As Patty perfected a quick pat down, the man from the window crossed the room to stand some six feet behind Adam.

"Hands behind you," ordered Patty. She quickly slapped a pair of handcuffs on him.

"Turn around," said Father Ignatius.

Adam turned and a sudden light of recognition flashed across his mind. He had never known the priest or seen him before the night of the killings, but he had seen him almost every day of the trial and it was a face he could never forget. For a moment, Adam breathed a sigh of relief. This was not a cop out to apprehend him. This was a man of the cloth with whom he could possibly talk and con into an escape. The wheels in Adam's head were turning full speed.

"You people obviously have the wrong man. My name's Irving Walston. I don't know who this Adam person is that you keep calling me, but you can check my ID in my back pocket." Adam's words rang hollow in the empty library and as if running out of gas, he seemed to be at a loss for words.

Patty walked over to the bag and opened it. Inside she found the gun tucked under some changes of underclothes. She heaved the bag with its contents out the door into the main hallway and out of range of Adam. Father Ignatius took a step towards Adam and then stopped. He knew exactly what it was he wanted to say; he'd been rehearsing it for years, but as he stood within a few feet of the killer, the words wouldn't come and he could feel the tears welling up in his eyes. In his mind's eye he could see the face of Sister Therese. She was talking to him, telling him that what he was about to do was wrong, was against God's wishes.

"Get down," ordered Patty, prodding Adam with the gun.

At the sound of her command, Adam looked at her as if seeing her for the first time, so focused was he on the priest.

"Fuck you," he spat. "Fuck you, whore!" Suddenly, he made an off-balance lunge for the priest as if to bowl him over. Patty instinctively threw her body into the side of the moving killer, sending the powerful Adam sprawling to the floor. She threw herself on top of him and although his hands were manacled behind him, he fought her like an enraged gator trying to get a piece of her flesh in his mouth. Father Ignatius stood there, frozen in his tracks, unable to engage himself in the brawl. Patty pummeled Adam with her revolver but the blows didn't have any effect. As the two grappled on the floor, Sonny Brissette entered from the kitchen. He hastened over to where the two were struggling, came up behind Adam, and with hypodermic in hand, he stabbed the big man in the neck releasing a dose of sodium thiopental. In a matter of moments, Adam's body went limp and Patty was able to climb out from under the weight of the unconscious man.

She was thoroughly shaken as she got to her feet, trying to catch her breath. "My God, I thought that sonofabitch was going to kill me."

"Why didn't you shoot him?" rebuked Sonny.

"I thought we agreed."

"Not if you're life was in danger. My God, woman, this isn't a game where you play by a set of rules." Brissette was angry at how close Patty came to being overcome by the larger man. "You listen to me, young lady. You want to live long enough to serve the organization, you'd better use your head. You understand me?"

Without a reply, Patty walked over to Brissette, reached up to the taller man and planted a kiss of gratitude on his cheek. "I understand," she replied meekly.

~~~

They met in the eighth floor hotel of the Plaza. John Brown was pissed when he learned that Patty Walsh had involved herself in the apprehension of Adam Wicker. "I told you specifically that you were recruited to work with me in the position of administrator. I don't want you out there getting involved in field work. You almost put seven years of hard work in jeopardy!"

There was nothing Patty could say as she stood before him feeling naked and contrite. As an afterthought she knew that what she'd done was not only irresponsible, but could have jeopardized every member of the organization. *What a stupid way to get my feet wet*, she thought. But did the end justify the means? Wicker's body had been found in an alley in midtown Manhattan, his death making the front page of most of the newspapers. He had been shot twice, execution style. His death was meant to send a message to the criminal element at large that sooner or later justice would prevail.

Father Ignatius had never seen John Brown in such a rage in all the years they'd been associates. If Patty's actions raised his ire, the priest wondered how he was going to react with what he had to say. "I know Patty realized that what she did was foolish, to say the least, but unless someone took the initiative, we could have lost Adam Wicker. Time was of the essence and since your whereabouts was unknown..."

"Under the circumstances, my whereabouts took precedence," he said changing gears. He cleared his throat, took a deep breath, and avoiding eye contact he went on. "I guess now is as good a time as any to bring you up to date. I've got a cancer. I was not exactly incommunicado; I was at the Mayo in Scottsdale. I've been undergoing chemo for the past three months but it appears that I'm on the losing end of a long battle…"

The two associates stood in shock. It was obvious that John Brown's outburst was not only his disappointment with Patty, but also his bitter knowledge that his time was running out.

"We have much work to do before I leave." He turned to Father Ignatius. "Did Mr. Brissette make arrangements for Miguel Montero as promised?"

"Yes, sir. Weisman, the attorney who handles immigration cases is on it. He's the best and knows just about everyone in the system. He's taking Mr. Montero's case pro bono. He and Brissette have a long-standing relationship."

"Great." He turned his attention to Patty. "You and I will have to begin to clean house. There are too many unresolved names on the List, names that should have been removed long ago." His attitude suddenly softened. "Please, Patty, there's so much to do and so little time. I'm going to need your undivided attention to the List before I turn it over to you. No heroics, please."

"I understand," she said, trying her best not to display her emotions.

~~~

The two years of incarceration had turned Warren Price into a different man. He had lost weight, spent time every day working out in the prison gym, and during the time he spent behind bars, he managed to create a totally new persona. Beyond just his physical change, there was a mental metamorphosis as well. He had plenty of time to contemplate how he could repay the female officer who had been so diligent in tracking him down and testifying. His sessions with the therapist in prison lessened to some degree his distorted sexual appetite, but in its place there grew a burning desire to seek a physical revenge, to pay back the policewoman who stole two years of his life. He was consumed with a sexual desire to have her, but in every instance when he dwelt on their sexual encounters, it always ended in an act of violence wherein he derived pleasure in physically choking the life out of her. Price had managed to change one anti-social behavior for the desire to commit another — murder.

Price was no stranger to Patty Walsh. His release from prison after serving his sentence was brought to her attention by Thurman Falk who kept a running tag on each and every name on the List. The two years since she last testified against Price did not temper her dislike for the man. There wasn't the slightest doubt in her mind that once back out on the street, Price would revert back to his modus operandi of accosting minor children for his sexual gratification. Falk put a shadow on Price from the day he left his incarceration until he signed in at the halfway house in San Francisco. Then Price's whereabouts suddenly went up in smoke. He disappeared from the halfway house from one day to the next.

"I don't like it," said Falk. "For the life of me, I can't imagine a rehabilitated Warren Price. He's a recidivist from the get go and all the therapy in the world is not going to make him into a model citizen with normal sexual desires. I don't care what the court or the penal system says, there's a time bomb out there just waiting to go off."

Patty was of the same mind in sharing Falk's assessment of Price. She took comfort in knowing that they were on the same page. Sooner or later Price had to be taken out. But more important than the urgency to find Price was the sudden news that John Brown had been rushed to the Emergency Room at St, Rose's Hospital. The chemotherapy had taken its toll and the man had become a skeleton of his former self.

Father Ignatius, Falk, and Patty met in the third floor waiting room of the hospital. Neither Brissette nor any of the other members of the organization had been informed of his condition and none were present. That was the way John Brown had planned to leave the organization – without fanfare. The transition would be swift and the torch passed on. Little did the three confidantes know how little time was left. As they gathered around his bedside with the sound of the monitor beeping away his last, precious minutes, Patty let the tears flow without embarrassment. She may have been an ex-cop, but that did not detract from her ability to feel the loss of someone who had taken her into his deepest confidence. She only hoped that she would be able to carry on his work with his same dedication and ardor. As the minutes ticked away, the floor nurse entered the room. She walked over to where the priest was standing and addressed him in a confidential tone. "They're here," was all she said.

The priest knew the implication and taking John Brown's hand in his, he held it up to his lips, placed a gentle kiss on it, said a few words in Latin and stepped back. Falk also took John Brown's hand, stroked it for a moment, and backed away as Patty stepped up, leaned over and gently kissed John Brown's cheek goodbye. The three exited the room without another word. They would never see John Brown again as he reverted back to his original identity of Martin Wolfson. There were three adults in the lobby waiting to be admitted into the room —the Wolfson children. The Priest stopped to extend his condolences as Patty and Falk passed on down the corridor to the elevator. As they stepped out of the hospital into the bright sunlight, the three were acutely aware that a whole new day was dawning, that the baton had been passed with the battle unrelenting.

~~~

In the month after the death of John Brown, four more names were stricken from the Guardian List. The membership of the organization had gained three new members, with eight more on standby pending investigation of their backgrounds. John Brown had proven to be a man of his word. A trust fund amounting to just over ten million dollars had been established with the corporation of Supreme Security as its beneficiary. Patty was listed as C.E.O. with complete control of the finances. However, what seemed to be the perfect transition period actually had some gaping holes that were yet to be resolved.

Thurman Falk felt uncomfortable having to broach the subject, but there was no other way to get around it. "I'd like to terminate my work with the organization," he said, knowing that there was no painless way to do this.

The resignation of Falk was no less than a slap to the face and Patty recoiled. She was almost speechless. "Is it because of me? Because you don't want to work with a woman?"

Falk had to smile. "My wife is a woman," he said, "and I don't have any desire to terminate my relationship with her."

"I hope it's nothing I've done. My God, Thurman, what you bring to the table is unique. Is there anything I can do or say that would make you change your mind?"

"I hadn't planned to stay on as long as I have, but with John's illness…well, I didn't want to add to his infirmity. I've been promising Cathy that we'd do some of the things I've been promising her these past few years. She's never been to Europe and we both need an overdue vacation. She's pregnant, you know. Once the baby comes it's going to be difficult to just take off whenever I want."

"Have you given any thought to a replacement, someone we can depend on to take up the slack?"

"I've used a couple of guys that I could recommend. Of course, they're just investigators and they don't know anything about the workings of the List, but for everyday investigation or tailing, they're good. I'll help with the transition, if that works for you. And, of course, I'll try to make myself available to help out from time to time but

Cathy and I are planning to get a place down in the islands…probably Nassau."

This is not good, thought Patty. Falk's timing couldn't have been worse, what with John Brown gone only a month. She wondered what he would say under the circumstances. "Have you talked this over with Father Ignatius?" she asked.

Falk appeared to be focused in on his hands as if there was a script written on them that he could refer to. "Damn it, Patty, but I hate to be the bearer of bad tidings but I wouldn't depend on the priest for much longer either. John Brown's death has given him pause to reflect on the whole organization, the whole concept and what we're about. I think he wants to return to the ministry, to be active again in the church as an act of contrition. After that whole episode with Adam Wicker, he's been questioning his role in the organization."

Patty could feel a buzz coming on. It was all looking so good when she stepped up to the plate and all of a sudden it appeared that the wheels were coming off the wagon. "We couldn't have terminated Wicker without his help. I don't understand where he's coming from."

"He told me he felt helpless when Wicker tried to escape and he did nothing. He feels that he's old and useless, that he's served his purpose with the organization and that it's time for him to 'prepare for his journey' as he put it. He's almost eighty years old, you know…"

Patty attempted to stand but her legs felt rubbery and her head was swimming in circles. "Thurman, I'm asking you, from the bottom of my heart to stay on with me until I can make some other arrangements. It would mean a whole recruiting program, but it will take time to implement it and I need your help."

How can I deny her? "I'll try to give you six, maybe eight months at the outset, but once the baby comes, Cathy will want me to keep some of the broken promises I've made in the past," he said. Besides, he really owed it to John Brown.

Chapter 31

Warren Price was on a mission. He was obsessed with the need to find the whereabouts of Officer Patty Walsh. Upon his release from the penitentiary his first order of business was to call the station where he knew Officer Walsh had worked in San Francisco. Once he established her routine, the rest would be easy. He was informed that Officer Walsh had tendered her resignation from the department and was no longer working in law enforcement.

"Do you have a number where she can be reached?" he asked.

"I'm sorry, but I can't give out that information. Is this personal or business?" asked the Desk Sergeant.

"My name is Trevor Dettre. I worked with Officer Walsh a couple of years ago on the Price case. I'm a bounty hunter and I just heard that Warren Price had been released from the penitentiary. Word on the street is he may be looking for her. I'd like to give her a head's up if I can just get a number where she can be reached."

"Last I heard, Mr. Dettre, she moved out of the San Francisco area a couple of years ago. That's the best I can do. If you want, I can let you speak with her Captain. He may be able to help you."

"No, that's quite all right. I've got the name of some of her associates and I thought I'd try the station first. Bye."

While serving his sentence, Price learned from another inmate that Patty Walsh had been a Metro cop in Las Vegas before transferring to San Francisco. *What the hell*, thought Price. He hadn't been to Vegas in years and he was due for a vacation.

~~~

After checking into the Sun Coast Motel just off the Strip, Price checked the Las Vegas phone book on an outside chance that Patty Walsh was listed. No such luck. Ironically, had he checked the supplemental phone book for Henderson, he would have found a listing for Patty Walsh. Using the Yellow Pages, he found the listings for Private Investigators and picked out one at random.

Nick Sabatello was a gaunt sixty-year-old private detective that had been chasing lost persons and people with bad debts for thirty years. A transplant from the streets of New York he still managed to maintain his eastern accent. He claimed "if there's someone out there to find, Nick Sabatello is the man to do the job." He explained, "Vegas is a goldmine for missing persons. You got a gambling problem, you come to Vegas, lose all your money and when the shame sets in, you try to hide. But in the end, Nick Sabatello will find you," he said with no small amount of bravado.

"I don't have much time," explained Price.

"If you're lady friend is hiding out in Vegas, I'll find her. Guaranteed." He pulled out a legal pad and placed it on the desk. "Now, I'll need some particulars...you got a photo?"

"Not a recent one."

"No sweat. 'Patricia Walsh.' That's a pretty common name. It may take me a few days to run her down."

"I've got a few days," said Price.

~~~

It didn't take a few days for Nick Sabatello to run down the name of Patty Walsh. It took him about two hours. He ran the name in his computer database, found her listed as CEO of Supreme Security, and sat back to kill time and rack up the hours he'd charge his client. Usually, in a missing person's case, Nick wanted to know as many details as possible. He planned to get around to that and was surprised that he was able to find the Walsh woman right out there as if she had a sign painted on her chest. This guy Price...Nick Sabatello didn't like him from the get go. Something about the guy, kinda sleazy with shifty eyes and a lot of loose skin around his jowls. Probably he'd lost weight at one time or another and didn't have the good sense to get a tuck. This Walsh woman was apparently a fellow investigator and Nick wondered if he should pick up the phone and let her know that someone was paying him to find her. Professional courtesy. Of course, that would be unethical, he mused. He'd already spent the money he was getting to track down the Walsh woman so Price's reasons were his own personal business.

Two days later and four hundred dollars lighter, Warren Price was parked in a rental car in the lot adjacent to the Real Estate office on Eastern Avenue. But after four days without a sighting, he decided to take a chance and call the number given to him by Sabatello. He was disappointed to learn that he'd been spinning his wheels for almost a week, that the receptionist rarely saw the Walsh woman who only came by infrequently to pick up mail or leave a package for someone to pick up. Price concluded that the place was nothing more than a front or a drop off point for whatever it was that the ex-cop was into. He had questioned Nick Sabatello as to whether or not he'd heard of a Patty Walsh with Supreme Security before his inquiry, but Nick assured him that if he knew anything about the woman, he would be obliged to divulge whatever it was he knew. The more illusive Patty Walsh became, the more intrigued was Price and the more determined he was to find her. After a number of hours of dwelling on how he was going to locate her and confront her face-to-face, he devised a plan. He remembered that while serving his time, he had read a newspaper article telling of the death of Mike Decker, a police officer who had been engaged to Patty Walsh. Perhaps it was time for Trevor Dettre to extend his condolences to the grieving fiancée.

He called the number Nick Sabatello had given him for the office. Using the name Trevor Dettre, he left a message with the receptionist at the real estate office saying that he had been out of the country these past few years and when he returned, he tried to get in touch with his friend, Mike Decker, only to learn of his unfortunate passing. He got Patty Walsh's name from Captain Craig with the SFPD. Could he possibly set up a meeting with her? He'd like to learn what happened first hand. He left a number.

~~~

Patty was nobody's fool or how else could she be in the position she held with the organization? The call from Trevor Dettre stunk to the high heavens, she told herself. Falk had already warned her to be on her guard because Warren Price was out of prison and his whereabouts were unknown. She had already decided to meet with this Trevor Dettre character but she had to cover her ass. She could turn to Marge on this one; use her as a backup just in case, but if Dettre did turn out to be Warren Price, Marge could be an obstacle to taking Price out. Then there was the other side of the coin: Just suppose this guy is legit. *Am I being paranoid?* One thing was for sure; she wasn't about to meet this Dettre person alone and unarmed. The meeting would have to be in a public place where there couldn't be a chance of her being ambushed or physically accosted. The office of Supreme Security was out of the question as was a meeting in an open field miles from civilization.

She dialed the number. Did the voice on the other end of the line sound disguised? Perhaps she had just awakened him. She couldn't be sure if it was or wasn't Warren Price. They agreed on a meeting place.

~~~

The Hole-in-One was a friendly neighborhood bar tucked away in the corner of a mini-mall behind a Shell Station just off of Green Valley Parkway and only minutes away from where Patty was living. She remembered how angry John Brown had gotten with her when she went into the field to bring down Adam Wicker and here she was, contemplating another hit when there were alternatives. But she knew Warren Price could identify him in a crowd where anyone else would have to go through a whole litany of tests trying to ascertain if Dettre was who he said he was.

She placed a call to Sonny Brissette in New York. He would be on the next flight.

The sound of her voice got the adrenalin flowing in Warren Price. He was amazed that the thought of sexually humiliating her was no longer a priority. He was overcome with a desire to mete out revenge and nothing more. If he could inflict pain for the suffering he went through, that would be perfect. But just the thought of killing her instilled in him a sense of power, a feeling of satisfaction in knowing that this bitch was going to pay for what she did to him. As he sat in his car at the end of the row of parked cars outside the bar, he was building a case to justify what he was about to do. He suddenly realized that he was getting sexually aroused at the thought of killing Patty Walsh. The meeting had been set for seven inside the bar but Patty arrived fifteen minutes early in the hopes that she would arrive in time to identify whoever it was that she was meeting. The early December evening was cool and she wore a sport jacket that concealed her service revolver holstered under her arm. She parked near the front door of the bar, did a quick glance around, then exited the car and began to walk up to the front door.

From where he sat, Price had no doubt that it was Patty Walsh and he quickly slid out of his seat in order to intercept her before she entered the building. She saw him out of the corner of her eye but even in the subdued lighting, just the way he moved towards her, she knew who it was. She reached inside her jacket but she was too late. He had already drawn his revolver and fired off two quick shots, the first hitting her in the chest and the second severing an artery in her arm. As she hit the ground she heard a series of shots before passing out. She knew that somewhere in the parking lot, Sonny Brissette was positioned to back her up. He stepped out of the shadow of one of the storefronts and fired off one shot, superficially wounding Price. Before he could get off another shot, Price turned and fired, a fatal shot hitting Brissette just below his heart. In a haze, Patty thought she heard a number of shots before she slipped into unconsciousness.

~~~

"She's lucky that someone knew to put pressure on that arm before she bled out," she heard someone say. She didn't know how long she had been out, but the pain in her chest was severe as was the throbbing in her arm. Her mouth was dry. She forced her eyes open only to find that she was in a hospital room. When she finally focused in, she could tell that the person standing bedside was a doctor with a stethoscope dangling from around his neck. "How are you feeling?" he asked.

"Thirsty" was all she could muster.

He held a glass with a straw up to her mouth and she sucked in the water almost causing her to choke. "Not so fast," said the doctor. "I've given you a sedative so you'll sleep. When you wake up you'll feel better…"

"My cat. I need to feed my cat…" was the last thing she said before slipping off into a drug-induced sleep. She slept for six hours before the drug wore off and still in a half conscious state, she tried to remember what had happened and how she got to the hospital. Through a haze, she could make out the form of someone sitting by her bed. As the miasma lifted, she could ascertain that it was Marge sitting alongside, holding her hand. "I'm sorry…" she managed before slipping off into a semi-fog in which she began to remember the events of the night when she was shot. An hour later, as the fog lifted, she began to remember clearly the events leading up to her ending up in the hospital. She focused in on Marge who looked as if she had lost her best friend.

"You scared the shit out of me," she said with no small amount of compassion. "My God, what were you thinking?"

That's a tough one, thought Patty. "What about Price? And Brissette?" she asked.

"Later. We'll talk later when you feel stronger. I'll wait outside. I've got to check in." She gently touched Patty's hand and exited the room.

Half-hour later, Patty was lucid and trying to put the pieces together. She remembered being shot by Price and then all hell broke loose. Was she able to get off a shot? Did she hit Price? Where was Brissette? Surely one of them must have gotten Price in that entire ruckus. Marge entered the room followed by Anthony Canu. They took seats by the side of her bed and again, Marge took up Patty's hand. "Think you're strong enough to answer some questions?" she asked, raising Patty's bed to a sitting position. "Better?"

"Yeah...much."

"At least you had brains enough to wear that vest. The impact from the bullet knocked you out and you lost a ton of blood from that shot in the arm."

"And Price?"

"I got him."

"You WHAT?"

"After he killed Brissette…"

"Oh, damn," was all she could utter.

"When it looked as if he was going to finish you off, I ordered him to drop his weapon. I had no choice."

"Hold it! Hold it! What the hell am I missing here? What were you doing there in the first place?"

"Yeah, well, that's another story."

"I'm listening."

Marge looked over to Anthony who sat with his head bowed as if in prayer. He raised his eyes and hunched his shoulders. "Guess now's as good a time as any," he said.

Marge cleared her throat and took a sip of water from Patty's glass. "I know about The List," she said almost matter-of-factly.

Patty could feel the air expel from her lungs. "Oh, jeez. How long?"

"Since a little after Captain Henning's death."

"You never said anything to me?"

"What was there to say? You weren't involved with the organization. You didn't even know anything about it until almost two years later after Mike got killed."

"And I thought I was protecting *you* by not getting you involved."

"I surmised that when we found out that you were going to leave the department and help Mr. Brown."

"You knew him?"

"We'd met a few times…"

Patty threw back the sheet that was covering her. She felt as if she were burning up. "This is too bizarre. Who else knows about The List and the organization?"

"Other than those on the inside, I don't know of anyone. After Captain Henning died I felt that we were missing something in the investigation. Anthony and I talked about the case for months trying to find a hook that would give us a break in the case. It didn't make any sense that a police officer of his rank would just turn rogue and kill Bienvenides just out of the blue. Then one day, Anthony called another case to my attention in New York where a retired police officer, Victor Vordenko, blew himself up in a restaurant taking out two suspected Muslim terrorists. The thing that caught Anthony's attention was the age of the police officer, again a retiree. We started to do an Internet search in which we were looking for retired police officers anywhere in the country that were involved in vigilante-type killings. Bingo! We hit the jackpot..."

"Why didn't you call it to the attention of the department?"

Marge looked over to Anthony. He took up the reins. "We weren't absolutely sure that what we found would hold up under intense investigation without more facts to substantiate what we suspected. After all, someone who was now deceased committed every assassination. Over a period of almost two years we had compiled a directory of no less than a dozen incidents in which retired police officers had been responsible for the killings of known criminals throughout the country. It began to smell of something more than coincidence. The more we probed, the more we felt we were onto something. We must have been getting close to touching a nerve because one day, out of the blue, we were visited by a priest."

"Oh my God. Father Ignatius?"

"That's him," said Marge. "At first it didn't ring a bell and then it suddenly came back to me. Remember the night you told me you'd met a man? It wasn't long after Michael's death and I thought it was too soon for you to start dating again, but you told me it was a priest, a Father Ignatius. How could I forget a name like that? I've known a lot of priests, but never a Father Ignatius. You said that he was the one who knew Michael and he could introduce you to the people who had made Michael the offer to go into private investigation if he decided to leave the department."

"Yeah, I remember, but how did you tie all this together to include me?"

Anthony responded. "I had your phone tapped."

"You WHAT?" Patty came off the bed as if shot from a cannon. Her head was suddenly swimming and she was just short of passing out when Marge grabbed her and helped her back onto the bed. "I'm not believing this," she blurted out. She was taking deep breaths to try to regain her composure. She hadn't learned a thing from the Adam Wicker incident and now she was responsible for the death of Sonny Brissette. John Brown had warned her, but she was just too pigheaded to listen. Now the entire organization was in jeopardy. *What would happen to The List?* She looked up at Marge, then over to Anthony. There wasn't very much she could say in the way of an apology or excuse. "I know this sounds sort of naïve, but are you planning to arrest me?" The question hung in the air like a giant riddle waiting to be solved.

"For what?" asked Anthony after making her sweat for almost a full minute.

"The killing of Warren Price. The death of Sonny Brissette."

"Actually, you weren't responsible for either of them," said Marge. "There was a fine line regarding your involvement in those two deaths, but with a bit of maneuvering, juxtaposing the truth, so to speak, those two deaths occurred in the line of duty. Quite simply, I shot Price after he shot Sonny Brissette and you. As for your possession of a weapon that you fired in self-defense, I think the District Attorney can close a blind eye to that minor infraction. But that still leaves the question of the disposition of The Guardian List. From what I could gather from the priest, there are still a number of members of the organization poised to strike once you give the word…"

"And you can't let me do that, can you?"

"Patty, you are one short step away from a long prison sentence should any of this come out in an investigation," said Anthony. "If the press gets a whiff of it…well, you can imagine what a field day they'd have."

"I get the picture. So where do we go from here? I mean, do I just close the door and walk away as if none of this every happened?"

"Anthony and I think we might have a solution. We've discussed it and we think that perhaps it's time you took a long vacation."

"How long?"

"A year, maybe two. Just until we're sure there won't be any repercussions that could reflect back on you. The death of Sonny Brissette has raised some questions in a number of quarters and it appears that his death is not being accepted as an isolated incident…"

"Did I tell you that Sonny saved my life?"

"You'll have to get out of the country for a while, Patty," said Marge, feeling empathy for her friend. "Have you ever spent any time in Mexico City?" she asked.

EPILOGUE

One year later...

Colonel Juan Rivera-Ortega was more than pleased and gracious to accept Patty Walsh into his home in Mexico City at the request of Father Ignatius. The Colonel would be forever grateful for what the Priest and John Brown had done in balancing the scale for the death of his daughter, Silvana. Her death left a void in the lives of the Colonel and his beautiful wife, but the presence of Patty in their midst compensated to some degree for their loss. To the Colonel's delight, he also found Patty not only a welcome addition to his family, but also a very enlightened and ingenious addition to the Colonel's work in fighting the drug cartels running rampant along the northern border of his country.

No sooner had Patty settled into the Rivera-Ortega estate than she contacted the bank that managed the Supreme Security account stateside. She arranged for the proceeds accrued from the interest on the account to be distributed among various charitable organizations. She was sure that was what John Brown would have wanted. She had no plans to return north, although the case regarding the death of Sonny Brissette and Warren Price had been cleared from the docket and closed.

~~~

Of the remaining twelve members of the organization, eight had died of natural causes in one year. Two of the four remaining members were suffering from dementia and remembered nothing of their association with the organization. The other two members had adjusted to the reality that they would just have to leave this life without striking a blow for the good of mankind.

~~~

Marge and Anthony were making plans to marry and if necessary, they would do so in Mexico City where Patty could be in attendance without difficulty. Marge and Patty kept in constant touch through the Internet and Anthony enjoyed the idea that once he married Marge, Patty would be included as part of the contract—sort of an adopted sister.

~~~

Now well past eighty, Father Ignatius spent his remaining days in deep contemplation and prayer. He had made his peace with God. He found comfort in reflecting on his past role in the organization and the fact that soon he would have to answer to a Higher Power for temporarily serving as the spiritual advisor in the course of meting out justice on a secular level. He looked forward to the day when he and Sister Therese would once again meet to share their mutual love for a compassionate and forgiving God.

~~~

Cathy Falk gave birth to a handsome baby boy whom they named Martin, in memory of the man who was responsible for many of the pleasures they enjoyed in their little retreat on Paradise Island only minutes from the north shore of Nassau. For the first few months, Thurman took pleasure in fixing up their modest home, painting, and installing shutters that would make island living a comfortable experience for the family. Thurman enjoyed his daily swims in the tepid waters of the island and for diversion, he and Cathy, along with baby Martin, enjoyed sailing in their thirty-two foot sailboat, exploring coves and sights of the numerous islands of the Bahamas.

But soon the experience of enjoying Paradise began to lose its edge and Thurman longed for the excitement of past undertakings with the organization. As the contentment of each passing day became repetitious, he managed to find the time to recount the past events in which he participated as an integral member of the dedicated society. It saddened him to think that upon his passing, the activities and accomplishments of such a passionate and dedicated group of men would be lost forever…unless, of course, he took it upon himself to record those events. And so was born the plan of writing his first novel: THE GUARDIAN LIST…

ABOUT THE AUTHOR

Lawrence Montaigne starred or co-starred in twenty-five films in the U.S. and in Europe and also appeared in more than two hundred television episodes.

Trained as a classical dancer, he appeared on Broadway in two musicals and in Hollywood performed with the Hollywood Bowl Ballet Company. In films, he worked as a dancer with such notables as Gene Kelly, Donald O'Conner and Mitzi Gaynor. He studied fencing both in the U.S. and Europe, which afforded him the opportunity to work as a stuntman on *Scaramouche*, *The Three Musketeers*, *Julius Caesar*, and in a series of low-budget swashbuckling films for Sam Katzman at Columbia.

Upon discharge from the Marine Corps, he studied Drama at The Dramatic Workshop in New York and was later featured in such films as *The Great Escape* (with Steve McQueen and James Garner), *Tobruk* (with Rock Hudson and George Peppard), *The Power* (with George Hamilton and Suzanne Pleshette), *Captain Sinbad* and *Damon & Pythias* (both starring Guy Williams), *The Mongols* (starring Jack Palance and Anita Ekberg) and *Escape to Witch Mountain* (with Ray Milland and Donald Pleasance). He starred in *Pillar of Fire* (made in Israel), *Mobby Jackson* and *Rapina Al Quartiere Ovest* (both made in Italy). He has worked in Italy, Germany, Yugoslavia, and Israel.

"Of all the films, television and theatre I've done, I can honestly say that the things I'm most remembered for are the two roles I created on the original *Star Trek*: DECIUS in "Balance of Terror" and STONN in "Amok Time."

Made in the USA
Las Vegas, NV
06 September 2022